THE ALIEN'S DEFIANCE

CALLA ZAE

PROSE & CONCEPTS

THE ALIEN'S DEFIANCE

NORAKIAN WARRIOR SERIES

CALLA ZAE

COPYRIGHT

The Alien's Defiance

Prose & Concepts LLC

210 Park Avenue, Suite #280

Worcester, MA 01609

www.proseandconcepts.com

This book is a work of fiction. All characters, places, names, and events are a product of the author's imagination. Any resemblance to events, locations, or persons alive or otherwise, is entirely coincidental.

Library of Congress Cataloging-in-Publication Data

Library of Congress Control Number: 2020949058

First edition Paperback ISBN: 978-1-952820-00-7

First edition Ebook ISBN: 978-1-952820-01-4

For those fighting for love and truth.

.

.

.

"Darkness cannot drive out darkness; only light can do that."

— Martin Luther King Jr.

Larion
Asteroid Karma
Mercami
Celeron
Terrakado
Asteroid Icarus
Tacitus
Raekos
Alarus Galaxy
Calla Zae

Orchaeda Ocean
N
NE
NW
W
E
SW
SE
S
Dellrae Bay
DELLEON
NURAK
Ashana Ocean
Karaya Bay
Kristic Bay
YORRI
SASSARI
FALERA
Bay of Catthor
Sovereign Sea
ENSAAB
KORBA
Aweawe Ocean
THE REGIONS
OF TERRAKADO
Jahdah Sea
Calla Zae

Jeeto

Cosmic Key

ONE

Aleeya

Inside her bathroom, Aleeya tried to shake the strange sensation that clung to her like an old relationship that refused to be forgotten. For the past three days, the cautionary chills had crawled down her spine in a slow motion that seeped into her bones. Was the energy caressing her? Or was it her imagination trying to convince her she was desperate for a spa treatment? Heaven knew she needed one.

She shivered from the rush of energy and knocked over her lotion-plant that also served as an air freshener. Cursing herself, she straightened the plant and cleaned up the mess. Clumsiness wasn't her thing at all. What was going on here? She was a warrior, a spectacular archer who knew how to aim. Precision was her forte.

Something was off, and that irritated her. She wasn't the type to let things slide like this.

"I don't have time for this," Aleeya said to herself as the cosmic codes on the side of her face, neck, and arms illuminated.

That wasn't normal. The cosmic symbols were like birthmarks, and only heightened emotions could activate them. What was affecting them now?

Could a spirit be playing with her? From chatting with her warrior sister, Andara, she knew spirits existed everywhere. Energies came in various forms, and sometimes they passed through searching for the thing that kept them around.

Was one passing through her home? She'd have to look into it later. Right now, she had to get ready for her trip to Delleon, the neighboring region, with Elder Kai and El Lara.

Excited for her first Galactic Coalition of Truth Convention, Aleeya rolled her shoulders, shaking off the tingles from her body, and stared at herself in the mirror as the cosmic codes faded. Yawning, she dug into her pouch of feminine products and took out her lip-pen. She tapped on the pen. A virtual screen popped up for her to choose from a wide spectrum of colors. She chose a muted pink that complemented her dark skin and sprayed her cheeks with a gentle kiss of blushers. Gathering her white hair, she created a side braid, stepped back, and reviewed herself. Satisfied that the makeup hid her exhaustion, she tossed her beauty products back into the pouch and zipped them up into the small luggage in her bedroom.

The strange energy returned, but it stayed subtle at the base of her neck, like a warm scarf.

Her gold vambrace, a high-tech communication device on her arm, buzzed with a message from Elder Kai, notifying her that his spaceship, *Nadial Starc*, would dock in a few minutes.

As a Norakian warrior, she had traveled to many galaxies, but there were too many within the Cosmos to visit. New galaxies were being discovered all the time, and this would be a great opportunity to meet new life-forms.

She wanted to look decent in case she ran into a stunning male. Not that meeting a male was her primary purpose for traveling or anything. It was just a fun possibility, and she enjoyed fun times. Who didn't? Being prepared gave her an advantage, and she liked advantages. Her past lovers never lasted long. The most recent relationship had her lover disappearing without a word after a couple of weeks. Why didn't he contact her to let her know it was over? It would have been the right thing to do. She contacted him once, and he didn't reply, so she left it at that.

She didn't understand the male species, which was why "noncommittal" was key. She glanced at herself in the mirror. She'd been told she was beautiful, strong, and powerful, but she attracted men who didn't appreciate those attributes.

A busy warrior had things to do, and she didn't have time for something serious that demanded commitment. Commitment meant being stuck together forever. Commitment wanted more than she could offer. She couldn't give what she didn't have.

Aleeya forced herself back to the task at hand. She straightened her purple uniform. The gold accents were composed from the Norakian alloy, fortisium. It was a mix of steel, chromium, and other rare metals combined for strength, hardness, and flexibility. She had personalized the engraved plates with a hint of lilac. Aleeya pulled on her knee-length boots, made from a high-performance fabric that modified itself around the muscles of her legs. She gave a few kicks in the air, testing her movement.

Finally, she grabbed Xmark—her bow and arrow—and with a thought that activated the size controls, shrank them to a third of their size and tucked them into the small quiver sewn into her uniform like a pocket.

Aleeya widened her eyes to make herself look alert. She'd spent last night researching her past. Like always, it brought her to a dead end. Her only memory was that her mother had died. Did she have her father's or mother's eyes? Who did she look like? What features did she inherit from them?

These were normal questions that any orphan would inquire. Why did her father leave her at the Cosmic Corra Orphanage when she was only five solar cycles old?

Why did he abandon her? And why did it matter to her now?

Because the present is nothing without a past. Because a warrior is only an empty shell without the substance that held her together.

She strode by a loving family the other day, and that triggered her desire to know hers. Even after all these solar cycles, she still hung onto the fact that maybe one day she'd find the answers she'd been looking for. That maybe one day she'd find out all about Aleeya. Who was she?

"Stop it," she scolded herself.

Thinking about her father brought on anger. She didn't want to ruin her trip before it even started.

She huffed out a breath. "Time to move on."

Her vambrace buzzed, signifying someone had docked outside on the private platform of her apartment floor. Every apartment on every floor in her tall building had its own docking point. She snapped her fingers, and her small luggage followed her out to the private platform composed of interlacing energy and neutronic beads. The luggage followed Aleeya up the ramp and into Elder Kai's sleek *Nadial Starc*.

A swarm of energy slammed into her from the crown down to her legs, almost knocking her off balance. The heat coursed through her bloodstream. She braced a hand on the wall of the spaceship as the energy circulated around her body and evaporated from her pores. For a split moment, an unfamiliar geometric shape flashed before her eyes. She blinked and it disappeared.

Blackened Stardust. What the hell was going on with her today?

TWO

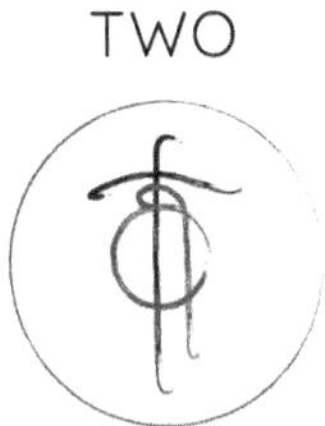

Aleeya

Aleeya inhaled a deep breath. The sensation faded as quickly as it had come. This was not her imagination. This was real. Her body hummed from the upgrade of energy. She'd never experienced anything so powerful in her life.

She'd have to ask El Lara about this odd occurrence. The Priestess of the Elseon Grove was more in tune with energies and a marvelous healer. She was an Official of the Norakian government and mentor to all the Norakian warriors.

Laughter drew her to the front of the spaceship. Her luggage joined the other cases in the corner. She inhaled another breath and admired the extravagant *Nadial Starc*. Luxurious fabric and innovative technology decorated Elder Kai's massive ship. The Elders were the top leaders of Norak, and they had a special connection to the Cosmos. Elder Kai was also a mentor to the Norakian warriors. Aleeya respected his wisdom and his service to the region.

The Elders had all the nice upgrades because they could

afford them. Aleeya ran her hand along the gun metal railing as she stepped up to the center station, where Elder Kai and El Lara sat in velvety chairs, looking at a virtual screen.

Aleeya placed a fist to her chest, tapped, and greeted them. They returned the greeting with a smile.

"Welcome aboard." Elder Kai gestured to a curved armchair. His braided white hair looked like a white snake down his back. He wore a white robe with gold accents. The whiteness of his ensemble made his orange, scaly skin appear like fire encased in snow.

"Are you ready for your first GCOT?" The star on El Lara's forehead glowed. Her white hair piled up neatly with floral pins that matched her light green robe.

Aleeya sat down on the velvety armchair and nodded to Peko, the pilot with the short pink hair and three ears. Like always, he was dressed in a black uniform. He sent her a wave and cheerful smile before turning to the monitors.

"We're off." Peko tapped some buttons, and a translucent screen sectioned him off, giving everyone privacy.

Aleeya sat back and crossed her legs. "Thank you for inviting me on this trip. I really appreciate it."

Elder Kai shifted in his seat, and the three gold bands that sectioned off his hair glinted. "It's a pleasure to have you. I wish I could offer this trip to every Norakian warrior, but the conference has limited seating. Furthermore, they're occupied with other responsibilities. It would be difficult to pull them away from their missions to attend a GCOT conference."

Aleeya lifted an eyebrow. "Are you saying I don't have a lot to do?"

El Lara's lips curved into a smile.

Elder Kai's green eyes glittered, but a seriousness overcame them. "No. I invited you for two reasons. One is because you've proven yourself a worthy warrior. So you deserve this extracurricular activity. Two is because our two suns and three moons wanted you here."

Surprise knocked into her. "What do you mean?"

El Lara flicked a glance at Elder Kai, waiting for an answer as well. Her blank expression revealed she just received the same information.

He rose from the chair and walked to stand in front of a large map of their galaxy, Alarus. "During one of my meditations, I received a message. They wanted me to take you to the GCOT. I don't know why. They didn't say, and I didn't ask. Even if I did, they wouldn't have told me. As you know, our suns and moons work in their own ways. They speak in riddles and metaphors. I believe this mission is important to you somehow. And that it is also important to Norak."

Blackened stardust. Was this what her body had been trying to tell her?

The Elders had powerful connections to the Cosmos. They could receive visions and messages that weren't privy to other star-beings. It reminded her of what Kazstrom and Teegan had gone through during the last solar cycle when Farra, one of the three moons, had chosen them to fulfill a mission that saved the Aurora Matrix—the sacred bridge in Norak—from being destroyed by darkness.

"Maybe this explains the energies I've been sensing around me."

Elder Kai faced her. "How do you feel?"

"Odd, off balance... they feel familiar and unfamiliar at the same time." She shrugged. "I don't know. I've never felt it before."

The star on EL Lara's forehead glowed. "Pay attention to it. Sometimes, the Cosmos delivers messages in subtle ways for us to decipher."

The Cosmos had chosen her, and that notion reigned supreme in her mind. Why was she chosen? For what reason?

"How did you get the extra ticket to the convention?" Aleeya asked.

"I had to pull a lot of strings," Elder Kai said.

What did the suns and the moons have planned for her? Nerves spiked in Aleeya's stomach and tightened the muscles around her chest. Her *corra* thudded like a cardio workout. She tried sensing that odd energy to see if it was still there. It wasn't. Was that energy sent from the Cosmos?

"I guess we'll find out what I'm supposed to do in Delleon. Whatever it is, I pray it's nothing like what Kazstrom and Teegan went through."

El Lara petted Sizzler, her green pet snake that slithered from her pocket. "They were fated starmates. They couldn't avoid their destiny even if they tried. We all have lessons to learn in life. Some seek closure. Some seek knowledge, redemption, forgiveness and other things. We can't dodge fate. You're a Norakian warrior. There's nothing you can't handle. Plus, you have us. You're not alone." The Priestess reached over and squeezed Aleeya's hand.

"I know and thank you. I'm telling you now that it will not be another fated starmate deal. I don't believe in it." Aleeya lifted a shoulder. "Everyone knows my relationships don't last long. I mean, doesn't the Cosmos have more important things to worry about than connecting lovers?"

Elder Kai and El Lara exchanged a smirk.

There was one male who had a crush on her during their time at the orphanage, but she wasn't interested in him. Rellok had tried to kiss her, and that action had gotten him in trouble. Even back then, love and affection were thing she didn't fully grasp.

"The Cosmos is a mystery to us all." Elder Kai sat back

down and expanded the virtual map floating in front of them. "Love is the most powerful frequency in all dimensions. It creates many realities that can save us. Or destroy us."

The love of family was something Aleeya lacked. Did that taint her perspective on every other relationship? A headache throbbed in her temple. All this talk about love and relationships wasn't what she expected when she prepared for this conference.

"Maybe the Cosmos wants to introduce me to Delleon fashion and food. Those things have been running through my mind all day."

Elder Kai laughed. "Only you would say such things."

Aleeya worried she might miss the clues from the Cosmos. Had it been sending clues all along and she dismissed them without knowing? She had to pay more attention. What if the Cosmos delivered a destiny she didn't want? She felt like she had just been assigned an important cosmic mission. One she knew nothing about. As a warrior, she didn't like not knowing the lay of the land. How could she plan a good defense?

Regardless, she had to put that aside and concentrate on the convention.

"What do you normally do or discuss at these meetings, anyway?" She grabbed a small fruit tart and poured herself a cup of Neptunian coffee from a pitcher labeled *Bound Together Bookstore and Café*. It was Teegan and Kazstrom's shop. She made a mental note to stop and visit when she got home. Kazstrom was the Prime General of the Norakian warriors, her brother-in-arms, who found his starmate with a human female.

Teegan and Kazstrom married six months ago inside the Elseon Grove. Aleeya was happy for her warrior brother, who had settled down after years of bachelorhood. She also got to meet Teegan's brother, Maverick, and her best friend, Steffani. Both of them stayed for a week and vowed to keep quiet about

Terrakado until NASA discovered the planet on its own. There were some things that humans needed to uncover at their own pace. The last thing the Norakians wanted was to create a panic on Earth.

El Lara sipped her green drink, which was probably some herbal blend. Aleeya had tried it before and decided she preferred something sweeter. "I don't get to attend the GCOT conference that often either. I'm actually replacing Master Churnar. He was pulled into another conference."

Aleeya couldn't keep up with all the conferences the Officials had to attend. Some were private and others were public knowledge.

"The Cosmos is busy these days," Aleeya said. She'd heard about the wars outside of her galaxy. There were extremely dark forces out there that required the joint forces from several galaxies to contain them. Those kinds of battles required other warriors to take part. Aleeya was happy to serve her home region.

"The battle between Light and Dark never stops." Elder Kai swiped to another map Aleeya hadn't seen before. "There's darkness here." He pointed to a circular section on a map. "It's growing stronger. Pockets of darkness are popping up all over the place. We're not sure why or how." He rubbed the green gemstone ring on his middle finger and rose to face the panoramic window that opened to a sea of clouds.

El Lara joined him. "I sense it is escalating rather than decreasing. Let's hope the Infinitii warriors can resolve this fast."

The Infinitii warriors dealt with major galactic conflicts. She'd overheard stories about the galactic wars, but paid no attention because that took energy away from her tasks in Norak. What could she do about a war on a planet that was outside her galaxy?

Aleeya was curious. "What can we do to stop the spread of darkness?"

El Lara offered a simple answer. "By spreading light."

"If there's no darkness, there wouldn't be a need for us, right?" Aleeya stood beside them as the spaceship lowered, and a dry landscape came into view.

Peko glanced at her from his seat. El Lara flicked a warning gaze a mother would give her child for an insensitive remark.

"That came out wrong. What I meant to say is that we exist to fight the dark. That's our purpose."

"It is, and it has been for eons." Elder Kai kept his eyes focused on Delleon.

They remained quiet as they stared out at the orange glow from the red, sandy terrain. About half of Delleon was composed of desert and open fields. The region wasn't as lush as Norak. But Norak was blessed with the Aurora Matrix, which fed the land beneficial energy that allowed various life forms to thrive. However, Norak gifted its neighbor with divine energy from the Aurora Matrix.

That benefit showed when they passed over lush mountains of colorful forests and grasslands. The metropolitan city of Phyllus came into view. Vegetation of blue, purple, and green trees surrounded the city.

"I'm happy to see they took advantage of what we gave them." Aleeya pointed to the glowing ball of energy sitting inside a massive, transparent dish. Colors flowed out and down into the soil.

"It's good to share resources when possible," Elder Kai said. "At the end of the day, everyone wants a decent life for their families. Life is crucial no matter what region you live in, no matter what star race you are. When society can go to bed on a full stomach and feel safe, there will be fewer crimes."

Understanding, Aleeya nodded. Fewer crimes in an adjacent region meant the reduction of immigrants looking for safety in Norak as well. No one would leave their home unless their lives were threatened.

Peko landed the spaceship in Phyllus's Aero Terminal. Five minutes later, Aleeya sat in the front seat of an oblong-shaped carrier heading toward the Clova Hotel. Elder Kai and El Lara claimed their comfortable spot in the back seat, while Peko drove on concrete roads to their destination.

The ride gave Aleeya a chance to enjoy the view. She admired the tall, glass buildings with pointed tops and the hexagonal structures that were stacked on top of each other. Her eyebrows climbed when the carrier entered an area of the city that contrasted the clean and sophisticated setting she just witnessed.

Trash scattered on the streets. Buildings in dire need of renovations appeared as she passed broken streets that required new pavement and beggars wandered back and forth on the sidewalk.

This section of the city was still part of Phyllus. What happened to it?

She thought about the citizens of Norak and was glad there were several shelters created for those who needed a bed.

"Why did the city abandon this section?" Aleeya thought out loud.

No one responded. Maybe the same question floated in their minds.

Peko steered the carrier up and over to avoid a plastic bin that rolled out of nowhere, blocking their path. He continued hovering above the road until he came to a stoplight that blinked in the air. Several longships, personal riders, air-bikes, and carriers passed them by on the other side.

Twenty feet from her carrier, two dark-haired children with filthy, nervous faces ran up to a passerby who was dressed in a pricey suit. The image clutched Aleeya's corra. The male star-being opened his palm, and the children gave him a little pouch. In exchange, he offered them coins, which were used for smaller purchases.

What were they selling? The pale, blue-skinned boy and girl about eight solar cycles old took the coins and rushed up to a male with a green face that matched his jacket.

Aleeya pressed a button, and the window slid down, allowing her to hear the conversation better.

He pushed himself off from the wall. "How much did he give you?"

The children opened their palms to show the coins. He scowled at them and said something that made them tremble. The green-faced Delleon star-being lifted his hand, prepared to attack when the boy pushed him. The male stumbled back in shock. The children ran down an alley. Shouting, the green Delleon ran after them.

"He better not." Aleeya burst out with her objection. "Take the carrier down there, right now." She pointed to the alley where the children fled.

Peko made a right turn and went down the alley, shadowed by old buildings and dumpsters that reeked of death. About halfway down, Elder Kai lifted his hand, signifying Peko to stop.

Aleeya pushed the door open and stepped outside, searching. She didn't see the children or the Delleon star-being. She didn't hear any screams and prayed the kids had escaped unharmed.

Where were their parents? Did the Delleon star-being force them to beg?

Anger boiled in her blood. Her chest heaved with concern with all the scenarios that popped into her head. She couldn't wait to get her hands on Green Face and let him know what happened to adults who mistreated children.

Would she be in the same situation as those kids if she hadn't lived at the orphanage?

Aleeya stood staring down the alley, as if an answer would appear.

Elder Kai stepped out of the carrier and broke the silence. "Get back inside, Aleeya. This isn't our jurisdiction. We *cannot* intervene like this." The firm directive pierced her.

Aleeya whipped her eyes at him. "But this is wrong. How can we sit here and let those children suffer? That male wanted to hurt them."

"We have no proof; we have no cause. What you and I witnessed was a portion of the story. We can't assume without having all the information. You know this." He sighed. "We're guests in Phyllus. We need to remember our place."

Aleeya returned to the carrier as Peko circled back onto the main road. Anger scorched her, but she contained it.

El Lara spoke in a calm tone. "Elder Kai is right. This is Delleon territory. There are certain lines we can't cross. We have to respect our neighbors and their regulations."

Understanding their words, Aleeya held back an angry comment. She wouldn't like it if someone entered Norak and created their own law and order. But those terrified children carved an unforgettable image into her brain. Where did they go? Were they safe? What did the green being want from them?

"I'll contact the officials and ask them to look into it. We must be careful with how we interact with our neighbors. Right now, our relationship is cordial. Let's keep it that way." Elder Kai opened a screen from his vambrace and began typing. "Also, we can't be late to this convention. It's a coalition of galaxies, planets, regions, provinces, and countries that are here to discuss ways to improve the Cosmos in which we all live. Our presence represents Norak and its integrity, its contribution. We have to go now."

She glanced at her vambrace to check the time. They would definitely be late if she went after that bastard.

Later, she promised as she scratched an itch on the back of her neck. She curled her fingers into fists and catalogued the green face, green jacket, and red hair into her mind.

One way or another, she would apprehend him.

THREE

Kenzo

Kenzo Kwan purchased a sandwich from Charmi's Lunch Cart. The meat reminded him of a steak and cheese sandwich from when he lived on Earth. He inhaled a deep breath and tried his best to calm the muscle tremors running down his arms and hands. Tremors spiked in him every time he fought a criminal. He thought he had the issue contained, but recently they'd been occurring more often and with no triggers.

His life in the military had been full of stress and pressure, but it never bothered him until he arrived on this planet. Was it time for him to see a doctor or someone who could assist with these psychosomatic issues?

As if Jeeto sensed his discomfort, his furry pet peeked out from his jacket pocket and crawled up to hug his arm. Jeeto had been the friend that comforted him when the emotional demons were too much for him to handle. Kenzo patted the pouf of blue hair, and Jeeto squished his face.

Jeeto sniffed. "I want some." The pink tongue snuck out

from his mouth, tasting the delicious smell. Jeeto was the size of a bunny with large ears, a tail, and eyes that could get a man to do anything.

"Is that a 'he' or 'she?'" Charmi had green skin and curly brown hair.

"It's a 'he.'" Kenzo met Jeeto's puppy green eyes. "You just ate. I'm not having you puke all over me again."

No one could understand Jeeto's words except Kenzo. The bizarre communication still baffled him to this day, but he was grateful for the friend who helped him adjust to this new planet. God knew Kenzo's mental state could've gone a different route if Jeeto and his roommate, Tab, hadn't been there for him.

Charmi laughed, and her curly hair bounced like a sponge. "He's so cute. My kids would love him. What animal breed is he?"

Kenzo shrugged. "No clue."

Charmi handed over the sandwich with a bag of colorful fries he couldn't resist. "These are fresh. I know you love them."

"I don't know what I would do if you weren't selling food."

"My food is the quick stuff, which you should cut back on. I appreciate your credits, but you need to eat well to stay well. You look happy today. Joyful news?"

Delivering two bounties had earned him a lot of credits. "I'm just happy to see you. Thank you. I will cut back on the oily fries."

"So, I take it the bounty life agrees with you?" Charmi asked.

"It's keeping me going. It's been five solar cycles since I was abducted, escaped, and made this region my home."

"I know. You've mentioned it every time I feed you up! I'm glad you're here, human."

"Yeah well, some days I'm worried I'm gonna wake up and be home, then I wake up and I'm still here."

"So, is that a good or bad thing?"

"A good thing. I have some unfinished business to attend to before I can go anywhere."

"Well, here are some extra fries to keep you going. Take care and come back."

Funny, Kenzo would have thought Charmi was the one who should take care, especially on this side of Phyllus. The tremors in his hand subsided as he gave her his universal credit badge.

Living in the city of Phyllus had taught him that Earth would never catch up to the technology of these aliens, who preferred to be called star-beings. Which made sense to him since they lived amongst the stars and could basically visit any planets and galaxies with ease.

Kenzo had made connections that could've taken him back home to Earth, but he stayed on Terrakado for two reasons. One, vengeance for his military brothers' deaths. His biological brother, Terence, was among those killed. Kenzo had been their admiral and failed at protecting them. Two, there was nothing back on Earth for him. He enjoyed the unpredictable lifestyle and living on a new planet gave him that unpredictability. Impermanence suited him. It was what he was used to.

He'd always wanted to be part of something bigger, something that represented honor, respect, integrity, and courage. Something that gave him a purpose. But all that changed when his brothers died. Their deaths fueled a new purpose in him. He had to obliterate those monsters who had tortured them. Were there other humans locked somewhere being abused and mutilated right now?

He should've died too. Why didn't he? That question continued to gnaw at him with no clear answer. It didn't matter. His mission was to find out who was behind the abduction and kill them all. Anyone who had a part in the torture would fucking die.

Perhaps their deaths would also destroy the post-traumatic stress disorder plaguing him. He never imagined these symptoms could disrupt his life this much. But he learned to deal with them, and Jeeto had been the unexpected friend that helped him along the way.

Kenzo strode down to the bench, sat, and bit into his sandwich, which didn't look tasty anymore. He broke a piece off the sandwich and gave it to Jeeto. "Here. Don't say I'm never nice to you."

Jeeto gobbled it up and swallowed. "I'd never say that." He jumped out of the pocket, wagged his tail, sat on Kenzo's lap, and dove into the bag of colorful fries. He scooted closer to Kenzo's side, leaned in, and offered his adorable smile that eased the vengeful thoughts.

"Eat slowly. You can have the entire bag. I don't want to hear any complaints about a tummy ache."

Jeeto smiled with a mouthful of fries. Kenzo snuck one for himself. These colorful fries tasted better than the ones on Earth. They were made from some Norakian root that came in various colors that boosted your energy.

As a bounty hunter, Kenzo apprehended the criminals, delivered them, and got paid. He landed the job by accident. He had seen a felon he knew from the media outlets, followed him, and rescued two female star-beings from rape. Detective Ahlex thanked and paid Kenzo credits for the assistance. Kenzo wasn't the only bounty hunter in Delleon. The detective appreciated all the help he could get, and an occupation was born on that day.

It had been five years since the abduction, and he wasn't any closer to finding out who had orchestrated the torture that killed his brothers. But he vowed to find him, her, or them.

Vengeance had a flavor, and the bitterness and distaste ruined his appetite. *Fuck.*

He gave the rest of his sandwich to Jeeto. "You better not puke in my jacket."

Jeeto grinned and devoured the sandwich. That thing could really eat.

A message blinked on his leather vambrace, which was like a mobile device strapped to his arm, versatile and light.

"Brock's in the vicinity." An image of the drug dealer popped onto the screen from Tab, his savior and his roommate.

Brock sold the orange pills called Bliss, a popular street drug in Delleon. Kenzo remembered being injected with a bright liquid during his capture. Maybe Brock could lead him to the star-beings responsible for his torture and his brothers' deaths. Members of the drug world knew each other, didn't they?

Though Kenzo didn't have a bounty on Brock, he didn't mind eliminating a criminal for Delleon free of charge.

FOUR

Aleeya

On their way to the Clova Hotel, Aleeya studied the tall towers and dome-shaped architecture of Phyllus. Multi-leveled roads allowed the longships, autobuses, and air-bikes to reach their destination without crashing into each other. Small spacecraft flew amongst the monowheels. The streets became wider and cleaner as they entered the busy city. Lovely trees aligned the sidewalks made of glistening stones.

No children begged on these streets. Instead, families laughed as they strode on the wide sidewalk. Peko shot a glance at her, probably checking to see if she was still angry.

The storefronts were just as busy as the Shopping Plaza of Norak. The Clova Hotel looked like an abstract tree with a fat trunk. Large branches extended out from it. Windows and balconies filled those branches. Aleeya would have liked the image a lot more if her first impression wasn't ruined by what she saw in the poorer sections of Phyllus.

Peko dropped them off, went to park in the garage, and had the day off until transportation was required.

Aleeya made her way to the tenth level. From her suite, she could see the Dellrae Bay. The spacious room welcomed her with warm colors of peach and ivory. She strode into the bedroom with lilac walls, opened the tall screen door, and stepped out onto the private balcony. The soft ivory curtains danced with the gentle breeze. The balcony offered a spectacular view of the city and its architecture.

She strode back inside and surveyed the kitchen. A plate of Delleon fruits sat on the counter. She'd never tried the cactiberry, citrus-grape, or a Delleon purple-pear. Next to the kitchen was an enormous bathroom with all the amenities she expected from a luxurious hotel.

Pleased with her suite, Aleeya sorted out her luggage, and the image of the frightened children popped into her mind. She performed a quick search on Phyllus via the Galacto Net, an extensive galactic network that anyone could access for general information. But as a Norakian warrior, she had access into areas reserved for investigators. Two hours later, she discovered that there were many missing children and adults in Phyllus. What happened to them?

Questions bombarded her as she headed to the conference area on the fifteenth floor. Elder Kai and El Lara sat at a round table closer to the front with other attendees wearing a gold badge. The gold badges signified invited members only. Aleeya grabbed her silver badge—which allowed her general clearance —and took a seat at a table near the back.

To her left, three two-headed star-beings with orange skin nodded at her. Aleeya greeted them and discovered they were from the Coronal Sector galaxy. There were too many galaxies out there for her to remember. To her right, a GCOT warrior offered her a nod. She had never met one before. The gold insignia displayed on his uniform identified him as an Infinitii warrior. His cloud-white skin stood out against the gold and gunmetal uniform, and the disheveled blue hair completed the powerful appearance.

"Do you attend these conferences often?" Aleeya asked, noticing he had a gold badge. Why wasn't he sitting in the front?

Fierce blue eyes, darker than his hair, stared at her. "I do," he said. "Is this your first conference?" His eyes shifted in a way that made the corners tilt up, and the white skin glistened with visible scales.

"You're a shifter?"

A smile formed. "It's a pleasure to meet a Norakian warrior. I'm Pheon from the Cierra Cluster, and yes, I'm a shifter."

She had never met anyone from that galaxy before. There had been no missions that required her to travel that far from Terrakado. "I'm Aleeya," she said. "It's nice to be acquainted with one of the GCOT warriors. What's your alter ego?"

The corners of his eyes crinkled. "A dragon."

Aleeya gave him a once over and couldn't wait to share the news with Andara, who had a fascination with dragons. "If my warrior sister were here, she'd hound you with dragon questions."

He laughed.

She didn't know if Pheon could help, but he was an Infinitii warrior who had access to a lot more information, and as part of the GCOT, he didn't need to follow the same regulations as she did.

An idea percolated in Aleeya's mind. "Have you been to the other side of Phyllus? The poorer sections? The disparity between the poor and the wealthy is profound, wouldn't you agree?"

"I haven't," he said, considering her. "Why do you ask?"

Aleeya remembered what Elder Kai had said about being

careful. She didn't know Pheon, but she needed information. She grabbed two pastries from the large plate and placed them onto her dish. "I'm just curious. On my way here, I saw children begging for food. I thought it was a strange contrast to this area."

"I believe Delleon is working on improving the living conditions in their cities," he said. "In every galaxy, there are children who need our help. Children are the most vulnerable."

"They are, and they need adults who can help them." She bit into her sweet tart, chewed, and swallowed.

Pheon stared at her. "You're bothered by something. How can I help?"

Aleeya smiled at his straightforwardness. She leaned in and whispered, "I'd love any information on the missing children and adults in Phyllus. Can you help with that?"

Pheon's blue eyebrows quirked. "I'll do what I can."

"Great, thank you. Let me know if I can help you with anything." Aleeya tapped her vambrace to his, giving him access to her information, and vice versa. As an Infinitii warrior, Pheon was vetted by the Galactic Coalition of Truth that upheld cosmic laws. So, she gave him the benefit of the doubt.

"Will do." Pheon's attention turned to something in the front, and he rose from his seat. "I have to go now. Be well, Aleeya."

Glancing at the front of the room, Aleeya tried to spot Elder Kai, but didn't see him as more star-beings filed in. Did he get a reply from Phyllus officials regarding the boy and girl?

Aleeya sat through several virtual screens sharing information about the Cosmos, the increased solar flares, the frequencies of Alarus and its surrounding galaxies, the current wars and battles in other realms, the list of galactic fugitives, and how all the galaxies were moving toward that magnetic location called, The Great Vortex. This enigmatic area within the Cosmos had always interested her. She didn't know of anyone who had gotten near it. She recalled studying its potent pull from the Intergalactic Library and was in awe of its power. The Great Vortex could bend time and space, warping realities, illusions, and energies.

An itch irritated her neck, and she reached back to scratch it. Was she allergic to something in Phyllus? She'd been itchy ever since she stepped foot in the Delleon region. Maybe she was allergic to their crimes. She scratched again, and though the itch diminished, it lingered beneath her skin like an annoyance. She needed a better moisturizer!

Aleeya focused her attention on the podium. A star-being with several arms and an elongated face spoke. "The Great Vortex is a massive gravitational anomaly, and it's part of the Cosmic Plan. A plan where all of us are small players. Collectively, we are being pulled towards it whether we want to or not. This is our divine evolution. Change is a constant, and we must adapt to this constant. Or we fall."

Silence hung in the room as she glanced around at the serious faces that understood the magnitude of his statement. This was where critical changes, uproars, and evolution within the Cosmos were revealed. The Galactic Coalition of Truth encompassed powerful star-beings from various galaxies who came together to maintain the balance of the Cosmos. Right now, darkness was expanding rapidly. It was an enormous task, one too large for a Norakian warrior like herself. She preferred something tangible that she could relate to.

During the intermission, the Zeta Meida Band performed their new reggae album while Aleeya sipped the Orion Mojito and nibbled on delicacies of cacti-flavored fowless meatballs, spongy fishcakes, and sweet rainbow-apple tart.

An energy brushed across her, getting her attention. A knowingness she couldn't explain validated what she had been thinking. If listening to all this galactic knowledge had taught her anything, it confirmed that she had to stand up for what she believed in.

The Cosmos was vast, and everyone had their part in it. She could contribute to this fight against the darkness by protecting the children. They were the light of the future.

Truth had to be maintained. She had to be authentic to herself, even if that defied every local rule and regulation before her. To ignore injustice was an injustice to herself. Motivated, she used her universal badge of credits and rented a Bug-Z coupe, a white rider with ears that mimicked an adorable animal. She punched in the coordinates and headed back to the alley, where she last saw those children.

FIVE

Kenzo

Kenzo parked his gunmetal Bullet T53, which was like a sleek bulletproof modern sports car on Earth. He took Jeeto out of his pocket. "Stay here. Don't go anywhere."

"Where are you going?" Jeeto yawned.

"I've got business."

"You always got business."

"Business buys you food. Watch my car."

Kenzo's driver side door slid open. He got out and locked the car with a button on his leather vambrace. Drug dealers always had weapons, and he came prepared. As he made his way toward the alley, he ran a hand down his jacket, making sure his weapons were all present. Three blasters, two knives, and two smoke bombs the size of grapes.

As he neared the alley, the two suns descended like lovers settling down for the evening. The warm colors splashed against the buildings with crumbling bricks and broken windows. These abandoned buildings could be homes for the homeless if the city paid more attention to this neglected area of Phyllus. Businesses wouldn't thrive in an area like this, though. This was a place for crime. The stench of illegal activities crawled up his nose. He had grown used to places like this with every bounty he retrieved.

Kenzo glanced down at his vambrace and saw no more messages from Tab. Tab knew of Kenzo's mission and passed along information that could assist him. Did Brock know anything about the experiments on humans?

A child's scream echoed down the alley. With caution, Kenzo made his way toward the sound. As he neared, a female voice spoke in the universal language, "Give him to me."

Kenzo slid behind a broken autobus and studied the beautiful warrior standing at the mouth of the alley. He had gained the ability to understand the universal language because his abductors had forced a nasty liquid down his throat that burned his mouth and tongue and pounded his ears for days.

The setting suns cast shadows into the alley, making it more eerie.

He inched up to a dented delivery truck. She was an attractive, dark-skinned beauty with a posture that wielded power and determination. Her armor consisted of high-tech fabric that tailored to her spectacular body, revealing muscles in all the right places. Gold metal plates covered her shoulders, toned biceps, and a portion of her back. A pair of intricate vambraces protected her forearms, and boots made her legs appear a mile-long.

Her face portrayed a "no-nonsense" attitude that gripped and held him in place. Abstract symbols appeared on her face and neck like tattoos or birthmarks. Did she have more hidden under that armor? And why was he even thinking that right now?

"Let him go, or I will rip off your arm—the one you used on

that child. I remember how you terrorized the two kids yesterday." Her voice didn't rise, but Kenzo felt its roar.

Who was this woman? He had seen no warriors dressed like her in the area. She was probably from another region. But why would an outsider care about Phyllus's issues?

Kenzo recognized Brock from the image Tab sent him. He needed Brock for questioning. From the warrior's words, Brock abused that child. Kenzo clenched his fist, vowing to break Brock's bones before dropping him off to Detective Ahlex.

Kenzo inched closer and closer. A boy with light blue skin shuddered against Brock. He wrapped an arm around the boy's neck, pressed his blaster to the kid's head, and spat, "Get out of here before his brains splatter all over your pretty uniform."

The female cocked her head. "You move the blaster one more inch, and I'll feed you your brain."

Kenzo recognized the dark-haired boy as Raskaa, one of the missing children he'd seen on the media. Where was his twin sister, Jella? His parents had pleaded for their safe return.

"Who the hell are you? What do you want?" Brock glared at her with yellow eyes that took up most of his green face.

"I'm here to stop you." She jutted a finger at him. "Pick on someone your own size. I'll give you an opportunity to fight me."

Brock laughed and curled his lips. "No."

"Are you afraid to fight a female?" The warrior crossed her arms.

Brock flared his nostrils. "I'm not afraid of you, bitch."

"Oh, is that how you fight females? With name-calling?" She narrowed her eyes at him. "I've been called worse, and none of them bother me."

"Shut up or I'll blast his head." Brock pushed the blaster into the boy's temple. The boy winced and trembled.

The female swung a leg into Brock's knee. It cracked and he shrieked. The blaster dropped to the ground. Raskaa stumbled away from Brock and ran to hide behind a dirty couch. Brock limped toward the female star-being with a clenched fist. Obscenities poured from his mouth, but the warrior only smirked. She blocked his attack and twisted his arm. Bones crunched and Brock wailed like a baby.

While the two battled, Kenzo snuck over to Raskaa. "I'm here to help you. Where's your sister, Jella?"

Raskaa trembled as he considered Kenzo. Kenzo saw fear and suspicion in the kid's eyes. "I work with Detective Ahlex, and I'm here to bring you home. This is you and your sister, correct?" He pulled up an image of them from the media on his vambrace.

Hope and tears gleamed in Raskaa's eyes. "They still have her."

"Where did they take her?"

"I don't know. They separated us yesterday." Raskaa wiped his eyes with the back of his hands. "There are other kids, but I don't know them."

"Okay, that's excellent information. Let's get you home now." Kenzo offered his hand, and Raskaa took it. Though Kenzo wanted more information, the frightened kid needed his parents more.

Kenzo recognized the fear on Raskaa's face. Kenzo had experienced it firsthand when brutal star-beings abducted and experimented on him. But he was a well-trained Navy SEAL who could tolerate fear and pain better than children like Raskaa and Jella. Kenzo couldn't imagine the trauma they had experienced and what it would take for them to heal.

Hell, to this day, he was still trying to fight those nightmares.

As Kenzo assisted Raskaa out of the alley, the female warrior shouted after him. "Leave the kid alone! He's only a kid, you piece of *poogul!*"

Kenzo paused at the curse, calling him shit from the ugliest and stinkiest animal on this planet. He turned and met her glaring eyes as she slammed Brock's body against the wall with one hand.

Brock tried to wriggle free, but she clamped her fingers around his neck and glared at him. "Don't move, or I'll kill you right now."

If Kenzo didn't have the kid with him, and if he had more time on his hands, he would have stayed and enjoyed a duel with her. Something in her fierceness—in her absolute determination—intrigued him.

"I'm taking the kid, thanks for the distraction." Kenzo would've stayed to help her, but a warrior like her didn't need his help. She was handling the criminal well.

Initially, Kenzo came for Brock, a drug dealer of Bliss. But Kenzo ended up rescuing a child that was missing.

The fire in the warrior's eyes showed she thought he was with Brock. Kenzo gave her a smirk, turned back to Raskaa, lifted the weak kid into his arms, and fled out of the alley.

"*Malastrom!* Come back here!" Her voice echoed on and on.

For the first time in his life, Kenzo smiled at curses thrown at him like an array of daggers. Curses that were laced with a promise for retribution, no doubt.

What had he gotten himself into? All he knew was that Raskaa needed to get home and that his sister, Jella, was in dire danger. He'd find a way to question Brock if he didn't die today. If Brock died, then Kenzo would uncover his enemy by different means.

Kenzo reached his Bullet T53 and Jeeto's squished face greeted him. Raskaa sat in the back seat while Kenzo pulled out a virtual screen from his vambrace and alerted Detective Ahlex at the Phyllus Crime Division. Kenzo informed him about Brock's involvement with Raskaa's kidnapping. He alerted the detective that Brock was currently bothering a female and left an address to the alley. Detective Ahlex would send his team right away.

Kenzo typed on the virtual screen. "I want five minutes with Raskaa."

Though he should focus on his mission, something about this case lured him. Perhaps he could help locate Jella while also searching for his enemy. That would take extra work, extra time. He'd make his final decision once he understood the entire situation better.

He turned and found Raskaa occupied with Jeeto's silliness. Kenzo sped off, and his mind wandered back to the female warrior with fire in her eyes. He had made out with several beautiful star-beings, but none had made his heart thud erratically, especially from a distance.

He dismissed the sensation. He didn't have time for thudding hearts. He had children to save and vengeance to seek.

SIX

Aleeya

The next day, Aleeya wasn't in the mood for any conferences, so she excused herself. Her brain focused on Brock's murder, the missing boy, and the human male with the wild black hair who stole the kid from right under her nose.

Yesterday, when Aleeya hauled Brock to the edge of the alley, Phyllus officials showed up just in time to retrieve him. How did they know Brock's location? Detective Ahlex, a scaly green star-being with a wide head, two pointy ears, and orange hair, was happy Aleeya had captured him.

While the detective was busy with his team, Aleeya interrogated Brock regarding the two children. Where was the girl? However, Brock's head blew up during the interrogation. Blood and gore flung into her face and body. Detective Ahlex and his guards didn't escape Brock's splatter, either.

Who had done it? Why? What kind of information had to die with Brock? Did the human male have anything to do with this murder?

The detective didn't give her any details because she wasn't part of his department. She understood the protocol and didn't press on.

But that didn't mean she couldn't conduct her own investigation.

Aleeya made her way through the crowds of attendees and passed a green star-being with iridescent green scales and slicked back red hair. He wore a silver tailored jacket with matching pants. His posture and demeanor demanded attention.

"It's wonderful to meet you, Malixx," said a star-being with a massive horn on his head. "We heard your company, Atrium, has created several medications. Congratulations. When will you release them to the public?"

"Soon. You'll see them soon." Malixx's voice sounded like a hollow wind in some dark cave. When his gaze met hers, he lifted his glass filled with purple liquid.

She returned a casual smile and walked off. Her body shuddered from his presence. The cautionary energy clawed at her. Was it warning her about Malixx? Who was he? She kept his image in her mind for future reference.

A lot of things had tumbled inside her ever since stepping foot onto Delleon. Did the suns and moons send her to the city of Phyllus to rescue the children? Or did they want her to do something else?

Had Elder Kai heard on his inquiry regarding the children? Elder Kai and El Lara had been in private meetings all day.

If Elder Kai found out she had defied his orders and inserted herself into Phyllus business, he'd fire her from her Norakian responsibilities. She would no longer be a Norakian warrior. The thought squeezed her corra. She placed a hand on her chest and relaxed the tightness.

Aleeya slid into her Bug-Z coupe and leaned back on the

leather seat. She couldn't fathom what she would do if she weren't a Norakian warrior. Being a warrior had saved her life, her mindset. Growing up in the Cosmic Corra Orphanage with her warrior brothers and sisters had given her a sense of family when she had none. The orphanage was the home to all the Norakian warriors. That home trained her to be the warrior she was today and being able to serve the citizens of Norak had given her a purpose, a sense of self-worth.

She knew her responsibilities and took them seriously. She knew how she served.

Most of all, being a warrior taught her to acknowledge injustice. To grab it when it taunted her, even when covered in thorns.

How could she stand aside and do nothing when injustice spat her in the eye? If she didn't save those kids, she would go against everything she believed in.

Fully aware of her situation, she pulled up a virtual screen from her vambrace and contacted her warrior brothers: Kazstrom, the Prime General, and Magnetti, Captain of the Norakian warriors. They grew up with her in the orphanage, so they knew her character.

When their faces popped onto the screen, Aleeya placed a fist to her corra and tapped it two times, greeting them.

"How are you and Teegan?" she asked Kazstrom.

There was a beautiful energy to love. Kazstrom and Teegan emanated that vibration. Aleeya could see it on his face, his eyes, his entire body appeared more relaxed and at ease with life. A small part of Aleeya envied them. Would she ever find that love with anyone? Teegan stayed in Norak because she loved Kazstrom. She fought beside him, saved Norak, and became a successful bookstore owner. Would anyone sacrifice for Aleeya the way Teegan gave up her life on Earth to stay here in Norak with her love?

"We're well. And yourself?" Kazstrom sipped from a cup engraved with Teegan's shop logo. "How's the convention?" The bookcases in his background showed that he was at Bound Together Café & Bookstore.

"Are you causing trouble there, little sister?" Magnetti teased. He was promoted to Captain when Kazstrom took the Prime General's position.

"Me? Trouble? Are you referring to someone else?" Aleeya lifted a shoulder. "Phyllus is an interesting city. There's a huge disparity between the wealthy and the poor, but we've seen that in our travels. I wasn't expecting to see it in our neighboring region, though. I saw something that really bothered me in Phyllus. I want to help, but I know it's not our jurisdiction."

"You did the right thing by stepping back," Magnetti said. "Regional laws are tricky."

"I know." Aleeya made sure her voice carried a casual tone, not revealing any clue that she had other plans. She wasn't even sure why she had contacted them. Perhaps it was guilt. Perhaps it was her way of confessing, of letting her superiors know she walked on the edge of right and wrong. And hoped they'd catch her if she fell.

"What exactly did you see?" Kazstrom searched her face.

"Children begging in the streets. Children being abused. I saw a brother trying to protect his sister from an adult male who was about to hit them in public. These kids were dirty, and the alley they were in smelled like shit."

Kazstrom and Magnetti said nothing. They didn't have to. Kazstrom's cheek twitched, and he let out a breath. Magnetti's lips thinned into a tight line. Her brothers knew what life would have been like for them if they hadn't grown up in the orphanage. The orphanage gave them a home, and their corras were always on the side of children who needed help.

"Let me see what I can find out." Kazstrom was the Prime General. He had access to more information than she did.

"Elder Kai said he'd connect with the Phyllus officials. He's been busy in meetings, so I don't know the status of his inquiries. I don't want to bother you, Kaz. I'm sure you and Magnetti have things to do. I just wanted to keep you posted on current events here. Hypothetically, is there any way we can intervene on dire cases that are not in our region?" Though Aleeya followed rules, she wasn't against bending them once in a while.

Kaz lifted an eyebrow. "Rules are created for a reason, Aleeya."

"I know, but rigid rules will break absolutely. We both know circumstances change; they require a flexibility to encompass the situation on the ground."

"I agree with you," Magnetti said. "But we didn't make the rules. It's not a warzone, Aleeya. We can't enforce wartime laws. And we can't overrule planetary laws on a whim."

Aleeya contacted her brothers to talk about her issues. She hoped they could help her achieve a unique solution. But she should have known better than to place them in such a difficult position.

Malastrom! Blackened stardust! She wasn't thinking at all. She shouldn't have talked to them. She shouldn't have given them any inkling of her intention. Because if things blew up in her face, she didn't want her brothers going down with her.

Aleeya steered the topic elsewhere. "I've met a lot of interesting cosmic beings. I sat next to an Infinitii warrior, and I got to see a live performance by the Zeta Meida Band. I know they're popular in Norak too."

"They're outstanding." Magnetti busted out a song and started dancing.

Aleeya laughed. "With your moves, I'm surprised you're still without a mate."

He made a face. "Who says I'm without one?"

"I have met none of your female friends, so I can only assume."

"I can say the same about you, little sister."

He had her there. "Well, that's because they can't handle the extraordinary person I am. I have high standards. Who has time for dilly dallying, anyway? Warriors are busy."

"Kazstrom got lucky and found someone who could tolerate him," Magnetti said.

"You'll know when you meet the *one*." Kazstrom sipped again and looked at Aleeya. "You've always had high standards. You expect the best. You also give your best. Whatever it is you're facing, I know that you'll always do the right thing."

An indirect caution delivered with a casual flair. Kazstrom was a sharp knife that could cut through clutter with ease. He wasn't the Prime General for no reason.

Magnetti was just as brilliant. "Keep us posted on whatever you need. We're here for you."

"I will."

Kazstrom eyed her. "Regional laws are complicated. It's even trickier when you're there for an important convention and not assigned to a mission that's been approved and documented with the Elders. There's a big difference when a warrior goes on assignment that takes him or her down unpredictable routes and to other regions. Inter-regional laws are adjusted under rare circumstances. They are bent upon approval."

The approval she'd never receive and would never ask him for. Because asking him would disrespect El Lara and Elder Kai, who had already given her orders to stand down.

"Thanks for the reminder," Aleeya said. "Don't worry, I'll get over it. I'll be back in a few days."

Kazstrom and Magnetti both considered her, but said nothing.

"Anything else you'd like to add?" Kazstrom asked.

Aleeya didn't want to dishonor her legion. But she also didn't want to dishonor her beliefs. The mental struggle pounded her head until a sliver of logic slipped from her mind. *Sometimes you're pushed to the edge in order to right an injustice.* This was her choice to right a wrong. She'd take the consequences when they came.

"Yes, please have Teegan save me the new book releases from my favorite authors. And maybe some of those new moisturizing flowers El Lara prepared for the self-care section of the shop." Her hand went to the back of her neck, where the itch surfaced again.

Kazstrom smiled and nodded. "I'll let her know. See you soon. Stay out of trouble."

"Contact me if you need *anything*. I mean it." Magnetti placed a fist to his corra, and the two warriors clicked off.

Aleeya didn't waste any more time contemplating the "what-ifs." She made her decision, and she'd deal with the repercussions later. She drove to a clothing store and bought a few casual outfits of knit tops and high-tech pants. Going out on her own to probe a case wasn't in her plan when she packed for the convention. She didn't want to wear her Norakian warrior uniform while investigating. She was already defying orders and wearing her honorable uniform would add another layer of shame and dishonor. That kind of weight was too much for her to carry around.

In minutes, she changed into a high-tech denim and a purple jacket that had a back pocket for her bow and arrow, Xmark, and went to search for the human.

SEVEN

Kenzo

Kenzo stared at the virtual screen inside the Crime Division that displayed Brock's data and his death report. He hadn't expected Brock to die the way he did. Detective Ahlex mentioned the attack came from a roof of a nearby building while the female warrior spoke to Brock.

Who killed him? Who had been following him? Who was he working for?

Jeeto peeked out from Kenzo's chest pocket and narrowed his eyes and examined it.

"Who wanted him dead?" Kenzo muttered to himself.

"Well, it's obvious. It's someone who doesn't like him." Jeeto pointed his fuzzy finger at the image of Brock's desecration.

Kenzo shook his head and looked down at his blunt friend. Kenzo had wanted to interrogate Brock regarding Jella's whereabouts, besides his source for Bliss, but now he had to find another way. Where was the child? Was Brock working for a group of criminals?

A knock sounded on the conference room door, and Kenzo swiped at a different image on the virtual screen. Jeeto ducked back inside the pocket as Detective Ahlex ushered in Raskaa and his exhausted parents. Raskaa's mother and father sat on either side of him like bodyguards protecting their son. The parents inhaled a breath and straightened their backs, a move Kenzo had seen too many times from frightened parents who drew inner strength from the well of hope that their other child would be found soon.

Detective Ahlex nodded at Kenzo, signifying that he had ten minutes alone with them before the other Phyllus officials entered the building and cut off the interview. Kenzo appreciated the detective's help in allowing for this conversation to take place. They'd been working together for a while, and there was trust between them. No one else in his department knew about Kenzo's contribution to the city, which was fine. He didn't need the notoriety or the gratitude. Dangerous criminals needed to be punished regardless if he got paid for it.

The dirt on Raskaa's face and hair had been cleaned off, and he wore a fresh set of clothing.

Kenzo sat across from Raskaa and looked at the frightened kid holding onto brittle hope. In that moment, Kenzo decided he'd retrieve Jella. His brothers would want that child safe too.

"Thank you for letting me talk to you. I'm going to do my best to get your sister back home safely. To do that, I need your help."

Raskaa swallowed and tears welled in his eyes. "They separated us when we ran away from Brock. They injected her with something and took her in a dark autobus that zoomed above the city."

"Before they separated you, where did you stay? Do you remember anything about the location? Was there anyone else with you? Any other kids?"

Raskaa looked at his parents, and his mother rubbed his back. "Tell him what you know so he can get Jella back."

Raskaa met Kenzo's eyes. "We stayed in a dark room. There were a lot of beds... and bodies." His lips trembled. "There were other adults and kids there too, but I don't know them. They were sleeping." Tears streamed down his face. "They injected them with a glowing liquid. It glowed yellow. Some kids and adults fainted, and others went crazy. Everyone reacted differently to it. They separated us from those who showed..."

"Showed what, Raskaa?"

Could the glowing liquid be the same one that was injected into him during his abduction? This couldn't be a coincidence.

"Strange side effects." Raskaa shuddered. "This girl—she was younger than me—her chest glowed right before it exploded. There was this boy, he was a lot older than me, he gained extreme strength, and they ordered him to do stuff."

Silence hung in the room for a second, long enough for everyone to ground themselves for what came next.

"They told him to kill the ones who didn't show any side effects. And he listened. His eyes glowed and he strangled them. I closed my eyes and Jella's too, but we heard the screams." Raskaa swallowed and tightened the grip around his mother's hand. "The kid came to us, but when he looked at Jella, something changed in him, and he left us alone."

What the fuck were they doing to these kids? Kenzo clenched a fist. "I know how hard this is for you. You're reliving it while you're telling me. You're very brave, and that bravery is going to save your sister and all the others."

Raskaa pressed his lips together and nodded.

Kenzo exchanged a glance with Detective Ahlex. The anger in his eyes reflected the fire burning inside Kenzo. Something bigger was happening here, and Kenzo had to find out what. Could this case also be linked to his abduction? Maybe the same criminals were experimenting again, or maybe they never stopped. It was time he stopped them.

"Did they inject you with the same glowing liquid? Did you show any side effects besides sleepiness? Do you know or recognize the individuals who hurt you or the others?"

"They made us take Bliss to keep us sleepy. They were the same pills Brock made us sell. I heard them talking while I tried to stay awake. They planned to inject us with the glowing liquid in a few days. They didn't have time with me." His voice lowered. "I hope Jella is okay."

Kenzo whipped his gaze over to Ahlex. "We need to make sure his body is free of Bliss. It's more dangerous in a youthful body that can't process it quickly."

The detective nodded and typed into his virtual screen.

The detective settled the concerns on Raskaa's parents. "He'll be fine. We have the best doctors. I'll get a room set up for him right now."

Raskaa and Jella had been missing for only a week, and that was long enough for trauma to sink into their souls.

Kenzo reached across the table and tapped Raskaa's hand. "Perhaps someone is helping your sister right now."

Hope filled Raskaa's eyes. "I saw a colorful ribbon. It's bright and beautiful. It was just a flash. Jella is my fraternal twin, so I'm connected to her. I can sense her in ways my parents can't." He turned to them, and they smiled. "I can feel her fear, but it's not as strong as before. I think they gave her a lot of Bliss to keep her asleep." He pointed to his head. "Jella has a telepathic mind and can heal herself quickly."

Maybe her ability kept her and Raskaa safe from that boy. Kenzo would love nothing more than to continue asking questions, but fatigue weighed on Raskaa and his parents. Kenzo had enough to work with for now. Bliss was a sedative for the children. But what was the bright liquid that was injected into their bloodstream? It had to be something potent that could alter the body so significantly. Could it be the same solution he had received during his torture?

"Thank you for all the details. You're very brave. Everything you've told me is extremely helpful. If you remember anything else, let me or Detective Ahlex know. This is my contact information." Kenzo sent his data over to the parents' smart bracelets. "In a few minutes, the other Phyllus officials will want to hear what you've just told me. Tell them the truth, but mention nothing about me. I like to work alone. It's how I get things done."

"We understand." Raskaa's father rose from the chair. "We know how you work. That's why we'd like to hire you to get Jella back. We'll pay you anything."

Kenzo lifted a hand. "Don't worry about the payment. I'll do my best to get her back." *I promise*, was what he wanted to say, but he learned promises were tricky. He had promised to keep his younger brother safe and failed. So he was careful with that kind of pledge now.

Fifteen minutes later, Kenzo left through the back door of Ahlex's office so he wouldn't have to bump into the other detectives. He slid into his Bullet T53 and his vambrace buzzed with a message from Tab.

"I've located a facility that's producing Bliss for Atrium. Want to check it out?"

"Absolutely. You have perfect timing. Send the address over."

Tab replied, "Okay. Do you need me to go with you?"

"No." Kenzo clicked off before Tab could ask another question. He didn't want to worry his friend since he didn't know what awaited him at the facility.

Jeeto jumped out of his pocket and plopped onto the passenger seat like a stuffed toy. Kenzo appreciated that his pet-friend had remained quiet during the chat with Raskaa. Normally, the nosy animal wanted a piece of the action.

"Why are you smiling? This is serious stuff." Kenzo read the address Tab sent through, searched for the facility's location on his screen, and steered his Bullet T53 in that direction.

"I know something you don't."

Kenzo lifted a brow. "Do you know where the missing kid is? Because if you do, and you're not telling me, I'd be livid."

Jeeto angled his head. "No, I don't know where the kid is. What kind of animal do you think I am? I love kids. Keep your face on the road." He pointed to the windshield. "You have somewhere you need to be. You have things to do. The plan is in motion, and you can't avoid it."

Did Jeeto accidentally eat something he wasn't supposed to? This talk was out of character for him.

"What are you talking about? Why are you acting so strange? And why are you talking in riddles? What can't I avoid? I should stop feeding you so much food. When you're full, your brain goes missing."

"Now that's absurd. Food and I are best friends, okay?" Jeeto rubbed his round belly. "If you stop feeding me, I'll stop helping you."

Kenzo laughed. "Help me with what? Right now, you're helping deplete my credits from all the food I feed you."

"I'm helping you find the answers you've been waiting for. It's been over five solar cycles, my friend." Jeeto's voice sounded years wiser. His mischievous expression changed into a serious face that Kenzo didn't recognize. The gleaming eyes appeared like they could see things he couldn't.

What the fuck is going on with Jeeto?

Kenzo turned his attention back to the road, but stole a few glances at his pet-friend, making sure he was okay.

Jeeto jumped onto the dashboard and looked ahead. "I'm fine, don't worry about me. Worry about your ass."

"What?" Kenzo would have laughed, but the humorless expression on Jeeto's face told him something unexpected was about to happen.

Right now, he wasn't in the mood for unpleasant surprises.

EIGHT

Aleeya

Aleeya drove to the Crime Division, hoping to ask Detective Ahlex a few more questions regarding Brock. Then she saw the human male and thanked fate for the timing. He scowled as he entered his sleek sports rider and sped off.

A wave of energy slammed into her and tingled her skin. No, the tingles came from *underneath* her skin. It was tangible, yet intangible. Blackened stardust, she wasn't making any sense. The energy massaged her scalp until warmth bloomed around her head and neck. The warmth flowed down her body like liquid heat, igniting her cells and nerves. His face flashed in front of her and lingered for a few seconds before disappearing.

What the hell was happening?

This sensation was stronger than anything she'd ever felt. It was not a discomfort like the itching on her neck, nor was this the quiet energy that had clung to her at the beginning of her trip. That energy was a gentle warning that chilled her bones.

This frequency echoed in her memory. She couldn't grasp how she understood that. She just did.

What was it trying to tell her? What was it about this human male that knocked her senses alive? This odd vibration soothed her like a poem. How did she even connect to that analogy? She didn't know. It came from an ancient place, somewhere deep inside her she didn't know existed.

This human called to her on a strange level, and she needed to find out why. His actions in the alley rendered him a kidnapper, whom she wanted to kill, but the energy he gave off illustrated a new aspect that intrigued her. Was he the reason for her presence in Delleon? Or was her mind playing tricks on her?

No, it couldn't be. As a Norakian warrior, she trained to cut through the muck to find that clarity. Distractions could be the difference between victory and defeat. His frequency wasn't trying to distract her. It was trying to... *remind* her.

Of what? Was that possible? *Anything is possible.* That was the mantra that she recited during her years in training. Possibilities were limitless.

She forced herself to stop analyzing to deal with practical matters. Where were the boy and his sister? Everything else could wait.

Aleeya followed him, giving him enough distance so he wouldn't spot her. What was he doing at the Crime Division? Was he there for questioning?

Regardless of his unique frequency, if she discovered proof that he was a child abuser, she'd kill him. Children abusers were the worst scum in the Cosmos. These children could've been her. She thought back on her days at the Cosmic Corra. That place truly saved her life, her corra, and her soul. Her teachers became her parents, her orphan brothers and sisters became her true siblings. It wasn't until her teen years that she fully embraced every one of them. They filled her void. They made her better.

They were the reasons she had to rescue these kids, despite the consequences.

An itch sparked on her neck and she reached back to scratch it. She made a mental note to buy a different moisturizer on her way back.

The shiny gunmetal sports rider headed into a section of the city with busy traffic. Aleeya's Bug-Z coupe with its cute ears couldn't move as fast as his. She allowed a few autobuses, long ships, and personal riders to cut in front of her.

Where was he going? Was he leading her to the child?

NINE

Kenzo

Kenzo drove around and surveyed a street filled with distribution centers for paper goods, pet supplies, cyber security analysis, and other businesses. He eyed the white brick building with a metal plate that read "Office Management" company, which really described nothing.

He steered his car past the building and entered an adjacent parking lot. He activated the cloaking mode on the Bullet T53, making it invisible and parked on the ground level, away from the rest of the personal riders, delivery vans, and autobuses. A docking station for spacecraft appeared on the upper level.

"You stay here and monitor my car." He patted Jeeto's tuff of blue hair.

"Okay." Jeeto stretched out on the dashboard. Though the serious demeanor from earlier vanished, Kenzo wondered what had happened to his pet. He'd dig into it later.

He made his way toward the brick structure by cutting through the woods separating the two parking lots. He sat on a large rock that gave him an open view of the three-level building with barely any windows. Three visible cameras covered the front entrance. The back area and the interior would have cameras too, no doubt.

At a glance, the facility didn't appear open for visitors or even workers. Only two personal riders were parked near the front entrance, probably belonging to the security guards. Or were they decoys? An empty warehouse was the perfect facade to hide illegal things. He checked the time on his leather vambrace. He'd wait another ten minutes to see if anyone would leave for the evening before he made his move.

Was this facility only creating Bliss? Or were they producing valuable medicine that was stolen, manipulated, or used for other purposes? Even decent medicine could be lethal with an incorrect dosage.

The silence brought his mind back to the female warrior. The face and the fire in her eyes increased his heart rate again. *Fuck.* What was wrong with him? He wasn't moving a muscle, and yet his heart pounded like a cardio workout.

Was she looking for him? That theory appealed to him. Despite his better judgment, he wanted her to find him.

A vision of his brothers' body parts flashed before him. Chills rushed down his body, and pain gripped his chest as he remembered the torture. Grief clawed at his heart. His hands shook as he took in deep breaths to help control the sudden symptoms that crippled him.

I will avenge you. I won't forget you.

He repeated those words in his mind as he breathed in and out. He'd never been more cognizant of his breathwork until now. It quieted his mind and helped him release unprocessed energy, or whatever it was. He convinced himself that the only way to heal—to eradicate this illness—was to get his vengeance. It was the closure he needed. Vengeance was the medicine to his disease. The irony of it sickened him, but it was the truth.

A few minutes later, his body calmed as if nothing had happened.

Kenzo turned his attention to the evening sky that arrived with dark pinks and purples. The bugs from the woods buzzed and annoyed him. He swatted them away. But unlike the tiny and pesky mosquitoes on Earth, these Terrakado buggers were the size of a wasp that didn't budge until he squashed a few flat on the rock's surface.

Compared to the one moon on Earth, the three orbs glowing before him portrayed a different portrait. One glowed pink with a light blue aura, another illuminated yellow with a golden rim around it. The third one radiated blue with a purple haze encircling it. The magnificence and magic of them mesmerized him. One day, he vowed to take a mini vacation and visit one of them. That kind of galactic trip wasn't difficult to attain on this planet.

Ten minutes passed, and no deliveries arrived, and no one exited the building. Kenzo wasted no time, jumped off the rock, and maneuvered along the edge of the woods, trying to find a spot with no cameras. He wandered around the back to a window above a dumpster. One camera pointed toward the side of the building with the wide doors.

Kenzo leaped onto a dumpster lid, cracked open a window, and waited a moment for an alarm. When nothing came, he climbed into a storage room. Empty plastic tubes, bottles, paper supplies, towels, and other miscellaneous things packed the metal racks, bookcases, and cabinets. He strode to a door, and it creaked slightly as it opened into a large laboratory. Plastic containers filled with the drug, Bliss, sat on the white countertops. More containers with the orange pills crammed the cubicles behind the glass panels.

Kenzo strode to a desk with a stack of folders that hadn't

been filed away. He grabbed the top folder and flipped through the data. He was grateful that Tab took him to a doctor who activated the language codex within his brain via a beam of energy. The human brain was an undiscovered masterpiece. Humans hadn't mastered the full potential of their brain. Now, Kenzo could read the universal language simply because that mechanism, that ability, was now active.

He opened to a page listing the ingredients of Bliss, categorized as a sleeping agent. The document showed a long list of chemicals only a scientist or doctor could decipher. He flipped to the next page, and his eyes locked on the document with the letters "C.S.". Someone handwrote the word "dangerous" in a small penmanship at the bottom corner. He would've missed it if he hadn't been searching for clues.

Questions bombarded Kenzo. What did the "C.S." stand for? Was it a new drug? And who sat at this desk? Was it a doctor concocting something he knew was dangerous? Was the danger intentional? Or was it a side effect?

Kenzo found a map at the back of the folder, detailing sections of the building. He checked the other folders, and they all had an imprint of the building's layout, which meant these folders were for important individuals who needed to know the blueprint. Someone had highlighted the basement area. He didn't know what it meant, but his gut told him something informative was there.

Kenzo followed the map, and sure enough, the basement held a massive translucent tank filled with yellow, glowing fluids with a robotic claw stirring the liquids. At the far end of the basement, orange Bliss pills traveled on a quiet conveyer belt that dumped them into a large cart.

Was this the glowing chemical "C.S."? If not, then what was it? A feeling told him these were harmful liquids. He didn't know how he knew it, but he trusted his gut. Why wasn't anyone monitoring this production? A couple of scenarios crossed his mind. Maybe they'd been producing them for so long, they had confidence in their machines to produce without hiccups? There could be hidden cameras monitoring, and if so, they had images of him.

It didn't matter. The vibes in this place made him cringe. He was going to destroy it. But first, he had to make sure there was no one else in this building. What if there were hostages? What if this location was a hideaway for more deadly experiments?

He glanced around and discovered a computer by the wall. As he approached, it sensed him and turned on. A virtual monitor expanded, giving him glimpses of several camera angles. He noted two cyborgs in gray uniform with red vambraces. They carried blasters wandering around at the front entrance. Other than that, he didn't see or hear anything.

Satisfied that there were no innocent civilians, Kenzo pulled out the blaster on his belt, shot holes into the tanks, and liquids spilled out onto the floor. The chemical came in contact with the air and hissed as part of the substance turned into steam. The toxic fumes smelled like gas and tightened his throat. He knew he didn't have much time, and if he were to fire another blast, he'd die from the explosion.

"Where's the child?" The female warrior appeared in front of him.

Shock and delight slammed into Kenzo. He faced her and didn't reply. Explanation took time, and he had none.

She eyed the blaster in his hand. "What are you doing here? What is this substance? It's flammable." She covered her nose with her hand.

"I'll explain later. We need to get out of here. Now."

She didn't object as the fluids seeped over the floor and

hazardous fumes steamed up the room. "You're difficult to track down. Where did you take the child?"

"We'll talk about that later. Go. This place is about to explode." He let her go first and sent a blast into the room. He rushed out, shut the door, heard electricity crackle as he ran back to the storage room, and jumped out the window. A boom erupted as the warrior landed with him on the ground. "This way." He fled toward the woods as the building blew up in flames.

The tension and anxiety sent a wave of tremors down his body. The muscles on his legs cramped, but he pushed forward. *Fuck, not right now.*

Images of his torture flashed in and out, bringing back the fear, the pain, and the hopelessness of what he'd endured. When would he be able to remove these physical and emotional symptoms? When would he no longer be a victim?

He didn't want her to see him this way. It was a stupid thought, given the dire circumstances, but it was there. Once they were three feet inside the woods, he braced a hand on a tree trunk, and his breathing increased. He released heavy exhale for every inhale.

She eyed him. "Are you okay?"

When he didn't respond, she stepped closer. Something peculiar happened at that moment. The muscles on his legs relaxed, and his breathing calmed. His heart rate slowed, and the muscle tremors faded. A strange calmness soothed him.

Kenzo looked at her and felt her energy envelop him. Her presence eased his ailment. Why her?

She waved a hand across his face. "Hello? Are you okay?"

He blinked, blew out a slow sigh, nodded, and straightened himself. "Yes. The toxic fumes got to me." That wasn't a complete lie. Besides, how was he supposed to explain everything to her? He didn't even know her. Would she even care to listen?

Did she sense this odd connection between them? Why was she concerned about his well-being instead of demanding answers?

"Where's the child?"

He spoke too soon. He admired her persistence, but this was not the time to chat.

"Later. Shh." He held a finger to his lips and gestured to the two cyborgs who ran out of the front entrance of the building. Fire engulfed them as they dropped to the ground.

He should rush to his Bullet T-53, but he feared the action would cramp him up again. As long as he was out of immediate danger, he could spare a moment for his body to calm.

"What's going on here? What are *you* doing here?"

Up close, she was even more attractive. Her white hair was in a side braid like twisted clouds. Heavenly. A few strands swayed across her face like angelic whispers. Abstract codes adorned her forehead and the side of her face like beautiful hieroglyphics. They glowed when she narrowed her eyes at him.

He didn't know why, but he wanted to see that fire in her eyes again. "It's none of your business."

As expected, fury sparked in those brown eyes. "You're going to tell me, or you're going to get hurt." She glanced at his legs where the muscles had cramped.

Kenzo crossed his arms and smirked. "I can ask you the same question. What are *you* doing here?"

"Looking for you."

His heart thudded. "I guess I'm no longer a poogul? I have to admit you're the first female to associate me with the ugliest and stinkiest animal on this planet."

A smirk slid onto her face. "Well, I'm honest. I say it how I see it. What's a human doing in Delleon?"

"What's a female warrior doing in Delleon?" he retorted.

She stared at him and his skin tingled. He swore the silence hissed as it seduced the energy between them. Then she smiled, and his bulge hardened. *What the fuck?*

His body was no longer in traumatic mode, it had moved onto something entirely different. He preferred the latter any day, but the sudden change baffled him. How could she make him react this way?

This was out of his sphere.

Kenzo had no control over what his body did when it came to her. He didn't even know her, but he wanted to kiss that determined face that demanded answers. He wanted to thread his fingers in her heavenly hair. He wanted to see a different fire in her eyes. The kind that lured a man to hell, and he'd go willingly. He should get back to his car, but an invisible pull kept him anchored.

This powerful attraction perplexed him.

"Why are you kidnapping children?"

The question broke through the insanity in his mind. "I don't kidnap children."

"Then where's the child from the other day? You took him from me."

"I *saved* him."

She angled her head and the abstract symbols on her face glowed. "Then where is he?"

"Home with his parents."

She gave him a suspicious look. "Where does he live?"

"You don't trust me."

"I'm cautious. You haven't proven yourself trustworthy. For all I know, you could be lying about everything. I've met you twice. The first time you took a kid away. This time, you blew up a building. At the moment, the evidence doesn't support you."

Kenzo admired the clarity of her mind. Based on that, he knew she wasn't a simple warrior sticking her nose in other people's business. This warrior was sharp and had an unwavering standard that some would call stubbornness.

Damn him for finding that attractive. No matter what he told her right now, she wouldn't believe him. She needed time to study and dissect him. He saw that in her eyes. The thing was, he didn't have time.

"Tell me, why do you care what happens to that child? What's in it for you? Do you have permission to run around Phyllus looking for missing kids?"

She glared at him. "I don't need permission to do what's right. If more people cared, then fewer children would suffer. Nothing is in it for me. Children are the most vulnerable, and we need to keep them safe."

He read the truth in her words and in her demeanor. The calm and firm tone could command a king. She didn't wear her warrior uniform today. Dressed in a casual jacket and high-tech denim, she still looked stunning, seductive, and powerful. Her metal vambrace peeked out from under her sleeves.

"Then we have something in common. I don't like to see children suffer, either."

She studied him. "Why did you blow up that building?"

Kenzo glanced toward the fire and knew the officials would arrive soon. Someone in the adjacent building would have called it in. Or the cyborgs could have alerted their leaders before they died. Whatever the reason, it wasn't safe for them to remain there any longer.

"We need to go. It's not safe to stay here."

"Give me the location of the child." Stubbornness had to be her nickname.

"I'll give it to you later. Believe me, I'm not a kidnapper."

Sirens echoed, and he strode back toward the other parking lot where his Bullet T53 parked.

"Says every kidnapper on the planet." Twigs crunched as she followed him.

Kenzo whirled around to face her, and her fist came flying at him. He blocked it, swerved, and threw a fist back at her. She dodged it successfully, and a smile bloomed on her face.

Though time was scarce, he dueled with her. Their bodies slammed into each other, and powerful punches whirled at shoulders and necks. Arms windmilled, and legs swung and kicked. She was a spectacular fighter.

One thing occurred that hadn't happened in five years. His muscles didn't tighten during the fight. Horrific images didn't intrude his mind. In fact, his mind was clear, allowing him to focus. Was it possible that she could tame his PTSD symptoms?

When their arms intertwined, he stared into her brown eyes, where the gold rims of her irises glistened. The air stilled, or did he forget to breathe? *Fuck.* This star-being was messing with his head. Energy sizzled between them. He'd never experienced that odd sensation before. In that sudden stillness, nothing else existed but her. Her presence, her breath, her scent; they overwhelmed him. Something familiar and something unfamiliar came together all at once, confusing the hell out of him.

Curiosity flashed across her eyes, and she swung, buckling his knee. Confusion muddled his brain, and he crashed to the ground on his ass. Shock and embarrassment washed over him as a victorious grin spread across her face.

Worry about your ass. Jeeto's words rang in his head.

Did Jeeto know? This couldn't be a coincidence. This entire scenario was too bizarre. Kenzo jumped to his feet and met her amused look.

"You caught me off guard."

"In battle, always be on your guard."

Damn it, he didn't need her to teach him how to fight. This odd event was throwing him off balance, irritating him. Sirens blasted closer.

He walked up to her, testing the energy between them. She sucked in a breath, revealing that she also felt this inexplicable chemistry. "Maybe I wanted to fall. Maybe I wanted to look at you from that angle." His voice was low.

Her eyes widened and she shifted her heels.

The statement unsettled her. *Good.*

She eyed him. "Why?"

"Because I like your face. I like your hair." He lifted a hand to brush away a loose strand. For a moment, her cautious demeanor softened. He used the opportunity to swipe a leg, causing her to fall.

Then Kenzo took off like the wind, wearing a wide smile on his face.

"Malastrom! You poogul shit!" She cursed as she rushed after him.

He could've told her everything, but she wouldn't have believed him. After what he just did, he was on her shit list.

"You're not going anywhere!"

The tone had him turning back. She pulled out an energetic bow and arrow from her back. They grew in size as she aimed a golden arrow at him. *Fuck me.*

"Catch me if you can."

Derangement and psychosis were the only plausible explanation for his taunt. Why the hell did he say that? What brain cells activated that stupidity?

It was too late; he gave the challenge.

Kenzo ran as fast as he could out of the woods, but the storm of arrows sprayed everywhere. The energetic arrowheads intrigued him. They maneuvered around the trees and shrubberies with flexibility, like they had their own mind and knew what to do, where to go. One punctured him in the right arm. The energetic arrowhead stung, dug into his flesh, and dissolved.

As he made his way out of the woods, he yanked out the wooden arrow spine and tossed it. He'd never been hit by an energetic arrow before, and it hurt like hell. Sirens blasted in the distance, suffocating the sounds of her chasing after him. He headed to his car, slipped inside, and reclined his seat in a horizontal position.

Jeeto jumped onto Kenzo's stomach.

Though his cloaking modality was on, Kenzo had to be cautious. "Keep quiet. We need to talk later."

Jeeto's ear perked, searching for something. "She just left."

His pet had a good radar for that. But why would the warrior leave without searching for him? Did she think he was dead or was close to dying? She wasn't the type to give up easily.

But relief settled in Kenzo. At least all he had to worry about was the wound on his arm. He remained still for a few minutes to catch his breath. But he didn't want to wait too long before the officials blocked the street off. He pulled out a small care kit from his side door and began soaking up the blood seeping through his jacket. Jeeto assisted him by placing a wound-clamp over the injury to stop the bleeding and patched it up. That would do until Tab could assist him.

"Thank you." Kenzo gave his pet a playful rub on his tummy. "I'll get you something delicious tonight."

His pet offered a cute face.

Kenzo looked at Jeeto's smile. "You're acting strange today. What's going on?"

"This is exactly how it's supposed to happen." Jeeto snuggled into the blanket on the seat.

Kenzo inclined the seat, drove out of the parking lot, deactivating the cloaking ability that used up energetic fuel. He passed several city officials as they rushed to the explosion. Several aircraft also flew by.

Three miles away, he asked, "Did you know I was going to get hurt today?"

Guilt swam in Jeeto's eyes.

"Tell me."

Jeeto's eyes widened. "Does it really hurt?"

"Are you referring to my ass or my arm?"

Jeeto giggled. "Both. The arm was an unexpected addition that you added. You have free will. It was your decision that got you injured."

"Okay, pal. You need to disclose everything. How did she know I would be here today? Do you know where she went? How did *you* know I would fall on my ass?"

"I don't know where she went, but I'll talk better after dinner." Jeeto pulled the little blanket up to his chin, looking all cute and innocent.

"Fine."

Kenzo didn't press on. He needed time to let things sink in. Ever since he became a bounty hunter, he never imagined he would be the hunted. And now, he had challenged a lethal warrior to catch him.

What was he thinking?

TEN

Kenzo

Kenzo didn't know why, but he sent the female warrior Raskaa's home address. Maybe if he had given her that information at the beginning, his arm wouldn't be stinging right now as he sat in the kitchen waiting for Tab to retrieve the care kit. During their duel, Kenzo was close enough to access her vambrace's identification from his own.

Jeeto rushed to the living room, jumped onto the couch, and snuggled into a pillow, avoiding Kenzo. Nothing was going to stop Kenzo from getting the answer from his pet. But right now, he had more dire things to worry about.

Kenzo took off his jacket and shirt and examined the wound on his right arm. Tab placed the care kit on the table and removed the wound-clamp. Blood oozed from the wound, but he cleansed it with a sterilizing cloth, and sewed it up with a stitch-up device. Then he sprayed a flexible sealant over it, allowing his arm to move without irritating the wound.

Tab placed a hand on Kenzo's shoulder. "Take it easy on

that arm."

Tab had dark skin, a bald head, a white goatee that matched the eyebrows, and a sharp mind. Kenzo knew little about Tab's history, and Tab only knew about Kenzo's abduction and his desire for vengeance. Men didn't want to talk about pain and misery. Despite that, a mutual trust and friendship existed between them.

Kenzo thought about Jella and his mission. Both glared at him with urgency. Both mattered to him.

"It doesn't look that bad." Tab's brown eyes warmed. "I've seen worse."

Tab referred to the injuries Kenzo had obtained from the alien abduction that brought him to his planet. Gashes, puncture wounds, and scars covered his back, stomach, and legs. Those fucking bastards had prodded his body and injected him with many chemicals. It had taken months for his body to recover. Those experiments had also toyed with his mind. Maybe that was how he understood Jeeto's way of communication, which to anyone else was just random animal noises.

Kenzo's ability to speak and understand the universal language was the only beneficial thing that came from his abduction. Despite all the scars on his body, the worst wounds were the ones that were unseen. The ones that lived in the dark with the power to disable the mind.

The scar twitched on his abdomen like it remembered the trauma. A part of him believed he deserved all the misery. Guilt crept up his spine, reminding him he was alive, but his brothers weren't. The night Kenzo escaped his captors, Tab rescued him from the alley and gave him a place to stay. Kenzo owed Tab his life.

"You're right, it's just a minor wound. It'll heal fast." Kenzo slipped his arms carefully into the sleeves of his shirt.

Tab limped to put the care kit back into the cabinet. "A

wound is still a wound. You need to treat it with care otherwise it could turn into something drastic."

The apartment they shared had two bedrooms with soft yellow walls and a kitchen spacious enough for two bachelors. A ripped couch with colorful pillows, two worn armchairs that were still comfortable, and a round coffee table with dents and scratches furnished the quaint living room. Two bookcases filled with books sat along one wall. Several piles of books were on the floor, all of which belonged to his friend.

Tab returned to the kitchen and sat down. He scratched the back of his neck and let out a long sigh filled with worry. The wrinkles on his face deepened.

"What's wrong?" Kenzo asked.

"There are more facilities like the one you went to today. They're all over Delleon. There's one in a neighboring region. I'll let you know the exact locations when I get them."

"Which region?"

"Norak." Tab's long dark fingers curled into a fist on the table. A movement Kenzo hadn't seen before. "Atrium is creating more deadly drugs, which means Malixx knows something. It's his company."

Kenzo had never met Malixx, the star-being that started Atrium, the largest pharmaceutical company in Delleon. It created top-notch medicine and vitamins that were distributed all over Terrakado. Kenzo researched Malixx and found him intelligent, arrogant, and cold. But those qualities didn't make an individual a killer. However, based on the recent events, things had changed.

His suspicion that Atrium was responsible for his brother's death solidified, but he needed proof. "I have a feeling Malixx, or Atrium, is responsible for my capture and my brothers' deaths. I think they injected a similar glowing liquid into me back then. That's the connection I'm going by."

"Perhaps we have a common enemy." As a mail clerk at Atrium, Tab had access to critical information since he wasn't a threat. He worked in a small department that carried out simple responsibilities. With his limp, Tab preferred something easy on his body.

"How did you find out about the locations?" Kenzo asked.

"I placed a tracer on one of the secretary's computers. She monitors all the properties owned by Atrium."

"Are you sure no one saw you? I don't want anything happening to you. I thought you were taking your time investigating the company."

"I'm running out of patience." Tab's eyes locked onto Kenzo, and a fierceness glimmered in them.

Patience was one of Tab's virtues. Something must have escalated his actions.

"Did something happen? I never asked about your family. I figured you'd tell in your own time."

"And I thank you for that." He rubbed a hand over his face. "Talking about a dark past brings it back to life. Back then, I didn't have the strength for it, but I'm ready now."

Kenzo understood because he had monsters he didn't want to deal with either. "What changed?"

"A strong feeling? An innate knowing?" Tab lifted a shoulder. "I'm not sure. Maybe I'm sick of waiting, of working for a company that I know is creating harmful products. They're responsible for the missing children. I just know it in my gut, but I can't prove it. What is Atrium's purpose?"

Tab's jaw tightened, and sadness weighed on his face. The last time Kenzo witnessed this sorrow was many years ago, when a little girl was crying from the news that her parents recently died. That little girl's yearning for her family had broken Tab. It took him several months to recover.

"Malixx is an intelligent scientist and a shrewd

entrepreneur," Tab said. "He has his hands in several high-tech businesses. He's smart and inserts himself with the important crowd."

Kenzo had seen Malixx on the screens promoting his new business ventures and products that could improve lives. He'd seen similar promotions when he was on Earth, where companies tried to sell their innovations with pretty pictures and promises without disclosing the side effects. There was no such thing as a perfect product. Yes, they'd list cautions on the bottle in tiny letters with scientific wording that only the few would understand.

"I'm going to find out if Malixx works alone or with someone else," Kenzo said.

"There's not a lot of information about him available. He keeps a low profile."

"We'll find a way. I have my own way of investigating, remember?" Kenzo told him about his day, hoping to cheer up his friend. "I rescued a child today, but his sister is still out there. They're twins, so he has a special connection with her. He sees flashes of what she sees and feels. I want to dig further to see if I can locate her."

Tab's eyebrows pinched together. "What does he see?"

"A pretty colorful ribbon of light. That could be anything."

"It can't be..." Tab looked at Kenzo and hope filled his eyes. "I think I know what he's talking about."

"What?"

"There's a powerful bridge in Norak called the Aurora Matrix. It's a massive ribbon of light that gives the land its energy. That could be where the little girl is."

Kenzo flipped through his memory. He had seen images of the bridge on the screen, but he never really paid attention to it because there were many extraordinary things on this planet that awed him. "Have you been there?"

Tab nodded. "I used to live there. It's a beautiful region. Norak isn't a small region, so it's going to take time. We can take a trip there and see what we can find out. Maybe you can ask Detective Ahlex if he has any connections with the Norakian officials. That'll make the search easier."

Kenzo could ask him, but politics could take time that the child didn't have. Besides, he preferred to do things his way.

Kenzo looked at his friend. "What happened to your family?"

"An assassin killed them, and I came to Delleon looking for him."

"Did you find him?"

Tab nodded and gestured to his leg. "I killed him and earned this limp."

Jeeto's snore pulled Kenzo's attention over to the couch. It had been a strange day full of surprises.

Tab changed the subject. "How did you get injured?"

"A female warrior," Kenzo said.

Tab cocked his head. "Really? Who is she? What did you do?"

"She thinks I'm one of the kidnappers. It's just one of those incidents where I need time and patience to explain everything. I didn't have any of that. Neither did she."

Tab waved a disapproving finger. "That's a dangerous game you're playing. If she is a true warrior, she'll be after you."

If only Tab knew about the challenge. "She's not from this area. Fierce like a lioness." Very attractive, Kenzo wanted to add. But he kept that thought to himself.

"You need to be extra careful. You don't know who she is. Maybe she works for Atrium."

Tab was right, but something told Kenzo she wasn't. It was the way she demanded information about those children that told him she cared.

"I'm aware of that."

"Did you destroy that facility?" Tab inquired.

"I did. They were making Bliss pills and glowing chemicals."

"I heard the scientists at Atrium whispering about harvesting organs or something like that. I'll keep my ears open and let you know what I find out."

"Good. We'll need to destroy all their facilities."

Something beeped on a small screen underneath the kitchen cabinet. Tab strode over, pressed his thumb on the screen and swiped it.

He whirled to Kenzo with a smile. "I have the facility locations in Norak, and I have two in Phyllus."

"Sync it to my vambrace. I need to survey the area in Phyllus first before we decide to do anything." Kenzo rose from his chair.

"You're going now? You're still injured. It's dark out."

"Exactly. This is the perfect time to play ninja. I'm fine. You did an exceptional job tidying me up." Kenzo flexed his arm.

Tab frowned. "You never listen."

"I do. I listen to you. But I've learned to listen to my gut as well. If I had done that more often, I wouldn't have so many regrets."

Normally, Kenzo preferred to keep his emotions to himself. But something about the moment inspired him. "I haven't said this enough, but I owe you a lot. You took me in when I didn't have anyone. You taught me about your world, about star-beings and how to adapt to life on this planet." He walked up to Tab, and they stood eye to eye. "Life for me would have gone sideways if it weren't for you. You gave me the mental drive to survive. So, thank you for watching over me."

Tab pushed his eyebrows together. "Why are you getting sentimental? Are you planning to do something stupid?"

"No, I just want you to know that I appreciate you."

"You were never a talker. And now you're spewing out long sentences like you're some poet."

Kenzo chuckled. "What's wrong with poetry?"

"Nothing." Tab narrowed his eyes. "But from you? It's... strange. Did this woman kick you in the head?"

No, but I fell on my ass for her. Literally and figuratively.

"Consider yourself lucky, old friend. I guess you have a way of making me talk. You would've been a great interrogator."

Tab barked out a laugh of disbelief.

"You were a reporter before, so you're good at investigating. You know how to unlock people." Kenzo went over to the couch where Jeeto slept.

Tab stiffened as something flashed in his eyes.

"Sorry, I didn't mean to—"

"Nothing to be sorry for. The past is hard to forget sometimes. You know how it is."

Every man had his own secrets.

When Jeeto opened one eye, Kenzo said, "You stay home. I'll be right back. I'll postpone our chat until later. Tab, can you give him the special entree tonight?" Dinner that night consisted of flavored meat and vegetables.

"I'll take good care of him. You be careful."

Kenzo grabbed his jacket and slipped into it. The rip on the sleeve needed repair and the bloodstain needed cleansing. Both tasks could wait.

Outside, he inhaled the cool night air and strode toward his car. The female warrior leaned against his Bullet T53 like she owned it.

How the fuck did she track him down?

ELEVEN

Aleeya

Aleeya crossed her arms as she leaned against the fake kidnapper's gunmetal sports rider. It was an exceptional form of artwork that probably cost as much as a spacecraft. He approached with wide strides, wearing the same high-tech denim and tailored jacket as before. It shouldn't make him seem rugged and sexy, and yet that was the result.

The powerful energy that gripped her when she trailed him in her Bug-Z coupe grew prominent when they battled in the woods. During that time, she swore the consistency of her body shifted, like her blood flowed faster and her corra beat to a rhythm she didn't recognize. How in the hell was all that possible?

When he braced against the tree trunk in pain, she should have demanded answers from him. He was in no position to fight her then. Why didn't she? The vibration radiating from him kept her at bay. Not only that, but his energy also mingled with hers like they knew each other.

Why was she so drawn to him?

As he approached, the lights from the building allowed her to study him. He stood about six feet, a few inches taller than her. He had an angular face with high cheekbones and a square jaw marked with scars. His tanned skin showed he'd been kissed by the two suns. The brown eyes slightly tipped at the corners were lined with dark lashes that added a layer of mystery and mischief. He had a mouth that sent her mind swirling with a wild imagination. The wild black hair along with the focused eyes rendered him a tiger looking for its prey.

"How did you find me?" The tone was more curious than annoyed.

"You offered a challenge that I couldn't resist."

The challenge surprised her. He had an edge that could cut dangerously deep if she weren't careful. She'd never met prey who wanted to be hunted. That excited her.

Her eyes ran over his arm, where her arrow had punctured him. The blood had dried, and, given the confidence of his stance, shoulders back and chest out, she concluded he was feeling no signs of discomfort. His defiance in revealing the boy's location had infuriated her, and she channeled that infuriation into her arrows when she aimed them at him, guiding them to puncture, not kill.

"That doesn't answer the question." He tucked his hands into his denim pockets and considered her.

The moment pulsed as they stared at each other, and a quiet understanding passed between them. If she could see energy in solid form, it would sparkle and hiss right now. Perhaps that was why she didn't give her bow and arrow, Xmark, the lethal intention of killing him.

She wanted answers. When she received his message on her vambrace, she went to check out Raskaa's home. Not only did she see him well, she also had a brief chat with the boy and his parents.

"Why didn't you tell me the truth from the beginning, Kenzo?" She discovered his name from the parents. "That would've saved you injury."

"Like someone I know, I can be relentless and stubborn." He eyed her. "Maybe I wanted to see how far you'd go." He lifted his injured arm, moved it up and down. "But I'll definitely reconsider my decision next time."

Aleeya let out a half laugh. "Stubbornness is friends with trouble."

"Does that mean we're friends now? Friends against a common enemy?" The brown eyes sparkled with another challenge.

That wasn't what she meant, but he smiled, and her stomach flipped, catching her off-guard. He was definitely trouble in a different arena. Her brain lost focus, and her legs wobbled. She shifted and stabilized herself against the sports rider. She didn't want to make a fool out of herself by stumbling.

This sudden reaction to this human was unfamiliar to her. "It's a start."

"You're welcome."

Her brain slowly climbed back up to her head. "For what?"

"For giving you the answer you've been waiting for. Did you visit Raskaa?" He gestured her aside as the doors to his sports rider slid open.

"Yes, I did. And thank you. His parents are grateful for what you did." Aleeya had discovered he was a bounty hunter who often did pro bono work. "Sorry for the injury."

He shrugged. "I taunted you. I deserved it."

"You did. On both counts."

He chuckled. "You know my name, yet I don't know yours."

"Aleeya."

He nodded slowly. "Aleeya, would you like to join me on a mission?"

Her eyebrows quirked suspiciously.

"If you've spoken to Raskaa's parents, then you know that their daughter, Jella, is still missing. The kidnapper injected a glowing agent into their captives. Raskaa was lucky to escape them. I've discovered a new facility that's producing this lethal chemical. I figure you'd want in." A sly smile curved on his lips. "Or you can consider this adventure as a date with me."

Aleeya brushed off the flirt as his energy continued to disturb her bodily systems. She had to concentrate on more important matters. She recalled the worry and anxiety from Jella's parents. They didn't give Aleeya a lot of details because they didn't know her. Kenzo knew more about the case. Could she trust him? She didn't know.

Kenzo slid into his seat and glanced back at her. "Coming?"

She looked around at the dark sky and quiet streets. More than half the region was probably asleep. Concern for the little girl coupled with this inexplicable curiosity to know him urged her into his rider.

Inside the compact space of the sports rider, energy pulsed. His presence wasn't one to ignore. It swirled around her like a seductive snake. She desperately wanted to investigate this enigma. It wasn't in her nature to let things go, especially when it piqued her interest. She had been bombarded with two distinct energies in the past few days. One appeared like a gentle warning of some sort. Malixx's face popped into her vision. What role did he play in all of this? The other energy belonged to him. It made her body aware of itself the way nothing had before. Why were these energies noticeable now?

She leaned back on the leather seat and examined the carved name on the dashboard: Bullet T53. She studied and admired the high-tech amenities. It was time to upgrade her personal rider to something more stylish. Not that she needed one to do her job. Her spaceship, *Sentra Five*, took her anywhere she wanted to go, but its size didn't accommodate for certain situations that required something smaller. Her cloud-mobile could transport her at the ground level, but it wasn't enclosed. Sometimes she just wanted a simpler form of transportation—not that Bullet T53 was a simple machine—she longed for something different and fun when she wasn't on duty or on some faraway mission.

"You never answered my question." Kenzo's voice brought her out of her reverie.

How did you find me?

Aleeya tugged at the hem of his jacket and retrieved the pin-point tracker she had placed there during their battle.

Disbelief washed over his face. "I guess we're even." He pulled up a virtual screen with a map.

She didn't forget he had accessed her vambrace without her permission, which annoyed her. "Perhaps." She grinned and enjoyed the shock pasted on his face. "No one has ever outmaneuvered you the way I have?"

He flicked her a gaze that held a remark he didn't share. Instead, he tapped his fingers on the steering wheel. "Would you believe me if I told you that it was all part of my plan? That *I* maneuvered you to tracking me down?"

She rolled her eyes. "I'd rather believe that we have four moons staring at us, and one had suddenly grown ears."

He barked out a laugh that was loud, genuine, and perfect. The kind that was let loose amongst friends, people you knew well. They didn't know each other, and yet she felt an odd connection to him. This spark occurred somewhere between their duel and her discovery that he did pro bono work for Phyllus citizens. She had met other human males before, but none had intrigued her the way this man had. In fact, no star-beings had ever stirred her this much.

What was his story? How did he get to planet Terrakado? Why did he stay?

"You're a spectacular fighter. Where are you from?" he asked.

She remembered their battle, and how his strength, precision, and swiftness made him a great opponent. "You're not so bad yourself. I'm a Norakian warrior."

His head whipped up in bewilderment. "This isn't a coincidence."

"What's not a coincidence?"

"You. Norak. What my friend, Tab, and I just talked about." Kenzo shook his head. "Every damn thing that has happened today. Things are relating in strange ways. Even my pet, Jeeto, is acting weird."

He has a pet. Something about that made her smile. However, the seriousness on his face stopped her from inquiring further.

"I've never believed in fate. But there are unexplainable things that are nudging me in this direction, and I can't seem to figure it out."

She resonated with that statement. "Someone once told me certain things weren't meant to be figured out. The Cosmos has its own plan. A plan within a plan within a plan. I stopped wondering because it gives me a headache."

He looked at her. "You say that now, yet you're investigating too. I see it in your eyes."

Blackened stardust. He read her like an open sky.

It was no use trying to hide the truth. "I convince myself now and then that I'm just a small piece in the cosmic puzzle. It makes things easier to grasp. Are you going to share this 'coincidence' with me?"

"Can you show me around Norak? I need to get there."

Aleeya pursed her lips. "Why? I want to know everything. Why do you want to go there? If you're bringing trouble, then I'm the first to stop you."

"Trouble is already there. Raskaa's sister might be trapped somewhere in Norak."

"What?" A thought bloomed in her mind. If Jella was in Norak, Aleeya had every right to investigate all she wanted. Norak was her jurisdiction. A plan formed in her head. She'd send orders and details to her soldiers to start a search. Each Norakian warrior had a faction of soldiers to assist them. "How do you know this?"

A virtual map popped up and red dots blinked. He swerved down a dirt road and activated the cloaking modality of his sports rider. It was the same brand her spaceship used to become invisible. Three dots moved on the virtual map.

Aware of her surroundings, she glanced at the darkness. "Where are we? And why are we stopping here?" She peeked out the window. Pebbles, dirt, and shrubberies. Her ears picked up on noise in the distance.

He focused his attention to the front of the main road. A second later, a longship and two personal riders drove by.

When they were long gone, Kenzo drove back onto the main road. "We're in Phyllus's Conservation area. I doubt the city has workers out here in the middle of the night. The sensory system told me we had company."

Still in cloaking mode, he pulled into the parking lot of a four-story brick building. He moved to an area away from the parked personal rider and one autobus. He stopped at a spot without the glow from the light posts, and they exited his rider.

"What's in this facility?" Aleeya followed him, staying in the shadows, using her vambrace to light a path. Her eyes scanned the area for danger.

"Bliss and other drugs. Bliss are the pills you saw in the facility I blew up, and Brock forced the kids to sell them to the public. There are other production sites throughout Phyllus. Maybe we'll find clues here that'll help find Jella. I want to look around first before we do anything."

The light from the glass entrance cast out into the darkness.

Aleeya clicked off the light from her vambrace as she circled toward the back of the building with Kenzo. The present moment showed her what a difference the past few hours had made to her attitude. Just earlier, she had been fighting with Kenzo, and now they were partners. Sort of.

She'd allowed nothing to distract her goal, and right now, Kenzo disrupted her mind with his presence and energy. She needed to find Jella, who was probably terrified. Aleeya understood that terror in her bones and knew what it could do to a child's psyche.

She wanted to trust Kenzo, but she had to be cautious. Besides her brothers, she couldn't depend on any other male. Her father abandoned her, and her ex-mates never stuck around. She had good reasons to be protective of herself. Yet, this yearning to understand him gnawed at her.

Pushing that thought away, she focused on the current task. A warrior should never deviate from her mission, especially during a critical moment. A tiny diversion could be the difference between life and death. She glanced at the two cameras on top of the building and wondered how many more were inside.

Kenzo took out his blaster and went up the stairs to the second floor. Aleeya drew her own blaster and stood ready, prepared for anything. Through the large window, she could see a cyborg in gray uniform with red vambraces, gripping the arm of a pink-skinned female with blue hair and could make out her fear through the glass.

"Please don't hurt me. I'm just a cleaner."

"What did you do with the documents? You're stealing data, aren't you? Don't lie to me." The cyborg squeezed her arm and waved his friend over.

"I'm not. Can't you tell the difference between organizing files and stealing documents? Why would I want your documents? Let me go!"

The cyborg lifted his arm and swung it at the female. Aleeya hissed, blasted at the two cameras on the top corners of the building, and activated an alarm. It screamed and the building flashed with lights. The cyborg pushed the female aside and shouted something into his vambrace. As he rushed outside, the pink-skinned female hid behind a desk.

Good, stay there.

Aleeya turned to Kenzo. "I'll take care of him, and you can save her and survey the area for other civilians."

Kenzo nodded, took off, and entered the building through the front entrance.

Aleeya fired at the cyborg, and his chest flashed a yellow glow. His body stumbled and blood oozed from his chest wound. Unfazed by her attack, he charged at her again. She fired at his head and flung a fist at his face when he came too close to her. She broke his nose, but no pain showed on his face. He whirled a powerful arm at her, and she blocked and kicked him. The force sent him skidding a few feet away.

Why wasn't he dying?

His chest glowed again, and she fired several more shots, aiming at the brilliant corra. A snapping sound came from his chest, and the glowing died. He thudded to the ground, but seven more cyborgs came from around the building.

Malastrom! She reached for Xmark and fired a golden arrow at them. Her bow and arrow connected to her energy. With her eyes, she captured a snapshot of her moving targets. With her mind, she told the arrow to multiply and amplify. *Target the corras. Aim to kill.*

The energetic arrowheads speared through their corras and dissolved, leaving the metal shaft of the arrow sticking through them. Unlike the wooden spines from the arrows she had steered at Kenzo, these were more powerful and made from the Norakian alloy, fortisium. Calling them forth required more energy from her body and mind.

Electricity crackled from the thudding bodies. What was in their corras?

One cyborg escaped her arrow and leaped at her. Aleeya didn't want to waste a golden arrow on him, so she fired with her blaster. He required three shots in the corra before he collapsed.

A sound pulled Aleeya's attention to the building. The pink-skinned female grabbed a lamp from a table and whipped it at the cyborg. The lamp broke, and the cyborg went after her. Kenzo sent several blasts into him as more cyborgs arrived.

Fear spiked in Aleeya as she rushed in to help.

TWELVE

Kenzo

Kenzo sent three more blasts into the cyborg's heart, and electricity sparked from his chest before he dropped to the floor. The chest cavity burst like a flower of flesh and metal. A blue heart of abnormal size bled out purple blood. It was bigger than two of his fists put together.

"Find a hiding spot." He gestured to the female who tried to help.

Aleeya charged in and fired a golden arrow at the three cyborgs. The single arrow replicated into six arrows. Two arrows penetrated each of the cyborgs.

Aleeya kneeled and examined the cyborg's body. "I've never seen a blue corra."

Kenzo was accustomed to this planet's word for heart. Most of the ones he'd seen were purple. "Neither have I. The size is bigger too."

"Are there any other civilians around?" Aleeya looked down the hallway.

"No."

The female star-being stood beside Aleeya. She wore a white uniform with a cleaning company's logo. "Those are engineered corras. They're not natural."

Aleeya got to her feet and checked the star-being's arm. "Are you all right? Did they hurt you? What's your name?"

"Lila. I'm fine." She rubbed her arm where a bruise bloomed. "Thank you."

Though Lila's body trembled, her eyes revealed a resilience that spoke of inner strength. Here was a survivor who had endured something tragic.

"You should go. They'll send a team over any minute now." Lila looked at the dead bodies.

"What's in this building? Do you know why there are so many cyborgs here? Are they producing the same drugs as the other facility that was destroyed?" Kenzo asked.

Lila pressed her lips into a tight line. "Worse."

Aleeya exchanged a glance with Kenzo. "What are they doing?"

"They're creating this dangerous drug called the Corra Spark. It's a change agent."

A connection clicked in Kenzo's brain. "Was that you who left a clue in the documents in the other building? I saw something with C.S. Was that a clue to the Corra Spark?"

"Yes. I know I'm just a cleaner and I should mind my business, but I can't unsee what I've seen. I have a daughter and I wouldn't want anything that cruel to happen to her. I saw what the drugs did to the individuals they tested on. I couldn't bear their screams. I left clues in all the facilities I was cleaning at. I know I'm risking my job, but it's so wrong..."

"Doing the right thing can be hard, but we need individuals like you to call it out," Aleeya said. "What kind of change agent is it? What does it do?"

"It changes the corra and the mind somehow. There was a lab in the basement of this building. I saw an experiment on an adult star-being a few days ago. He broke out from the restraints and fought the cyborgs, but then his body just burst. There's no one in the basement right now."

"Then it's the perfect time to demolish this shithole," Kenzo said. "Aleeya, can you accompany Lila home? I'll take care of this and come get you after. We need to hurry."

Fury sparked in Aleeya's eyes. "You can escort Lila home. I'm trained in blowing shit up."

"Look, we can stand here and debate all night long. I know you want to obliterate this place, but I'm a resident of Delleon, and I'm working with Detective Ahlex. So if I get caught, it'll be easy for me to explain why I'm here. But how would you explain it? This isn't your jurisdiction. Besides, I still need a partner to help find Jella."

She flared her nostrils. "The last thing I need is to drag Norak into this mess." With a calmer demeanor, she turned to Lila. "Is it okay if I accompany you home? You don't know me, but I'm asking you to trust me. I'm not one of them. We're trying to stop them."

Lila's brown eyes glowed slightly, but enough for Kenzo to notice. "I trust you." The firm words carried no hesitation. Perhaps it was because they just saved her life.

Once Aleeya and Lila were out of harm's way, Kenzo inspected the building once more. He found a lab with beakers, flasks, and tubes of bright liquids. Boxes of sealed tubes lined one wall, ready for delivery. He snapped a photo of the address with his vambrace and rushed to check out the other rooms. He broke into a locked room and snapped images of the diagrams posted on a wall. A virtual screen flashed when he entered, probably tripped by a sensor.

Kenzo swiped through the gut-wrenching images of kids

and adults being experimented on. Anger rose in him as he recognized some of their faces. These were the missing individuals he had been searching for.

His body shivered from the images of the sharp utensils. But it was the masks on the guards holding down the subjects that brought back his dreadful memory in vivid colors. A wave of sudden heat rose in him, and his body trembled from the muscle spasms.

When he was fighting the cyborgs, he should have experienced crippling symptoms like the unpredictable and uncontrollable violence, but they never came. Somehow, Aleeya's energy prevented that darkness from overwhelming him. She healed him without even knowing.

She was not here now, but just thinking of her relaxed him. He took in a slow breath and released it. Though the horrific images triggered his memory of what he'd suffered, he dug for inner strength to fight them. This was the first time in five years, where he successfully reached in himself and held something that could lead him to a way out. The idea that there was a way out sparked hope in him.

I won't let the trauma defeat me.

He inhaled and composed himself as the heat diminished and muscle spasms subsided. His body was his again.

With his vambrace, he accessed what he could on the computer. He didn't have time to analyze. His priority was obliterating this torturous hell. The somatic sensations rushed through him as realization piqued. The individual responsible for abducting and experimenting on him, his brothers, and these civilians was the same. His heart rate escalated, but it wasn't a psychosomatic symptom. This was fury and vengeance colliding in his chest, in his gut. He had waited five long years for a name and face. Now he had both. Malixx was a tangible answer that gave him a clear path. Malixx was culpable for his brothers' deaths and his torture.

Malixx will pay with every drop of his blood.

This revelation spiked a rage in Kenzo. He sat in his Bullet T53 and watched the fire incinerate parts of the building. He discovered a fireproof tarp and covered parts of the basement, leaving some evidence for Detective Ahlex. The incineration reflected the stormy vengeance for those he loved, and for those innocent lives Malixx and his company took.

As the fire burned externally, the internal fire burned his trauma, eating it away slowly. He imagined the flames devouring the agonizing memories that trembled his body. His brothers' screams, the icy blades cutting into his flesh, and the chemicals that tore through his body turned to soot. They became ashes floating in the air, taking one particle of pain away at a time. As the fire carried away his mental misery, he gained the ability to reflect with clarity. This critical moment severed the traumatic link between the past and the present.

Aleeya pushed his healing forward. When he silenced his mind, he sensed her energy lingering around him. A new flame sparked in his heart, but it had nothing do with the destruction in front of him. This kind of flame kindled something else, something that illuminated possibilities he never dreamed of.

With a rational mind, Kenzo steered his attention back to Malixx. What was the purpose of all his madness? Why did he create the Corra Spark? Was he simply a wealthy and insane star-being who wanted to play God? Or was he after something else?

THIRTEEN

Aleeya

As Lila drove away from the facility, Aleeya glanced at the rearview mirror. Darkness greeted them. Trees lined both sides of the road. One street light glowed in the distance.

A pair of headlights followed them for the next two minutes.

"Lila," Aleeya said in a calm voice. "There's someone following us. Don't panic. Listen to me and do as I say. I want you to rev up, then I'm going to jump out of your rider. I'll be fine. After that, I want you to speed up. Turn down a small street and stay out of view. I'll find you." She tapped her vambrace to Lila's gold cuff and retrieved her information.

Lila turned to Aleeya, revealing no fear. "Got it."

Aleeya jumped out and rolled to the side of the road full of trees. As the dark rider drove by, she saw the cyborg. She reached for Xmark and fired a golden arrow. She commanded her arrows to multiply and aim to kill.

A second later, she heard a loud crash and a ball of fire erupted, illuminating the dark road.

She glanced at her vambrace when Lila's message popped onto the screen. Aleeya ran forward and met Lila halfway.

Aleeya slid into the rider. "All taken care of." She continued to survey the streets for any unforeseen attackers. "Let's not go home yet. Give me a quick tour of your neighborhood. I want to make sure there's no one else after you. If there is, I'll stop them before they get close to your home. We don't want to place your daughter in danger."

Lila nodded. "Thank you."

FOURTEEN

Aleeya

Aleeya surveyed Lila's apartment building and made sure Atrium didn't send anyone after her. The cyborgs would have alerted their leaders after catching Lila tampering with the documents.

Satisfied the area appeared safe, Aleeya nodded to Lila to enter. Lila lived in a small apartment with her daughter, Embur, eight solar cycles old and sound asleep. Lila ambled over to the couch, where an older female star-being slept.

Lila tapped her shoulder. "Sorry, I'm late tonight, Granny Mona."

Granny Mona woke, smiled, and pushed herself up. "It's okay. I'm just down the hallway. Let me know whenever you need help."

"Embur and I are moving soon. Thank you for making our time in Phyllus wonderful."

"My pleasure. Please send Embur my best when she wakes

and please keep in touch." Granny Mona nodded at Aleeya before she left the apartment.

A blue-eyed girl emerged from a room, rubbed her eyes, and stared at Aleeya with keen interest. She had fiery red hair against white skin that glistened in the light. She didn't have Lila's pink skin or blue hair. Perhaps she had her father's features.

"Hello, I'm Aleeya."

She gave a slight wave. "I'm Embur. Where's Lila?"

Lila and not 'mother' or 'mom'?

Lila dragged two luggage cases out from the bedroom and placed them next to the one already in the living room.

"You're leaving now?" Aleeya asked.

Lila wrapped an arm around Embur's shoulders. "Yes. I already planned to leave when I started scattering the documents where others could find them. I knew I'd be in danger. It's only a matter of time before they figured something out. After what happened tonight, I need to get out of here. I sent the Crime Division a copy of the documents anonymously."

Lila placed her family in danger because she disagreed with her employer. Aleeya respected her ethics. "Thank you for your bravery. Kenzo works with Detective Ahlex, so we'll look at those documents too. Can I help you with anything now? How are you feeling?"

Aleeya imagined Lila's terror, but her composure showed that she'd been through this before.

"I'm okay, and we'll be all right. I've worked at their head quarters for a while. Most of the employees don't know what's really going on, or what Atrium is making. So I dropped hints and hoped someone would look into the company."

"Kenzo and I will."

Kenzo and I? Why did Aleeya talk about him as if she knew him well?

"We're currently searching for a girl named Jella. She was kidnapped. She has light blue skin with dark hair. Have you seen her?"

Lila placed a hand on her chest. "No. I pray she's all right."

"Me too."

Lila turned to Embur. "Do you want to watch something on your tablet for a bit? I want to discuss something with Aleeya."

Embur gave Aleeya a warm smile. Embur strode into her bedroom, her demeanor more mature than other kids her age.

Lila pulled out a chair in the kitchen and gestured to Aleeya. "Have a seat. I have something to share with you before I leave here."

"Don't you need to leave? Atrium could come for you."

A white glaze covered Lila's eyes for a second before returning to normal. "Not tonight. I don't sense that urgency in the air. I will leave after I say what needs to be said." She wasn't an ordinary civilian.

Curious, Aleeya sat. "Are you hiding from someone other than Atrium?"

"I have another reason for my relocation. We'll be fine, don't worry. Thank you for your concern, though. You have a wonderful corra. I sensed that at the facility, and that was why I allowed you to take me home." Lila placed a hand over Aleeya's. Lila sucked in a breath and her eyes glazed over and disappeared for a few seconds.

Lila didn't answer her question, and Aleeya didn't pressure her. "What happened to your eyes?"

Lila's face warmed. "I connected to your energy. When I first met you, I read your aura. A quick scan lets me know if you're someone I could trust. Just now, when I touched your skin, the energies showed me snippets of your future. I didn't ask it to. It just showed me."

Energy fields had always fascinated Aleeya, but she couldn't see the magnetic field or any of its variations. Her warrior sister, Andara, could see them though, that's how Aleeya knew they were real. "What did you see?"

"There's an authenticity to you. Your energy field is full of truth, integrity, and justice. Especially for those less fortunate."

"Those qualities have auras? Colors?"

"We often forget that everything is energy. I see the various levels of energies. Different frequencies have distinct patterns."

Did Lila want to discuss Aleeya's energy, or did she have something else on her mind?

"Do you have information on Atrium that I need to know about? If you know where they're performing their evil experiments, please tell me."

Lila intertwined her fingers. "If I did, I'd tell you. Check the company's other locations. I tried to do my research while keeping my distance. I needed the job to take care of Embur."

"I understand."

Lila twirled a finger around her blue hair and smiled, appearing younger. "You have a lot of loving energy around you. Some familial and starmate energies."

Caught by surprise, Aleeya didn't know how to respond to that. When she found her words again, she said, "I have many brothers and sisters. They're family to me. I don't know about any starmate, though. I'm not with anyone right now."

"Maybe I'm picking up on your warrior family. But there's one energy that's definitely blood family. Familial ties have a different frequency. Perhaps, a father, a mother, or brother."

Aleeya's corra pounded in her chest. Lila had to be wrong. She had to be. "My mother died when I was young. I don't have a brother, and I don't know where my father is. For all I know, he could be dead."

Lila pursed her lips and closed her eyes. "I don't know why, but I'm picking up on a powerful family member. Maybe you'll receive some news soon. It's just there."

Was Lila picking up on the father who abandoned Aleeya? Her memory of him had faded. She couldn't remember what he looked like. Sometimes, she'd see flashes of a silhouette that tightened her chest, followed by a deep sorrow that dragged her into depression for weeks.

Aleeya had been searching for him for so long with no results. Hearing Lila's prediction offered her hope she might finally find her closure.

If he was coming back after all these solar cycles, why now? Why didn't he come back when she really needed him? What had he been up to? Did he ever think about the daughter he left at the orphanage?

Stress, anger, and resentment battled inside Aleeya, and the struggle probably showed on her face.

"Don't worry," Lila said. "I don't sense this as a negative thing. I know negative energy, and this isn't it."

Relief quieted the nerves in her stomach.

Lila changed the topic. "There's love around you too. The kind that's forever." Her face beamed.

Aleeya snorted and threw her head back in a laugh that shook off her anxiety. "That message is incorrect. I'm not made for the 'forever' kind. In fact, I'm not made for any long-term relationships. Trust is an issue for me. The mates I've been with prefer short term too."

But deep inside her, she wondered if she would ever find her "forever" with anyone. It seemed unattainable.

Lila's eyes twinkled. "Well, then they're fools."

"I totally agree." Aleeya enjoyed the female chat. "I'm a Norakian warrior and I'm very busy. I don't have time for the relationship you're talking about. Commitment and dedication take up too much corra space. I don't think I'm capable of that. Plus, I like the freedom to do whatever, whenever, you know?"

Lila's face turned serious. "Just keep in mind what we've discussed. This is a new energy. Something you've never experienced before."

Aleeya forced herself to think. The first image that popped into her mind was Kenzo. His face intruded into her thoughts more than she liked. "This loving energy that you see; is it from the past, the present, or the future? Like, can you tell where it's stemming from? Is that possible to sense?"

"It's your present moment," Lila said. "I think you already know who I'm talking about. Dismiss nothing. Be open to possibilities. The Cosmos works wonders. None of us can truly understand why and how things work the way they do. When two souls are matched, like rare starmates, that's a divine intention from a higher place."

Love was an unfamiliar arena that Aleeya didn't have experience in. It could defeat her because she didn't know how to navigate it. She'd never even considered it. Was she capable of this type of emotion? Before she could love anyone, she needed to understand herself. Right now, she didn't even know her past. She had no solid ground to stand on. If she jumped into something serious right now, the unstable foundation would collapse. Where would that leave her?

So it was best to save herself from all the drama and pain. She didn't know why, but there was something about Lila's bravery and honesty that made Aleeya trust her like a friend.

"Maybe you were sensing my friendly affection for *you*. It's something new, something I've never experienced before, and I'm open to it."

Lila chuckled. "I also sense stubbornness."

"That's not new." Aleeya appreciated Lila's information and interpretations. She'd tuck it safely away to review again at a later time. "Thank you for telling me. I have a lot to think about."

Lila rose and placed a gentle hand on Aleeya's arm. "My suggestion is not to think about it. Just let things be. Let them play out the way they're supposed to. It's all any of us can really do."

"I will." Aleeya threw her arms around Lila. "Where are you moving to? Let's keep in touch. I'll let you know if any of your predictions come true."

"I've secured a place in Sassari. You have my contact and I have yours. I've moved up our departure. The carrier will be here any minute. Atrium will send their cyborgs tomorrow to check on me and everyone who had access to that facility. They'll come to eliminate any trail linking back to the destruction tonight."

Aleeya studied Lila and smiled. "You think like a warrior."

"Just survival skills kicking in." Lila's cuff blinked, and she called to her daughter. "Embur, we have to go. Grab your jacket."

"I'll escort you to your carrier." Aleeya assisted with the luggage, so Embur didn't have to.

The carrier waiting for her was a small craft that could fly them to Sassari quickly. Aleeya waited for the spacecraft to disappear into the sky before she collapsed onto a bench on the sidewalk. The hectic evening, coupled with what Lila shared, exhausted her.

Life could be so comical. It had dumped startling things on her just to see if she'd laugh, cry, or throw a tantrum. The storm of emotions inside her wanted to do all those things, but the trained warrior reeled it in. The law of cause and effect applied to everything within the Cosmos. As Lila said, everything has a reason, a purpose.

As much as she'd like to ignore the information Lila gave her, she couldn't. It struck a chord in her and a flood of emotions surged.

She glanced up at the three glowing moons, Farra, Jarra, and Yarra and prayed they could hear her. She asked for their guidance. *Show me the way, show me clarity. Show me how to move forward.*

A tingle ran up her spine like a confirmation. She shivered and convinced herself that it was the night's chill. She looked at the moon again and faced a painful truth that had been eating her up.

Show me how to forgive him. Forgive the father who left her. That was the only way for her to find closure and move forward.

Her vambrace buzzed with a message with no video from her friend, Pheon, the dragon shifter whom she had met at the convention. "Sorry, I can't be of help right now. My schedule has changed. I have an urgent issue to resolve. I'm cutting my time in Phyllus short. Perhaps we'll meet again. Be well."

Aleeya forgot that she'd requested the Infinitii warrior's assistance. "No worries. Good luck with your issue."

A second later, Kenzo pulled up in his Bullet T53 and warmth filled her, chasing away the chill from earlier.

Aleeya got in and faced him. "Did you annihilate that place?"

"Parts of the facility are up in flames. I left some areas intact for the officials." He searched her face, and his eyes flickered.

"What?"

He shifted in his seat and gripped her chin with his thumb and index finger. "There's something on your face."

"What is it?"

His mouth closed over hers. Instinct had her pushing him

away. She stared at those intense eyes, and need and curiosity coursed through her. She yanked him back to her. His lips were gentle, seductive, and comforting on hers. All the things she needed at the moment. His kiss smoothed out the rough edges of her day. Anxious nerves replaced by a desire that pounded in her chest. Her hands gripped his jacket, pulling him closer.

When he intensified the kiss, Aleeya moaned, opening her lips so they could taste each other. She forgot all anxiety and fell into the kiss. She broke for breath and his corra hammered against her palm.

Kenzo skimmed a thumb over her lips. "Dread was on your face, and I didn't like it on you. Are you feeling better now?"

She didn't know what to think about the sudden kiss. There was so much distress around her that the intimacy was the contrast she needed. "I used to push distractions aside to get the job done, but today, various emotions have bombarded me and thrown me off course."

His eyes pinned her, making her corra drum faster. *You're the primary reason.* A whisper inserted itself into her mind.

Kenzo grabbed her hand and held it to his corra. "There's nothing wrong with feeling an emotion. It's the difference between a spaceship and the individual conducting it. The conductor gives it a purpose." He lifted her hand to his lips. "Just like how you give me reason to feel. You're healing me in some strange way."

She healed him? How could she be someone's purpose when she didn't even know what her own goal was? Perhaps this entire ordeal was messing with his mind too.

"Sometimes you have to believe that there's a higher purpose to everything you do, to the people you meet. When I was on Earth, I didn't believe in God, or any higher power. But when I landed on Terrakado and saw things that had never occurred to me, I wondered that, perhaps, we don't know everything."

Kenzo's philosophical words gripped her. She liked how he expressed himself to her. The more she understood him, the more she realized he was teaching her so much about life and survival. Things she thought she already comprehended. Each moment with him, the cautionary barrier she built up dismantled.

She offered a warm smile. "I haven't heard you speak this much before."

"Consider that a privilege."

"Look." She pointed down.

His attention followed her finger to his boots.

"Your ego is too big, it just dropped."

He laughed. "Do you believe in a God or a higher power?"

"It's complicated. A deep part of me believes in it, and sometimes that's what I turn to when I face a dead end. In Norak, we pray to the two suns or three moons."

"Have you prayed to them?" Kenzo's eyes bored into hers, searching for something she didn't know.

"Yes."

"What did you pray for?"

Why was he asking these questions? Questions no one ever wanted to know. It was an opportunity for her to share a deep part of her. Should she? What did she have to lose?

"To be loved and wanted." The honest words escaped her before she could stop herself. They made her sound like she was some neglected child. She was no longer that child, but that pain had dug an unfathomable hole in her.

Kenzo tugged her toward his lips and gave her a soothing kiss that promised her love. This man could really kiss her pain away. Her chest tightened and emotions roiled inside of her.

"You're not a bounty hunter... you're something else."

"I like that analysis." He pulled the Bullet T53 away. "It's been an odd day."

"I won't argue there."

Aleeya wanted to know about his day, but she feared the more she knew, the deeper she'd sink into the mystery of Kenzo. She preferred to stay grounded on the shore where it was safe, where she could retreat when necessary.

"I took some data from that facility. There's a warehouse in Norak that's holding the Corra Spark. We have to destroy them."

"Show me."

"I'll show you tomorrow. We both need some rest and sleep, especially you."

"You don't know what I need or want."

He shot her a look. "I know that kiss helped you forget whatever was bothering you. I know you enjoyed kissing me just as much as I enjoyed kissing you. And I *know* there's going to be more of it between us."

The bold statement of certainty, of absoluteness, annoyed her.

Aleeya wasn't in the mood to argue because that would take more energy from her. And right now, her well was spent.

She'd let the audacity slide for now. She ignored the fact that he was right. She loved the kiss between them, but she'd rather die than give him the satisfaction of that admission. His kiss did more than ease her harsh day. It stirred something mysterious in her. She loved the way he explored her mouth, and yes, she wanted more of it.

Malastrom! Blackened stardust. Kenzo knew her better than any previous mate and in far less time. That made him dangerous. The protective wall that had crumbled rebuilt itself again. She had to be extra cautious around him.

"Stop analyzing, stop thinking about me. It's just going to keep you up all night."

She didn't know why, but his inflated ego—in that moment—made her laugh out loud.

"Just take me back to my hotel so I can sleep."

"Okay, I'll see you tomorrow."

FIFTEEN

Kenzo

The next day, Kenzo joined a video call with Detective Ahlex. Kenzo informed him of the grim news and identified the names of the missing children and adults from the files. Kenzo and the detective reviewed the documents provided by Lila on the shared virtual screen.

"Take your DNA team to that facility and you'll find your evidence in the basement. Parts of the building are destroyed, but the important areas are still in one piece. Don't ask me how I know this. You'd probably arrest me. When we began working together, you knew I did things my way."

Ahlex had become a friend, but Kenzo kept his distance because he didn't want to mix business with a personal relationship. He had a history of tainting those close to him, and he didn't want his friend to end up like his brothers.

Ahlex nodded. "I did, and that's why I won't ask. I'll send my team there to gather more evidence."

"One more thing. I'm going to Norak to search for Jella.

Maybe she's there, maybe she isn't, but we have to try. There's a Corra Spark facility in that region. I'll track that down. Maybe someone can lead me to her. Time is ticking. I'll keep you posted."

Ahlex pursed his lips, thinking. "Don't do anything stupid that'll get you arrested. Because if you do, I won't be able to help you. You're not a Phyllus official, and you'll be in a new region. So, tread carefully."

Kenzo understood the lines he was crossing. He didn't have the approval to enter another region to investigate, but he wasn't working for the Delleon government. He was his own man, and that gave him more freedom than the detective, who was bound by regulations. However, a bounty hunter still needed to follow general laws and regulations that applied to all citizens.

"I'll inform you when I locate Jella. Also, do you have any information on Malixx?"

"I have some data on him, but it's classified. I'll give you access to view it with my ID." Ahlex sighed. "We've been trying to connect him to a couple of Phyllus officials, but so far we've been unsuccessful. Malixx is powerful because he has connections to powerful individuals. We need to find the link and proof so we can take him down."

Kenzo wasn't surprised by what he heard. "I'll find it."

"Do what you need to do. Help me sort this out. I'm swamped with meetings today regarding the two explosions. The region is on high alert. Malixx and his representatives are visiting the station to demand a thorough investigation regarding the damages to his properties."

Kenzo wanted nothing more than to scrutinize Malixx, but he didn't officially work for the city. He worked with Detective Ahlex under the radar. Besides, Jella needed him right now. His enemy wasn't going anywhere. If Kenzo wanted to destroy him, he had to ensure there were no loopholes, and that took time and calculation. "Be careful what you reveal to him."

"As far as I'm concerned, we're still investigating." Ahlex's ears perked and his gray eyes sharpened. "This is how it's playing out: Our department is thorough. The investigation will take time. Perhaps there were some faulty electrical wires that started the explosion. Or perhaps one employee was doing something he or she wasn't supposed to. We've seen these things happen."

Kenzo smirked. "Just don't make yourself a target. I can't always save your ass."

Ahlex laughed and clicked off the video conference.

Though Kenzo had lived in Phyllus for five years, he hadn't adopted the term "solar cycles" yet. He referred to it as years because it anchored him to Earth, linking him to his past. It was where he came from, and he didn't want to forget his origin.

Five years ago, if a psychic had told Kenzo that his closest friends would be star-beings—humanoids of various colors and a talking pet who knew strange things—he would've dismissed the outrageous idea without a thought. But now, his life sparked with outrageous phenomena.

It still baffled him he was living on an undiscovered planet with incredible wonders. Kenzo stared at the virtual screen, showing the Aurora Matrix. It was an exceptional bridge, with waves of energy circling Norak like a protective, energetic field. Norak had gifted Delleon a portion of its magic, which was encased and displayed at the center of Phyllus. Because of this gift, Delleon's vegetation and air quality had improved immensely. What did that say about Norak? It cared about its neighbors and wanted to help. Like Earth, Terrakado had its politics, and at the core of it all, these star-beings weren't that different from human beings. They had their own issues, even if their technology, magic, and abilities were way beyond a human's grasp.

Another phenomenon that enchanted him was Aleeya. He didn't know why, but the need to protect her overwhelmed him ever since he first met her. Each moment spent with her increased this desire and that confused the hell out of him. Kenzo didn't like complications. He preferred the straightforward lifestyle with no strings attached. But her presence saved him in more ways than one. What was he supposed to do now?

Vengeance and finding Jella were his primary missions. Could he allow himself to be distracted for a little while? Guilt sparked in him. Before she intruded on his life, he only had one goal. He never thought about what he'd do after that. Aleeya made him wonder too much.

God knew she didn't need his protection. She could probably whoop his ass. In fact, she had. But the idea of him submitting to her physically was intriguing. He could think of many ways of submission. The images brought a smile to his face.

Last night, the despair that weighed on her face had squeezed his heart. Something bothered her, and all he wanted to do was wipe that pain away. He'd only meant to distract her, but when his lips touched hers, his heart jolted awake. He hadn't realized his heart had been dormant until that powerful contact. Desire still pounded through him, and when he escalated the kiss, his brain cells burst like tiny bombs. At that moment, he didn't think, he couldn't. The fire, the passion in her had seeped into his body and shifted something in him.

He ran a finger over his lips, remembering the taste of her. He wanted more—any sane man would—but a cautious voice echoed in his mind. Those who were close to him always suffered. Was he cursed? He couldn't risk starting a relationship and placing her in danger.

The relationship he had with his parents dissolved when

they blamed him for Terence's desire to join the Navy SEALs, following Kenzo's footsteps. His parents had been right. If Kenzo had stopped Terence back then, his brother would be alive today, working at some corporate job, driving his sports car, and dating some desirable girl. Maybe he'd even be married with children to extend the Kwan lineage.

His traditional parents expected their children to grow up and take over the family real estate business. Kenzo and Terence had no interest. When they told their parents, it tore the family apart. They blamed Kenzo for influencing Terence's decision, for not being the role model they expected him to be. Conforming was never Kenzo's forte. He wondered what would have happened if he had been more flexible? Would Terence be alive? Kenzo would've switched places with his brother in a heartbeat.

The military would have notified his parents about their sons' disappearance. How did they react? He imagined the guilt they must have felt, and he couldn't bear it. One day, he'd visit them, give them closure. But he couldn't do that until he achieved his vengeance.

His chest tightened at the image of Aleeya's face. He wanted her, but at what cost? The need to keep her safe billowed in him. What if more prominent symptoms flared up unexpectedly? So far, he'd experienced heat waves, muscles spasms, and difficulty breathing. But he'd also pummeled his enemies from an uncontrollable tendency. These occurred when images of his dead brothers appeared in his vision. How many chairs and tables had he broken because of this illness? He could lash out at Aleeya for no reason. A barrier between them was the best solution.

Kenzo's mood soured, shifting from wanting to see her to having to stay away. For the next hour he kept himself busy, researching and planning his trip to Norak. He could go there to investigate without Aleeya. He'd go today.

His vambrace buzzed, and a message from Aleeya popped onto his virtual screen. "I'm heading over to see the data you retrieved from the facility."

Kenzo should have known she wouldn't forget something like that. A thrill rippled through his body at the thought of seeing her again.

"Do you need my apartment number?" Kenzo replied. "You shouldn't since you tracked me the other day, but I'll give it to you, anyway."

Jeeto jumped onto the desk and beamed.

"Why are you so happy?" Kenzo faced his pet. "We have things to talk about. You've been acting strange lately. How did you know I'd fall on my ass? What kind of friend are you for not preventing that?"

Jeeto looked at him with emerald eyes. "I don't intervene with the cosmic plan. You have free will, Kenzo. Your choices create the outcome. I get to go home soon."

There was wisdom woven in there somewhere, but Kenzo wasn't in the mood for deep digging.

He focused on Jeeto's face. "You're already home." Or did he mean a different home?

The longing on Jeeto's face showed that something else was going on. After all these years of being together, Kenzo assumed his pet was from the Delleon region. He didn't know his pet that well, after all.

"Where is your home?"

Jeeto's emerald-green eyes sparkled. "Norak."

That region again. What was the significance there?

"Then why are you in Delleon?"

Jeeto intertwined his hands. "I had a job to do."

That didn't answer his question, but Kenzo let it slide.

"What job? Eating?"

"Keeping you company."

"What?" Kenzo didn't need a babysitter, but Jeeto's companionship did help him survive this planet. "Why? Who sent you?"

Jeeto dangled his feet on the edge of the table. "You'll find out when the time is right."

"Why do you speak in codes? Why can't you just tell me? We've been through a lot; don't you trust me?"

"I trust you." Jeeto scooted closer and hopped onto Kenzo's lap, giving Kenzo the adorable look he could never resist. "But you must trust me too. You'll have your answers soon."

Kenzo sighed and wrapped an arm around his pet. Why couldn't Jeeto just tell him? Who was he working for? Or was this all something beyond Kenzo's grasp of understanding? Perhaps there were other forces at play he wasn't accustomed to? But why him? He was just a regular human being, a former Navy SEAL who didn't have a specific goal in mind.

A thought came to the forefront. So far, everyone around him connected to Norak. Jeeto, Tab, and Aleeya were all from that region. The search for Jella would take him there as well.

What was in Norak for him?

Jeeto's stomach growled. "It's someone's lunchtime."

Shaking his head, Kenzo took out a fresh bag of dried meat and dumped it into a large bowl that was twice as big as Jeeto. How could such a small body eat this much? He was the size of a bunny, but ate like a bear. Where did all the food go? The little round tummy didn't account for the amount of food that should have added another twenty pounds on him.

His vambrace buzzed with a message from Aleeya. "I'm here." Then a knock sounded on the door.

Kenzo welcomed her into the apartment. "You're early."

"I want to see your data. Then we can head to Norak. I

alerted my legion and gave them some details to start the search. They don't really have much to go on, but the information is in their ears. Maybe they'll hear something that'll resonate."

"You're efficient. Thank you."

"I didn't do it for you. I did it for the scared child."

"I know, thank you, anyway." He looked at her. "You're taking me to Norak?" he expected hesitation or something.

She flicked him a glance. "Based on what occurred last night, I assumed you'd want to go right away. You know more about this case than I do. And we both want Jella back. You'll be working with me, so don't go rogue."

Keeping his distance from her would be difficult now. He prayed his symptoms remained under the radar during their collaboration. He'd reevaluate his situation after they found Jella.

She glanced around and walked up to a soft yellow wall. "Interesting color choice. It's not a color I picture you with. You live here by yourself?"

"The walls were already that color when I moved in. I have a roommate, but he went out."

Jeeto stopped chowing and ran over, clearing his throat. "Hey, what about me?"

Aleeya chuckled and crouched. "Well, hello there. You must be Kenzo's pet."

"You can hear him? You can *understand* him?" Kenzo asked.

Aleeya scooped Jeeto into her arms and sat down on a chair at the kitchen table where he had two virtual screens open. "Yes, doesn't everyone? I've been around animals who can talk. We have them in Norak."

Kenzo knew there were certain animals that could communicate through the universal language, but in Jeeto's case, he had met no one who could. For example, Tab couldn't understand Jeeto at all. Was Jeeto speaking a different tongue?

"Besides me, you're the first person who can understand him."

Aleeya patted its head. "What's your name, little one? What language are you speaking?"

He gave her a wide smile. "Jeeto speaks Yarran."

Kenzo leaned closer to his pet. "What's Yarran? Why didn't you share this with me?"

"You never asked." Jeeto smirked.

Aleeya's face became expressionless, which was a contrast to the delightful look of a few seconds ago. "Are you from Yarra?"

Jeeto snuggled closer.

Kenzo didn't think it could get stranger. "Is he referring to one of the three moons?"

Aleeya nodded. "Farra, Yarra, and Jarra. They're connected to the Aurora Matrix. Last solar cycle, Farra appeared inside the Soulstar moonstone that saved Norak from darkness." She looked at him. "Has he told you anything? How long has he been with you?"

"He tells me things, but he speaks in riddles."

Jeeto jumped over to Kenzo's arm.

"The Soulstar spoke in riddles too." Concern filled Aleeya's eyes. "What message does the moon have for Norak this time?"

Jeeto climbed up to Kenzo's shoulder. "Look for the signs."

Aleeya turned to Kenzo. "We'll have to pay attention to all the surrounding details. Where's the data you have?"

He showed her the images from the facility. "These experiments are brutal. It appears they're harvesting organs. Lila said the cyborgs had engineered corras. Why is Atrium producing artificial organs?"

Her hands clenched, and she looked him in the eye. "It doesn't matter. We'll destroy all their facilities."

Her conviction slammed into him, and he recalled the kiss

from last night. He could still feel her soft lips. He shouldn't be thinking about them. They had important matters to attend to. But he couldn't help it.

Aleeya broke the trance. "I'm going to reiterate this. You come to Norak as a friend I've recruited to help me and not as a bounty hunter who's going to cause trouble in my region. Agree?"

Kenzo leaned back in the chair and grinned. "I'll agree to the date, if you agree to give me a tour of the Aurora Matrix. I heard it's not open to the public."

"It's not a—"

"Call it whatever you want. To me, it's a date."

What the fuck was wrong with him? Why was he teasing and taunting her? He blamed it on the bulge in his pants. It twitched and took over his goddamned mind. Whenever she was near, he lost control of himself. That confusion perplexed him. For a moment, he forgot about everything except wanting to touch her.

He scooted closer, and Jeeto jumped off his shoulder and ran off without a word. *Smart guy.*

Kenzo brushed a lock of that gorgeous white hair away from her face. "Are you afraid of me?"

"No." The word came out too fast. Veins throbbed on her neck, and her cosmic codes glowed against the dark skin. "No. Why would you think that?"

His fingers traced the code along her neck. "Your body is reacting as if you are afraid of me. Afraid of how I make you feel."

She shivered at his touch, and Kenzo smiled.

She sucked in a breath. "You don't know how I feel."

He stared into her eyes, light brown with gold speckles that resembled a beautiful star bursting. "You're attracted to me, and I'm attracted to you—"

She crushed her lips to his, kissing him like a true warrior claiming victory. She moved over to his lap with her lips still fused to his. She smelled like a wildflower and an untamed dream tumbling together, arousing him until his bulge ached. Her sweet taste blurred his mind as her fingers gripped his hair. He loved the feel of her exploring him. His hands went to her ass, so fucking firm and perfect.

She broke for breath, her eyes bright and filled with lust. "I don't want to play games."

He gasped for air and sanity. "Neither do I. We're attracted to each other, we're both consenting adults. So let's act on it, no strings attached. Agree?"

"Just sex."

What happened to the need to stay away? He decided she was safer with him nearby. He swore it wasn't logic that made that decision. It was sexual desire and something else. No more physical barriers between them, but the emotional barrier would remain up. "Fine with me."

"Anything else is just too complicated. I don't like complications."

"Neither do I," he repeated her words, and didn't know why his chest constricted a little more.

This was the best solution for him, wasn't it? It was just sex. Two adults with this kind of fantastic chemistry would no doubt create a sexual bonfire.

Only an insane man would deny such an offer. "We have a deal." His hands stayed on her ass, claiming. "I like you in this position."

"I'll show you several positions, but not today." Aleeya slid off his lap, tormenting him with every movement. He tried to yank her back, but her face turned serious. "We need to get to Norak."

Fuck. She was right. Logic and urgency glared at him as he scrubbed a hand over his face.

"Go pack what you need. I'm alerting my superiors that I'm skipping the rest of the GCOT convention to assist with a case in Norak. They weren't too keen on me inserting myself in Delleon issues."

"But you did it, anyway."

Aleeya shrugged. "I'll deal with the consequences when the time comes. My soldiers in Norak are already looking for clues about Jella and the Corra Spark. They can cover some ground before we get there."

An eyebrow lifted. "You've been working behind the scenes?"

"Always." She eyed him. "A warrior needs to be prepared for unexpected events. She needs to know her advantages and disadvantages to every course of action." She stepped closer. "She does not settle for defeat. She needs to maximize her time to ensure victory. To ensure her claim." Her hand covered his bulge and squeezed.

Fuuuck.

She defeated him with the one move. He surrendered. "Claim away, warrior."

She smiled.

Ten minutes later, Kenzo's small luggage rolled out to the living room and stopped next to Aleeya.

"That's it?" she asked.

"I'm a man. I don't have a lot of stuff."

"I thought I traveled light. Your luggage is a third of mine. I need to stop by Hotel Clova to retrieve my things. Peko is going to fly us back and return for my superiors, who will remain at the convention until the end."

"Will your superiors be angry that you left early?" Kenzo glanced around, searching for Jeeto.

"Not when I tell them about the missing child in Norak and a warehouse full of lethal drugs." Aleeya carried a bag of food with Jeeto's head peeking out.

Jeeto waved at Kenzo. "These are delicious."

"Be careful with him, he's going to eat you out of house and home."

Kenzo brought the luggage outside and placed it into Aleeya's Bug-Z coupe.

Tab strode up to him. "Where are you going?"

"I'm heading to Norak with my friend, Aleeya. I won't be gone for long. Aleeya, this is my roommate, Tab."

Aleeya smiled. "It's very nice to meet you."

Tab gawked at her for a few seconds, long enough to make it awkward.

Though Tab was a friend, Kenzo didn't enjoy sharing his woman with anyone. He cleared his throat. "You okay?"

Tab shook his head and reached a hand to the back of his neck, scratching. "I'm so sorry. That was rude. I blanked out for a bit there."

Aleeya waved it off and scratched her neck. "Don't worry about it. It happens when you're exhausted, and you look tired."

"I am exhausted." Still scratching some itch, Tab turned to Kenzo. "Let me know when you get there safely. Keep me posted on what you find out. I'll let you know if I discover anything else. By the way, Malixx missed two company meetings. They can't find him anywhere."

Did Malixx attend the meeting with Detective Ahlex? Or did he miss that too?

"I'll keep my eyes and ears open for Malixx. Go home and rest." Kenzo studied Tab, who appeared worn and exhausted, like something just took the wind out of him.

Inside Aleeya's Bug-Z, Jeeto fell asleep in the pocket of Kenzo's jacket. As she drove, she scratched the back of her neck.

It wasn't one quick rub. For the next five minutes, Kenzo watched her reach for the same spot again and again. She did this earlier, right after Tab scratched his neck. Kenzo didn't believe in coincidences, not like this. This was a glaring pattern that begged to be deciphered. This particular detail signified something significant. But what? They were both from Norak, so were they both allergic to something he was immune to? Were they connected somehow?

"What's wrong with your neck?"

"I don't know. It's been bothering me." She angled her neck to the side so he could look. "I think I'm allergic to something in Delleon."

A red bump sat at the base of her skull. With his fingers, Kenzo rubbed the spot and added a slight pressure. Something hard poked him. "You have a piece of metal in you. It's throbbing."

SIXTEEN

Aleeya

"What?"

Aleeya pulled her Bug-Z over to the side of the road, parked, and pulled out a handheld mirror from her glove compartment. She positioned the mirror behind her and pulled up a screen from her vambrace that captured what the mirror reflected. A bump embedded in her skin, surrounded by a rash. With two fingers, she added pressure to the bump. Something hard with a geometric shape pressed against her skin.

"Malastrom! Blackened Stardust! How did it get in me? How did I not feel a piece of metal in me? I would've known. I *should have* known." She put away the mirror and swiped off the screen.

"Do you remember any surgical procedure?" Kenzo asked.

Aleeya blew out a sigh. "No, I would remember someone putting a chip or whatever this thing is inside my neck. How long has it been there?" The question was more to herself. She gave the itchy area one last scratch and refrained from touching it again until she could contact El Lara to remove it.

No, she'd do it herself when she landed in Norak. If she got an infection, she'd deal with it. What was inside her?

The cautionary energy swirled around her neck. Was it warning her about this embedded device? She was more determined to get it out of her now.

Aleeya pulled her Bug-Z back onto the road. Peko was waiting for them at the Aero Terminal to take them to Norak, and she didn't want to be late. She also needed to return her Bug-Z rental. It had served her well while she was in Phyllus.

"It's never bothered you before?" Kenzo asked.

"No, not until I arrived in this region. I thought I was allergic to the food, air, or weather. But this metal thing inside me signifies something else. Who put it in me? What is the purpose of it? Is it a tracker? Is it something poisonous?" Nerves wrangled her stomach. "Can you help me take it out?"

"I'm no surgeon, but I'll do my best. Do you know a doctor who can remove this foreign object correctly?"

"I do, but El Lara is at the convention. I want it removed right now. It's like a parasite in me. I feel violated."

Kenzo reached for her hand. "I'll help you take it out when we arrive in Norak. Let me know if you feel dizzy or not yourself."

I'm not myself when I'm near you, she wanted to say. She blew out an exhausted breath.

Was that foreign device messing with her mind? Was it the reason she agreed to a casual relationship with him? Her body tingled from the memory of what his kiss did to her. A casual relationship was her forte. It was something she could control. Something that had an ending she could predict. Yet, that deep part of her veered its head and reminded her of the "forever" she'd always wanted. On the surface, she wanted the short-term relationship because it was all she ever knew. Could she have the long-term with Kenzo? Would he even consider that? He appeared delighted about the no-strings attached theory, so she had her answer there.

A simple relationship gave her the space she needed. There was no commitment or demands for anything other than physical pleasure. If that was the case, then why did thinking of him make her corra ache?

Being close to him melted the bones, making her feeble. She didn't like feeling weak. Kenzo had witnessed her vulnerability last night. She should back away before she made a fool out of herself. There was nothing wrong with needing help. However, she wasn't used to having a male supporting her. She wasn't talking about her brothers or mentors. They were her family, a different kind of love and support. She was referring to the males she was intimate with.

All of them ended quickly, and none of them showed her this kind of care. Like always, she took care of herself. She was the only one she could depend on to tend to her corra. Then and now.

Despite that, Kenzo was dismantling her comfortable foundation.

Did she want the deconstruction? Where would she find the energy for the *reconstruction* when the time came for that? Could her corra handle another demolition? The idea frightened her to the core. For all she knew, the unknown device inside her could kill her at any moment. She should lighten up a bit.

And why was she even thinking about all of this? She should concentrate on their tasks and what they had to do. She had to save Jella because she understood the fear, loneliness, and hopelessness that child was going through. Rescuing her was rescuing herself in some strange way.

These thoughts drained her energy.

Kenzo nudged her with his arm and brought her back to reality. "What's bothering you?" His concern spread warmth through her.

"Nothing." She wasn't in the mood to explain. "Just trying to make sense of the whole thing."

"With that look on your face, *I* must be on your mind." He tossed her a challenging gaze, full of confidence and arrogance.

She narrowed her eyes at him. "Overconfidence is one example of miscalculation of judgment."

"I didn't say I was overconfident," he retorted. "Overconfidence is a sign of psychological issues. Do you think I have psychological issues?—don't answer that." His expression softened. "I'm just a man fascinated by a particular female warrior."

Something in his eyes intrigued her, and she whipped his question back at him. "What's bothering *you*?"

"It's not a bother, it's an interest. I'm just wondering where all of this is going. Me, you, Norak, Jeeto. Our contact and interaction means something, and I want to see the complete picture. Right now, we're getting pieces." He gripped her hand, and his thumb rubbed the top of it. The simple motion soothed her more than she expected. This unfamiliar gentleness shifted something in her. Something she wasn't sure she was ready to face yet.

Kenzo told her the truth, but not the whole truth. As a Norakian warrior, Aleeya could detect when a statement was incomplete. A shift in the voice, in the eyes, or the body language could show that. And right now, the way Kenzo held her hand protectively, the way his eyes stared at nothing, and how his lips thinned into a tight line told her something else was on his mind.

What was he worried about? And why didn't he share it with her?

When they boarded Elder Kai's *Nadial Starc*, Kenzo wandered around, admiring the spaceship's interior and amenities. "I've never been inside a spaceship this fancy. This lounge bar alone would make me happy. I could live here permanently."

"What would you like to drink?" Aleeya asked.

"An Omega Vega, please." Kenzo leaned against the counter and stared at Peko, who was busy monitoring multiple screens while he navigated through the air.

"Peko, this is my friend Kenzo." Aleeya introduced the men.

Peko offered a cordial nod. "How long have you been on this planet?"

"Five solar cycles."

"I hope you're enjoying your stay."

"Thank you."

"Would you like anything to drink, Peko?" Aleeya asked. "Thank you for taking us back to Norak."

"I'll pass and thank you for asking. It's my job to take you wherever you need to go."

"Thanks for letting me hitch a ride." Kenzo lifted his glass to Peko.

"You're welcome."

Peko had worked for Elder Kai for several solar cycles. She heard nothing but good things about him. He proved himself worthy, which was why Elder Kai hired him to fly his ship.

"Can you please drop us off at my apartment?" she asked.

"Will do."

Aleeya pulled up a screen on her vambrace and sent a message to El Lara, requesting her help when she returned to Norak. Regardless of when the Priestess got back, Aleeya wanted to share the embedded device with her.

Once Aleeya settled in her apartment, she needed to touch

base with Kazstrom, Magnetti, and her soldiers about Jella and the Corra Spark.

Someone had infiltrated Norak with dangerous drugs, and a child had been kidnapped and hidden somewhere in her region. That horror—more than anything else—infuriated her. Children were the most vulnerable, and she detested anyone who would take advantage of that.

The cautionary energy raked down her body in a powerful jolt that stiffened her spine.

What do you want me to know?

Kenzo

The spaceship docked at a platform of an abstract-shaped building constructed of glass, fortisium, and white stones. It overlooked Nouridan, the largest city in Norak.

Kenzo and Aleeya strode across the energetic platform made of neutronic beads. A sleek spaceship slightly smaller than the *Nadial Starc* docked on the other side of the platform. As they approached the building, the door slid open to a wide hallway. Kenzo followed her into her fancy apartment and glanced around.

"You can use this room." Aleeya pointed to a spacious guest room with light blue walls and a bed with too many pillows.

"Thank you for the accommodation." He left his luggage against the wall and notified Tab of his new location. He tucked sleepy Jeeto between two pillows on an armchair beside the bed. Once his pet was comfortable, he ambled out to survey her apartment.

Lilac walls wrapped around the living room that was

furnished with gray, comfy sofas. A sea of soft yellow pillows decorated the sofas. Now he understood why she was drawn to the yellow walls of his apartment. A shaggy rug in the same soft yellow covered the marble floor. A dining table with six chairs—each a different color—sat beside a kitchen that was decked with unique cooking tools and equipment. A slider door opened to a balcony overlooking the city.

Aleeya's home painted her perfectly, where bright and soft colors blended, portraying an eclectic and fascinating woman. A woman who had snuck into his heart and carved out a spot without him knowing. The stealth technique earned his admiration. Her entrance into his heart was soft like her walls, yet distinctive, like a tactical maneuver he experienced as a Navy SEAL. She was creating her own special forces in his heart. He prayed he would remain whole.

She took out a care kit and lay it on the kitchen table. "I'm ready to have this device removed from me. Can you help me? I have a numbing agent balm."

Kenzo understood Aleeya's desperation to remove the chip. He'd react the same way. But he didn't want to injure her accidentally. He had patched up his brothers' wounds during combat before, but that was because there was no other way. Aleeya had an option to wait for someone more experienced, but stubbornness wouldn't allow that until he tried his best, which he'd do. If he discovered a foreign object inside his body, he'd want it out as soon as possible.

Aleeya sat down on the chair and twisted her mane of white hair into a bun on top of her head. She opened the care kit and took out the tool and a container for the device. "There's a scalpel, antibacterial spray, sealant, gloves, and other miscellaneous items you might need."

Kenzo looked at her. "I've bandaged wounds before, so I have some knowledge, but I've never patched up a star-being.

I'll try my best to do it quickly. If there's extreme pain, let me know."

"I'll be fine. I've gained injuries before; I can deal with pain. The numbing agent should ease the process and the blood-halt spray will help cease the bleeding. I just want it out of me."

Kenzo pulled on the gloves and stood behind her, reviewing the rash. The swollen skin throbbed against his fingers. He rubbed the numbing agent over her skin and added a layer of antibacterial spray. "Let me know when you're numb."

"Go ahead."

With the scalpel, Kenzo applied a slight incision into Aleeya's skin. Purple blood oozed out, too much blood. He used the blood-halter spray, but it took longer than normal.

"I'm sealing up your wound. You're bleeding too much. This wasn't a good idea. The device is at the base of your neck. I don't want to injure your cervical nerves. What if something worse occurs? Let's wait for El Lara." Kenzo moved to stand in front of her. "I don't want anything to happen to you. I know you want it out. I do too, but we have to be careful, okay?"

Disappointment weighed on her, and she sighed, "Okay."

Kenzo cleaned up the blood, sprayed a sealant over the cut, and tossed the gloves in the trash. "All set. Maybe you can ask El Lara to come back sooner?"

"No, I don't want to interrupt her conference. She should be back in a couple of days. I can wait. I've had it in me for solar cycles, what's another two days?" She rose and released her hair to cover the wound. "Thank you for helping me. Just let me know if something bursts out of my skin. If I'm acting erratic, you have my permission to knock me out before I do anything stupid or disgraceful."

Worry lines creased between her eyebrows, and he soothed them away with his fingers. "What's on your mind?"

She considered him, and he imagined what was going on

inside that mind of hers. The afternoon light streamed in from the wide windows and lightened her brown eyes to gold.

"I'm not sure. I just have these nerves inside me that won't go away."

Kenzo grinned. "Having a foreign object in your body can do that to you. Or it could simply be my inevitable charm."

Aleeya rolled her eyes, but she smiled a little. "Not those nerves. My gut tells me something awful is happening or about to happen."

Kenzo had encountered feelings like that many times. The best way to deal with them was to let them play out while keeping your feet firmly planted on the ground. Being secured when the storm hit prepared you for the unexpected.

Wanting to remove her anxiety, he pulled her in for an embrace. "There's not much you can do right now. The one thing you can control is your mind and how you react to whatever is happening. You already know this, but sometimes it helps to hear it from someone else. Sometimes it's hard to listen to your own advice." He met her eyes. "Be aware of everything around you. Your environment, your family, friends, neighbors. All those details matter. For me, I see them as actors in a play. Every detail has a part, and if you can be the watcher of that play, you'll pick out clues that don't fit in with the picture. The outcast is your first clue. It's where you start digging for details."

Aleeya drew back and studied him. "I get it. Be the powerful bird in the sky. Look at everything. Do more than just see. Watch where the wind blows. Observe how the animals move. Connect to all your senses because that's how victory is achieved. Is that what you're trying to teach me?"

He kissed her forehead. "Not teach you. *Remind* you. You're an intelligent woman, you already know this."

She smiled. "Are you sure you're the same bounty hunter I

shot? The one who fell on his ass? Because the person I'm talking to right now sounds wise."

He loved a sarcastic woman who challenged him both mentally and physically.

"There's a compliment somewhere in there, right?" His fingers tugged at a lock of white hair that had fallen loose. "A beautiful woman distracted me, and I lost all my senses. To where I fell hard on my ass for her. I pushed her to track me down because I wanted to see her again. And here you are in my arms, *exactly* where I want you to be."

She pushed him away. "You can twist things around to suit you. Makes me wonder how much I can trust you."

He heard the sarcasm and the concern in her voice. It bothered him she hesitated at his honesty. "You *can* trust me."

She met his gaze, nodded, and her vambrace buzzed. A soldier with neon purple hair, dressed in black and silver armor, appeared on the screen and offered the Norakian greeting. "We didn't locate Jella, but we discovered a warehouse with C. S. and Magnetti is at the scene. Do you want to look now?"

"Yes, send me the location. Thank you and excellent work."

When she clicked off, her vambrace buzzed again. "Magnetti, I was going to contact you."

A blue-skinned warrior with spiky blonde hair appeared on the virtual screen. "I just discovered something that has ties to Phyllus. Are you still there?"

Aleeya whipped a glance at Kenzo. "No, I'm back in Norak. What did you discover?"

"Dead bodies and a warehouse full of drugs."

Aleeya gestured for Kenzo to come with her as she strode toward the door. "I'm on my way."

EIGHTEEN

Aleeya

Thoughts jumbled inside Aleeya's mind as she navigated *Sentra Five* to the location. Did Magnetti uncover the same drugs or something else? What prompted this sudden detection? Did he find any information regarding Jella?

Kenzo sat in the other navigating seat, surveying her spaceship. "This is very you."

"What do you mean?"

He swiveled the seat around, gesturing to her colorful pillows. "You're bold, vibrant, and provocative." He strode over to the lounge area and ran a hand over the velvet couch. "Soft and sensual." He examined the plant with small yellow flowers growing in a floating vase, emanating a sweet fragrance. "Your ambience and high-tech gadgets make you irresistible, Buttercup."

"Buttercup? What's that?"

He looked at her like she had a huge pimple on her forehead. "You don't know your flowers?"

"I don't know every single flower I see. Can you name every plant you've ever seen?"

"This plant looks like a buttercup, it's a flower on Earth. Though this one has purple stamens." He pulled up a small virtual screen from his leather vambrace and showed her a simple flower considered a weed. It had five petals and looked remarkably like the one floating over her coffee table.

She had gotten the plant because of its cheerful color and sweet scent. She pursed her lips. "I'm not a little flower. I'm more like the passion flower."

"No, you're a *wild* buttercup.

She rolled her eyes. "Shut up."

Why did she find his crooked smile so sexy? She shouldn't enjoy his attention. She should concentrate on the important investigation and not discuss irrelevant things like wild flowers. This proved that she was spiraling out of control when he was around.

"Buttercups have healing properties. They're used to treat certain ailments on Earth like arthritis and certain skin irritations."

"I'm not rubbing that flower on my neck."

Chuckling, he sat back down. "That's not what I meant. I mean, you could, if you wanted to test it out. I was referring to the idea that small things have purposes too. Just because something is small, doesn't mean it's insignificant. Sometimes we don't realize how much something matters until it's gone."

Aleeya loved this introspective side of him. She'd never been with anyone who shared his deep thoughts with her.

"You have an interesting choice of words. Sometimes I wonder if you're a bounty hunter or a secret poet, creating rare poems for those fortunate enough to hear them." She never thought she was a romantic, but ever since she met him, she'd softened to the idea.

"I'm just trying to keep you grounded, keeping the mood light for both of us so we can do our jobs." His expression turned serious. "Stress and pressure can do a number on your body and mind. I don't want you to experience that."

That admission tugged at her corra. She appreciated his thoughtfulness—his protectiveness—more than he realized. What did stress and pressure do to him? Would he tell her?

"I wonder if your brother stumbled onto one of Atrium's distribution centers."

"Sounds like it." She docked her spaceship in a public Aero Terminal in Kirkwin, a city just outside of Nouridan. She ambled to the side door of her spaceship and climbed onto her cloud-mobile, a two-seater vehicle with a platform she used for ground travel instead of her personal rider. "Let's go."

He rubbed his chin and stared at the puff of clouds floating under and over the vehicle. "Is that thing safe? I don't want to step through the clouds and break some bones."

"I'm standing on a solid platform. These clouds are made from tiny neutronic beads that produce powerful waves of energy you can step on. Come on." Aleeya stomped, creating a loud noise that proved he wouldn't die.

"I've never seen a cloud-mobile before. It's cute. There aren't any in Delleon."

"Of course not. This is my creation. Well, I had an engineer construct it, but I sketched it out for him."

Kenzo sat on the seat, leaned back, and buckled up. Like an awestruck kid, he reached up and touched the soft awning she recently added. He waved his hand through the clouds that rose over his feet and legs.

"We're at the center of Nouridan." She pointed to the bluish green glow as they descended. "That's the Aurora Matrix."

They arrived at a three-story facility made of brick and glass. It sat in an industrial section that produced medical supplies to several hospitals in Norak, mostly the children's hospitals.

Aleeya hopped off her cloud-mobile and strode over. She nodded to three of her soldiers, who carried evidence boxes to the data carts. Two investigators from the Crime Division showed Magnetti something on a tablet and returned to their emergency autobuses. The Norakian shotel sword gleamed at Magnetti's side. His battle bird perched on the side lawn, pecking at something in the grass.

"Hey there." Aleeya stroked the bird's blue and orange feathers.

The bird made a sound and eyed Kenzo, who stared at her with keen interest. "That's one enormous bird."

"This is Amenti, she's Magnetti's friend." Aleeya gave the bird a hug and made her way toward Magnetti.

Kenzo said something to Amenti, but she only squawked.

"She can't speak like Jeeto," Aleeya said.

"You're so majestic." Kenzo brushed her feathers, and Amenti's blue eyes sparkled.

Aleeya tapped a fist on her chest to greet Magnetti. "What happened here? This is my friend, Kenzo. He's helping me find Jella, the missing child. Kenzo rescued her brother in Delleon."

Magnetti glanced over at Kenzo. "I'm Magnetti, Captain of the Norakian warriors. Aleeya's friend is my friend as well. Thank you for your help." He gestured them over to the autobus. "A delivery-service discovered the two dead doctors and four droids. I was on my way home and intercepted the call. I stopped by, and good thing I did." He flipped up the cover to a box and withdrew some tubes filled with the yellow, glowing liquid. "When we arrived here, the employees evacuated like they knew they'd be arrested. One of our crime techs tested the liquid, and one drop of this stuff is strong enough to force instant cellular mutations."

"It's the Corra Spark." Kenzo examined one tube and placed it back into the box. "The facilities that produced these were also testing them on hostages, mostly children."

Magnetti let out a curse. "There's a lab at the back. Come with me."

They followed Magnetti to a wooden door. He opened the door slowly, and a powerful smell slammed into them.

"Fuck." Kenzo wrinkled his nose.

The scent of decay churned her stomach, and she prayed the decomposition didn't belong to Jella. They entered the dark room, and Kenzo found a light switch and flicked it on. Two dead bodies lay on a wide exam table with jars of corras aligning a counter. Next to that was a cart filled with organs in sealed containers.

A figure jumped out in front of them. A young star-being about eight solar cycles old peered up at them with fearful eyes. He had dark blue skin, and a mop of brown hair that matched his eyes. He wore a loose white top and matching pants. Another child, an older one, perhaps fifteen solar cycles old, stepped out from behind a wall of boxes and stood beside the younger child. He had orange skin and blue hair. His eyes glazed over before they cleared.

"Are you all right?" Aleeya asked.

Their corras glowed yellow through their chests, through the white shirts. Their corras were brighter than the ones she saw on the cyborgs in Phyllus. The teen lifted his hand at them and offered a smirk that had her gripping for her blaster.

A shot of lightning came from his palm and hit the floor, cracking it. Kenzo, Magnetti, and Aleeya jumped back. The lightning was the same color as his corra. The little star-being trembled and tried to run, but Kenzo caught him with one arm.

The teen's face contorted as blood gushed from his nose. He lifted his arm again. "I can't stop it."

His corra brightened and dulled as if it was confused. His body shook, trying to fight off whatever controlled him. Then his body detonated, sending blood and flesh everywhere.

Aleeya leaped out of the way, avoiding blood spatter. Magnetti jumped behind a bookcase. Kenzo used his body to shield the kid with tiny ears.

The kid cried in Kenzo's arm. "I don't want that to happen to me."

Kenzo took the child out of the room to a medic while Magnetti directed the crime scene investigators to clean and gather evidence.

Fury rocked Aleeya as she did her best to clean her clothes of blood and flesh. The flesh of a young child that she failed to save. Her corra shattered. The child's bloodstains reminded her of her failure.

Kenzo tipped up her chin. "Are you okay?"

"No, I'm not. We're supposed to save these kids. But so far, we've failed. Look at me. I'm covered in a child's blood and flesh." Tears glistened in her eyes.

A muscle ticked in Kenzo's jaw. "We'll find the bastards and kill them all."

Aleeya gathered herself, because, in battle, a broken warrior was a dead warrior. She would not break. She had to be strong for these children. She had been one of them a long time ago.

Magnetti worked with the investigators while updating Kazstrom from a virtual screen. Kazstrom was on his way to a galactic meeting with one of the other Elders.

Aleeya brought over a water bottle and a snack for the kid, who clung to Kenzo. Kenzo wiped the kid's face. His gentleness with children surprised and warmed her.

When the boy had calmed down, Aleeya asked, "What's your name? Where are you from?"

"Baato. I live in Nouridan."

"Were there other children here with you?"

He nodded as his hand went to his chest. "Their corras burst. Can you take that stuff out of me?"

Kenzo and Aleeya exchanged a horrified look. No child should have to experience this trauma.

"The glowing liquid?" Kenzo asked.

"They injected it into us. It changed our corras. Gave us strange abilities. I don't have any, though. I don't think the injection worked on me. Why would they do that?" Big brown eyes looked at her for answers.

"I'm not sure," Aleeya said, giving him as much truth as possible without adding more trauma. "But I will find out, and I will stop all of them. I promise."

Baato nodded. "I heard they were going to do more tests on me, so I hid in the closet. An adult male wearing a black mask appeared and shot the two doctors. He took a girl with him. His pink hair sticks out weird." Baato pointed around his ears.

Who was this masked individual? There were many star-beings with pink hair. Could it be Malixx in disguise?

"These are all significant details that will help us catch him, and you're very brave for remembering that. Is this the girl?" Kenzo pulled up a picture of Jella on his vambrace.

Baato looked at the image and bit his lip. "Her corra is very strong. I'm not sure what her ability is. She cried for her parents and brother a lot." Tears rolled down his cheeks. "Can I go home now?"

"Yes." Aleeya rubbed his back, trying to comfort him. "Your parents will meet you at the hospital. The doctors will need to clear your body of that glowing poison. So you'll have to stay there until you're well, okay?"

"Okay." Baato looked drained and scared. "Will the doctors hurt me?"

"No." Aleeya gripped his shoulders and looked him in the

eyes. "These are excellent doctors who will take great care of you."

Aleeya had more questions for him, but he deserved rest and safety. Questions could wait. She got his information and alerted his parents.

The crime team rolled the dead bodies out of the lab. One tech pushed a cart filled with jars of corras and other organs. What was the purpose of all of this? Why did Malixx want to give non-gifted commoners abilities? It made little sense, and her brain was too exhausted to sort it out.

Magnetti strode up to Aleeya. "I'll take care of the reports and continue the investigation from my office. We'll touch base later." She didn't know if he had other missions on his plate. He probably did, but he was the Captain, so he could juggle them.

Aleeya waved her soldiers over. "Get me surveillance for this block. I need to review all recordings. The criminal could be on one of those videos. Also, increase the urgency on the missing children to the media and let them know there's an illegal facility that was just uncovered and that we need the public's help to locate the child and identify the kidnapper. Have a sketch artist work with Baato when he's ready. Don't overwhelm him right now. He's traumatized. We'll need the public's help with the masked killer with pink hair."

"Will do."

The cautionary energy poked at her and lingered around. *What is it? What do you want me to know?*

While Aleeya spoke to the medic who was accompanying Baato to the hospital, Kenzo surveyed the area around the building.

A blaster went off and Aleeya fled around the building, searching for him. She found him firing his blaster into the woods.

"What happened? Are you all right?"

"Someone just tried to kill me."

"What?" Aleeya looked into the woods. A powerful surge of protectiveness rose in her. Was the killer still lurking around? She sent a message to her soldiers to scour the woods for signs of the attacker. She turned to Kenzo. "We have to be extra careful."

He held up a yellow flower and tucked it behind her ear. "This saved me. I bent down to pluck it for you and avoided the shot. You saved me."

She covered his hand with hers and squeezed. The thought of losing him terrified her to the core. The unexpected emotion baffled her. She had things to think about when her mind wasn't cluttered with a missing child, dead bodies, and spies or stalkers wanting to kill them.

"From today's discovery, there's no need to search the Aurora Matrix to confirm Jella's presence in Norak. She's definitely here," Kenzo said. "But I still want to visit this divine bridge when you have time. It's not a priority now."

"Okay." She blew out a heavy sigh and noticed the cautionary energy had faded. Did it arrive to warn her about Kenzo's attack? Was the assault meant for her? All the questions fused into a massive headache.

Kenzo placed a hand on each side of her shoulders. "My warrior looks worn."

Aleeya made it back to her apartment with fear, irritation, and exhaustion pulling at her muscles. After a hot shower with six shower heads, each blasting water and colorful energetic streams that massaged her muscles, the irritation slid away. The sweet fragrance from the body shampoo-plant softened her skin and calmed her mind.

Dressed in a silky robe, Aleeya came out of the bathroom and found Kenzo and Jeeto out on her balcony. Kenzo looked at something on a small virtual screen floating above his vambrace.

The Aurora Matrix glowed in the distance, making the night dreamy, like a mystical haze that blocked out all the wrongs in the world.

She allowed herself to forget the darkness that surrounded them today. Kenzo's presence in her home felt natural, like he belonged there.

Belonged to her.

She stepped out to the balcony. Kenzo scanned her body, revealing he wanted to do more than just kiss her. Her body shivered from the intense gaze. "Feeling better?"

Aleeya was about to answer him, but Jeeto climbed out of Kenzo's pocket, jumped into the chair, and wagged his tail. His emerald eyes glimmered with joy.

Jeeto's body emanated geometric codes and colors she recognized. "Look. These are codes from the Aurora Matrix."

Kenzo glanced over at his pet. "He's connected to the bridge."

Jeeto pointed toward the bridge, but made no sound.

Kenzo turned to Aleeya. "Maybe we'll find clues for Jella there."

Aleeya was still waiting on the surveillance from the nearby streets and businesses for her to review. She prayed a camera had caught sight of Jella or the kidnapper. For tonight, there was nothing she could do until she reviewed the recordings.

In combat, it was important to understand that while chaos wreaked havoc, there were other forces at play. A trained warrior could pick up on these subtle hints, and Jeeto's simple gesture was that subtle hint.

"There's a message for us on the Aurora Matrix," Aleeya said. "You're getting that trip sooner than expected."

NINETEEN

Kenzo

As Kenzo followed Aleeya up the wide energetic steps to the Aurora Matrix, energy hummed and swirled around him. He thought he had seen everything since landing on Delleon, but this bridge in Norak opened his eyes to the vastness of possibilities on this planet.

From his pocket, Jeeto's eyes beamed with joy.

"Normally, only Norakian warriors are allowed on here. But you have my authorization to visit. We try to keep the energy as pure as possible. It rejuvenates the land and the air." Dressed in her Norakian warrior uniform of purple and gold, Aleeya walked the length of the bridge.

"You mean like an air purifier?"

"That and the power of thousands of rainforests. It produces divine energy that nourishes the land, from the soil to molecular properties that create life-forms. It shifts energy in a way that allows for healthy growth. You can consider the bridge as the sunlight and the rain required for all living things to thrive."

Kenzo's body shivered from the waves of energy circulating around him. "I feel like I'm standing in the middle of the Northern Lights. I saw the beautiful lights when I traveled to Iceland a long time ago. But this is a thousand times more magical. Has anyone trespassed on here?"

"Many have. Last solar cycle, we had a tremendous battle here. It took a long time for the bridge to recalibrate."

Jeeto jumped out of Kenzo's pocket, stretched his little arms up toward the moons, and said, "Yarra." He ran up and down the bridge, playing with the geometric codes that glowed and floated around him. As he fled down the wide ribbon of lights, the bridge brightened, and codes illuminated where they had been invisible.

An image flashed in his mind. "I saw these geometric symbols when I was wavering in and out of consciousness during my escape."

Aleeya searched his face. In these beautiful lights, her white hair glowed, making her a goddess. "Escaped from what? I want to know everything about you." She stepped closer, and the energy between them crackled, sending out a magenta spark like a shooting star.

Standing on this magical bridge surrounded by the quiet night, he opened himself to her.

"I was abducted along with my military brothers. My blood brother, Terence, died along with them. We were tortured and experimented on."

Their faces popped into his vision, reminding him of the vengeance that had somehow taken a backseat ever since Aleeya entered his life. He had *not* forgotten about them. He'd never forget. But at the moment, he and Aleeya were working together to find Jella. Once he found the child, his focus would return to vengeance.

"I'm sorry to hear that. Who tortured you?" Fierceness grew in her eyes.

It had been a long time since he'd spoken about what happened to anyone. The monster still lived in his mind, tormenting him. That monster often showed up as muscle spasms, violent tendencies, difficulty breathing, blame, shame, guilt, and so much more. He expected it to reveal itself while he spoke about it, but it didn't show. Not a single symptom. Why?

Because of Aleeya. That monster was afraid of her. Her energy swirled around him, and its power was more noticeable on this bridge.

"I escaped when Phyllus officials realized what was happening and came in to dismantle the rebel operation. I was drugged, but I was cognizant enough to know I had to escape. I didn't trust anyone, especially another group of star-beings. I didn't know where I was. The last memory I had was of Earth, and suddenly here I was, on another planet. You don't know what that did to my mind. I thought I'd finally lost it. I kept seeing these geometric shapes floating around me, and I followed them." He walked along the bridge, absorbing the energy that invigorated him. "Eventually, I wandered into an alley. Jecto was by my side when I passed out. Tab found me. He saved me. He took me in and taught me about this world, and I made it my mission to find out who killed my brothers and tormented me."

"Abduction goes against the cosmic laws, and those who break them pay heavily with the Galactic Coalition of Truth. But even then, it's hard to catch them all. I'm sorry that happened to you." She placed a gentle hand on his arm.

"Criminals exist everywhere. I've learned that life on Terrakado isn't all that different from life on Earth."

Aleeya nodded. "Similar issues on a different dimension."

"Terence—my brother—had joined the Navy to be like me.

But I failed to protect him. He loved sports cars. His birthday was May third."

Epiphany dawned on her face. "I've studied about humans and Earth. The third day of the fifth month. Bullet T53."

Kenzo nodded. "My tribute to him. It was the least I could do to keep something about him alive. With me."

Brown eyes stared at him. "I'm sure he appreciates it."

"It's also why I never wanted to return to Earth. Someone had to pay for what they did to us. From the data I showed you, I suspect Malixx is responsible. I want to know why. Was it just a game to him?"

Aleeya ran a finger along his jawline, soothing the anger rising in him.

"I received a message from Detective Ahlex earlier. Malixx never showed up to the Crime Division office. I also reviewed some classified files about him. Malixx is a sick man. Apparently, he's been experimenting for a long time. He has ties to top officials in Delleon, who probably helped him hide evidence and so on. Ahlex needs proof to connect Malixx to the officials."

"We'll find it." She looked him square in the eye. "You became a bounty hunter to hunt those causing harm. While you found nothing on the man who did this to you and your brothers, you hunted down other scum who dared to hurt people."

Aleeya understood him more than he thought. "I guess it was my way of dealing with my trauma." He lifted a shoulder. "We all heal differently."

"Based on your experience, you could've gone in several directions. You could have given into self-loathing and self-destruction, but you *defied* that darkness by helping others. You defied your personal pain by becoming a weapon that helped and not hurt. You're a warrior too."

Her perspective spoke to him. Kenzo hadn't considered her

angle at all, but now he'd contemplate on it further. "I suppose defiance isn't a bad thing when it's opposing darkness."

"I defied orders from my superiors to ignore the crime in Delleon because it wasn't my jurisdiction. My defiance led me to you. I guess rebellious energies have a way of finding each other."

"We're the yin and yang energies. Together we're complete and more powerful."

Her energy brushed against his face and neck, sending a thrill down his back. Somehow, she twisted the word rebel and defiance into something attractive.

Life as a bounty hunter often exhausted him. The job reminded him that there was too much dark in the world, and that his one act of removing filth was never enough. But in this moment, Aleeya made him feel that his small actions were worth it.

"What did those monsters do to you?" she asked, like she was taking notes. "How many were there? Do you remember what they looked like?"

Did she want to punish them for him?

"There were about four or five star-beings. I don't remember their faces. They wore black masks. I was having trouble staying conscious. They took my blood, cut me, gave me drugs, inserted stuff into me, and monitored my brain," he said, trying to remember what he could. "When I escaped, I stumbled on my brothers' body parts. Their organs were missing. That should've been my fate."

Reliving those memories was tough, but as Kenzo shared his horror with her, the weight lessened, as if she carried a part of that pain for him. Was that why his internal monster stayed hidden when she was around? It confused him that she tamed his traumatic symptoms. But how long would that last? Until the monster became immune to her?

Aleeya curled her fingers into fists. "I'll kill them."

Her eyes glistened with tears, and she glanced down, probably not wanting him to see her vulnerability. His chest tightened, not from the pain of the past, but from an awakening of something more, something hopeful. No woman had ever shed tears for him.

Kenzo lifted his shirt, showing a wide scar that ran across his stomach. "I don't recall what happened here or here." He twisted, revealing more scars from his back.

She traced her fingers over the wounds. Her gentle touch soothed him, and the concern on her face took more of the pain away. No one had ever shown him this much care or interest in his injuries. He'd gained many during his time in the Special Forces. The women he'd been with always wanted something from him, and because he never knew what that was—or cared to ask—they never stayed long. Right now, he would give everything up for Aleeya.

The thought shocked him, sending a thrill through him that originated from his gut, scattering out to the rest of his body. He shuddered.

Aleeya looked at him. "Is the energy here getting to you? It happens. The Aurora Matrix is good with clearing clutter from the mind and the body."

"I needed that." He tried to process what just occurred. She became significant in his life. A necessity he couldn't live without. The pace at which this relationship grew perplexed him.

"We'll get Malixx and anyone who had a part in cutting you, hurting you. I will help you. They'll pay for what they did to you." Her words were weapons that glinted with promise.

Just like that, the stones around his heart crumpled. Her offer was so simple, so powerful. She stood for truth and justice without question, and he loved that about her.

Curiosity clawed at him. "Why?"

"Why what?"

"Why do you want to help me?"

"Why not? Friends help each other out."

"Friends?" They weren't just friends. They were... he wasn't sure. Friends with benefits? No, that sounded temporary, convenient, and unimportant. He didn't like that at all. But wasn't that their initial agreement? Just sex?

Kenzo wanted more. But what if his internal monsters returned and accidentally hurt her? What the fuck was wrong with him? He couldn't have it both ways, could he?

"Do you help all your friends this way?" he asked.

"Yes, if I believe in the cause. In your case, I do, and we're more than friends." She smirked, then her face turned serious. "I love my brothers and sisters. They're like family to me. And if someone hurt them, the way someone hurt your brothers, I'd go after them without hesitation." She paused, letting the statement sink in. "I understand what you're feeling."

"Thank you." His gaze stayed on her, fascinated by what he saw. Hope, sadness, and wishes.

She narrowed her eyes at him. "Something's different about you tonight. You're very polite. Very *gentlemanly*. I'm not sure if my *unladylike* traits prefer that."

A roaring laugh escaped him, wanting to know all her unladylike characteristics.

"You should laugh more often."

"Why?"

"Because it's a blessing, a gift to those around you. It makes them want to open it, understand it, and receive more of it."

What was the Aurora Matrix doing to him? This insurgence of feelings overwhelmed him.

Time suspended, allowing her words to coat his heart. Something shifted between them, and his heart quivered from this new frequency. The geometric codes on her face brightened like a confirmation that this was exactly where he was supposed to be. On a logical level, he didn't understand any of this. On an esoteric level, he knew he had a purpose in Norak with Aleeya. For what? He didn't entirely know yet, but he was willing to let it happen.

Communication and trust were virtues in any relationship. It was time to take their "friendship" to a new level.

"What's been on your mind? Something has been stressing you out," he said. "I spilled my deepest secrets to you, please trust me with yours in return."

Aleeya strode to the edge of the bridge, playing with a tree branch with circular leaves. Kenzo heard Jeeto's delight as he jumped up and down farther down the bridge.

"Do you remember Lila?"

The star-being who had assisted them at the facility flashed through his mind. "Yes."

"She reads auras, like a seer. She saw something about me, and that brought up all kinds of emotions from my past."

Kenzo never had a psychic reading, but he was open to the possibility that unfathomable things could happen. His presence here on this planet proved the impossible was very possible. He also knew that free will changed things. Nothing was truly set in stone.

"What did she see?" Kenzo asked.

"That a family member would show up in my life," Aleeya said, looking anxious about the statement. "I'm an orphan. Since I was five solar cycles. My mother died, and my father dropped me at the Cosmic Corra Orphanage and disappeared. That part of my life ended. The idea that he might return? I don't know how to handle that." She pointed in the distance where tall buildings stood. "He told me he'd return for me one day. I remember that part. He never did. I don't even remember what he looks like now. I can't picture him. I can't picture my mother's face. My memories of them faded over time."

Kenzo studied her and understood that trauma often pushed memories into the darkness. He also understood her need for closure. To bring light to the darkness. It was a normal part of healing. "Lila saw all that from just looking at you?"

Aleeya nodded. "She saw other things too, but that stood out."

The desire to protect Aleeya and keep her safe billowed in him. Kenzo had a theory, a far-fetched idea that needed more investigation before he could share it with her. He'd struggled with this thought when it had occurred to him inside her Bug-Z coupe. He didn't want to give her hope if his suspicion turned out wrong. To give someone hope only to take it away would be devastating.

"I'll help you find him." As he added another thing to his to-do list, his vengeance moved down. Guilt bit into him. *I haven't forgotten.*

She flicked him a glance of appreciation. "We just made vows to each other."

"Because we matter to each other." Kenzo looked up at the three moons, each glowing in a different color. For a moment, the one with a yellow glow appeared to throb, as if wanting his attention. "Do you see that moon?"

Her face paled, like she knew what was happening. "That's Yarra, the moon that encompasses the balance of feminine and masculine energy. It represents balance and harmony."

He had just referenced that analogy earlier. "The 'yin' and 'yang' frequencies."

Jeeto flew into Kenzo's arms, glowing with a bluish-green light, and stared at Aleeya with emerald eyes swirling with tiny geometric symbols. "Keep it safe."

"Keep what safe?" Aleeya asked.

"Keep it safe for the Cosmos. The 'key' to everything." Jeeto's eyes returned to normal, the glow disappeared, and he collapsed into Kenzo's arm with a snore.

"What does he mean?" Aleeya asked.

Kenzo shrugged and cradled his pet. "Jeeto's been acting strange and talking in riddles ever since I met you."

"What did Yarra tell him?" she muttered to herself.

"The moon talks?"

"It communicates with those meant to receive it." Aleeya looked at him, and a revelation glimmered in her eyes, followed by a playfulness that aroused him. "I want to experiment with something."

Maybe she and Kenzo were the "key" to everything.

TWENTY

Aleeya

Inside her apartment, nerves nipped and nibbled at Aleeya as she tried to grasp the ideas bubbling in her mind.

The events of the day replayed in her mind. She discovered a foreign device in her neck, confirmed that Jella was indeed in Norak and was still missing, and her corra cracked hearing about Kenzo's torture and examining his wounds. She couldn't deny her feelings for him. Standing on the Aurora Matrix, she sensed her energy mingled with his and knew their connection had significance.

What was it?

That spark that had zapped between them on the Aurora Matrix signified something else was at play here. Nothing like this had ever happened to her before. Was it just the physical attraction between them or something more? Something cosmic. She wanted to explore it with Kenzo tonight.

The combination of need and something else twisted in her stomach like a delightful swarm of pretty petal-flies fluttering inside her. She couldn't remember the last time she felt this way. In the past, it had always been a surge of sexual energy that quickly faded.

When Kenzo reached out a hand and touched her braid, she froze at the delicate action.

"I love the color of your hair. It reminds of the snow during the winter months when I lived on Earth. There's a gentle beauty to it, especially when you're alone watching the snowflakes float down from the sky. They're like blessings, kissing the Earth and the person witnessing them." Releasing her braid, he met her gaze. There was no challenge in his eyes. Just honesty, a remembrance from a life far from here.

Did he know he possessed a poet's soul?

Kenzo tucked Jeeto into a makeshift bed inside a rectangular container she gave him. He faced her, and the energy simmered between them, hummed louder. She had thought it would've diminished by now, since they were no longer on the Aurora Matrix. Energy increased, highlighting the raging need inside her.

"What kind of experiment were you planning?" His gaze lowered to her mouth.

"The kind that involves explorations and the art of tactics." She traced a finger along his shoulder. "We're both accustomed to the battlefield. I'm applying my skills to you tonight."

His bulge thickened in his pants. "What is your strategy, warrior?"

Her fingers drummed down his chest. "One of the most important principles in battle is 'measurement,' judge the terrain and battle lines." Her hand pressed into his abdomen. "I love this terrain. It's rugged, hard, and sustainable." She palmed his bulge, and it throbbed against her hand. "Oh yes, this terrain can absolutely benefit me."

Kenzo chuckled and gripped her face for a passionate kiss,

exploring her with his tongue. Then he broke the kiss and scooped her up into his arms, carrying her into her bedroom. No one had ever carried her before—another "first" for her. She expected a hard and fast sexual session, but he had a novel idea.

She reveled in the strength of his arms. "You do this often?"

"Do what?" His voice came out low and husky, his eyes filled with lust.

"Carry females into the bedroom."

"No, only you." He dropped her onto the bed. The sea of pillows bounced, and a few fell onto the floor.

She pushed herself up and sat on the edge of the bed. "Why?"

"Because I don't think anyone has ever cradled you before. You deserve it. I want to be the first."

How could this man know her so well?

Kenzo's eyes darkened. "Another rule of warfare is appraisal. Estimate the necessary forces to ensure victory. I'm taking my time with you tonight."

She challenged him. "Evaluate all you want because before tonight is over, you'll *surrender* to me." She gripped his jacket, yanking his mouth to hers. Hunger and need fueled the kiss. His mouth dragged over hers and he nibbled on her face, then earlobe.

Aleeya frantically stripped off his clothes, wanting to see, to touch, to feel, and to taste. When Kenzo stood naked before her, she took him in with her eyes. The way his brown eyes tilted at the corners made her think of an earth lion. He smelled of spices, denim, and leather. So masculine, so hot.

She sucked in a breath as her fingers traced over the scars on his abdomen, the wounds on his back, and the raised skin on his legs. Despite these flaws, she didn't see a weak man. Instead, she saw a survivor, a man who persevered. A man marked with purpose. These markings made him more powerful, more beautiful.

He had the perfect framework with strong shoulders that could endure any burden. These were shoulders that enabled him to survive torture. Muscles packed powerful arms that could break or embrace someone. Impressively toned legs made her want to wrap her own around them, teasing and tangling. Her attention slid to the perfect ass that punctuated the stunning appearance. The ass that had literally fallen for her.

Aleeya's eyes landed on his erection, gloriously proud and aroused. Reaching out, she examined him with keen interest. "Another effective technique in battle is calculation. Estimating your interests. This, right here, is a powerful weapon."

She studied him, his smoothness, his texture. He gasped and his chest rose and fell at her examination. The length of him resembled that of a male star-being, but a different color. But his magnificent manhood called to her the most, throbbed for her. Her fingers tightened around him, answering the call, and he let out a marvelous moan.

"You're wicked." His voice came out husky. "You're still clothed." He pulled her from the bed to stand in front of him.

Unlike Aleeya, Kenzo took his time removing her armor. She admired his self-control. That was another efficient skill in a combat. As the barriers between them peeled off, she grew closer to him. That notion opened something in her.

His eyes darkened as he studied every inch of her body. Heat inflamed her cheeks as she met his gaze. The yearning in him matched her own. Sexual tension stretched and stretched until it snapped, and they came at each other like hungry wolves, dying to mate with mouths, tongues, and growls. She clamped her legs around his waist as her hands roamed his body, discovering, gripping, and claiming. Her pulse quickened, reflecting the drumming of her corra. Skin slapped against skin, but that wasn't enough. She yearned for closer contact, for a more profound connection.

Kenzo's hands captured her buttocks as he angled his mouth, deepening the kiss and tormenting her with his tongue. The sensations dazzled her senses, and stardust sparkled and hissed around them. The sparks resembled the colors around Yarra's aura.

He broke the kiss and looked at the stardust—or rather moondust—floating around them. "The Cosmos approves." A foolish smile stretched on his lips, making him irresistible and sexy. She smiled in return.

Kenzo lowered to the edge of the bed with her on his lap. He sampled her mouth, the column of her neck, shoulders, and arms. She shivered as each kiss woke her cells, and the cosmic codes on her body lit up.

"I love how you illuminate for me." He savored her skin, and she arched, giving him what he wanted.

His mouth left a fiery trail down her shoulders. He nibbled at her skin like a man sampling his way around a dessert table with an unyielding appetite.

"I love how I affect you..."

He cupped her breasts with his hands, and his thumbs worked their magic. The cosmic symbols pulsed as the sensations pounding through her escalated.

She moaned and ached for his touch. When his mouth closed over a nipple, her vision blurred. A jolt of pleasure coursed through her, pooled at her core, and drove her crazy. He worshipped her breasts, and she pushed him back onto the bed with her on top. Need slammed into need, and she panted out his name.

With a quick move, he flipped her over and under so that he was now on top. "The most important principle in warfare is victory." He gripped both of her wrists over her head. She'd never felt more vulnerable and more powerful than in that very moment. Both defenseless to his desires and in control of his needs. She relished that she was the reason for the wanton look in his eyes.

"You're my prey tonight." The breathy voice aroused her.

"Is that so?" She tried to bite him, but his powerful arms held her in place. His manhood throbbed between her legs, seeking for her attention.

She shifted, creating friction and torturing him in the most delicious ways. When he growled, she captured his lips. "Who's the prey now?"

TWENTY-ONE

Kenzo

He loved the way she devoured his mouth with such desperation. His tongue warred with hers as if she needed the battle just as much as he did. He might have called her his prey, but in reality, he was hers. He reveled in it, weak and willing for her, and only her.

"Do whatever you want with me," he murmured against her lips.

"Oh, I plan to." Desire filled her eyes, promising delectable things.

Holy fuck.

He'd never wanted anyone the way he wanted Aleeya. She tasted like a luscious siren come to offer him salvation. She was a dangerous temptation that drowned him, but in this moment, he didn't give a damn.

Need scorched through him as tension tightened his body. He didn't want this night to end. Kenzo savored her, took his time with her, and learned every crevice and secret to her. He broke the kiss and dragged his mouth along her body. Her skin was like silky chocolate he could lick and love all night. He loved how his tanned skin was shades lighter than hers. They were the same hue but different saturation, and he found that relationship beautiful. He couldn't get enough of her. She tried to wriggle free from his grip, but her movement only enticed him even more. This powerful female warrior was at his mercy.

Her cosmic codes glowed like stars against her dark skin. Their approval cheered him on. He felt like he was kissing the night sky. His hand found her heat, and she arched into it, moving and moaning and begging for more. Her response to his touch stirred something in him. Aroused at the sight, his fingers entertained her center. She spread her thighs wider for him, giving him the view of a lifetime. She was the most beautiful woman he'd ever seen. She even had cosmic symbols down here. He wanted them to illuminate for him.

Because of him.

Kenzo kissed her heat once, and she gasped as her symbols gleamed with celebration. Satisfied, he settled his mouth on her, tasting and savoring. He released the grip on her wrists to lift her buttocks. Aleeya's hands flew to his head, digging into his hair. He drove her wild and loved every second.

"Kenzo..." She moaned and his name became an antidote to all his problems.

Her desperation mirrored his own. He glanced around, searching for the Safe-Sex Spray. She pointed to the side table. In seconds, he had covered himself in the translucent protection. The colorful design and texture reminded him of a raised tattoo.

Kenzo aligned himself to her, met her gaze, and slid into her. Her muscles stretched and contracted, making room for him. Growling, he drove in further and further. Sweat gleamed on her forehead, and he brushed the wet strands of hair away as his mouth merged with hers.

Merged and united in two places, they moved in perfect rhythm. Long, slow strokes rendered their love like a silent poem between two people. This wasn't just sex. This wasn't temporary. This wasn't a convenience.

This was *more*. It was exactly what he wanted. His blood roared with recognition and he intensified his strokes. Aleeya reached her crescendo and shuddered, calling out his name. He could die happy with his name on her lips.

"You have my surrender, always." His heart raged with excitement as he climaxed, sending ripples of pleasure through his body. He rolled over and pulled her still trembling body to his side. Her breathing steadied as her head rested upon his shoulder. The safe-sex protection dissolved, and it was one of the most innovative inventions on this planet. She laughed as he said so.

Kenzo glanced at the sparkles still floating around the room.

"I've never seen magical moondust," Aleeya said.

"How do you know it's moondust and not stardust?" He wouldn't know the difference.

"Those are sparkles from Yarra."

That moon again. "What do you think it means?"

"It means my theory was right."

His eyebrows came together. "I don't understand. What were you trying to prove?"

"That we're connected."

"Well, I really enjoyed connecting with you. And I want to do it again and again." He gestured to his manhood.

Aleeya chuckled. "I meant connected by the Cosmos. Something beyond us. We were meant to meet, Kenzo. Yarra has a purpose for us. Maybe, we're the 'key' to everything like Jeeto said." She sat up and covered herself with the blanket.

"Last solar cycle, Farra brought Kazstrom and Teegan together. They saved the Aurora Matrix, but they were also…"

"Also, what?"

"Starmates. They fell in love, and she stayed here with him, when she could have gone back to Earth." Aleeya gripped the blanket tighter.

Kenzo wanted her to trust him with anything and everything.

"And you're afraid that we're heading that way?"

She flicked him a glance, and something flashed in her eyes, but disappeared quickly. "It's not just that. There's danger ahead, and I'm worried I won't be able to keep Norak safe. The three moons are divine entities, and their clues, riddles—or whatever you call them—mean something dire is about to happen."

Or is already happening, he thought.

She didn't answer his question directly, but he'd let it pass. A threat was brewing around them, he could sense it. He had to keep her safe. Moreover, he needed time to reflect on that question himself. Could it be true that their meeting was predestined? That would explain his inexplicable desire for her. Would he accept this mystical theory that a moon had the power to alter the course of life? He'd never believed in such a thing before. Why him?

Regardless, he had a choice. But what would he choose? Love was beyond him. He'd never experienced it before. But being with Aleeya stirred something unfamiliar in him. Was it love? She made him feel like a worthy man. She made him *want* to be a better man. In all these years, he'd never felt worthy or good enough for anyone. More so, being with her, his darkness dimmed and his need for vengeance took second place behind her.

She accepted his flawed body, but would she accept his flawed soul?

Everything that mattered to him died. His parents disowned him. Terence and his comrades were murdered. Kenzo didn't want Aleeya to meet that fate too.

"Let's just enjoy tonight and leave anything else for tomorrow, okay?" He wrapped an arm around her and turned into her hair. He inhaled her sweet scent and knew he could live the rest of his life wrapped in her embrace.

TWENTY-TWO

Kenzo

The next morning, Kenzo and Aleeya sat on her long couch and reviewed the surveillance her soldiers had gathered. "There's a lot to sort through."

"My soldiers already narrowed them down for us. They've removed irrelevant videos." She opened three virtual screens. "Let's divide up the tasks. I'll look at all videos from the day we visited the facility, and you can review the recordings from the day prior. How does that sound?"

"Sounds like an effective attack strategy." A smile curved onto his lips, remembering last night's sexual battle.

Her eyes glittered with amusement, but she made no comment about that. Instead, she focused on her work. "Move all videos with potential to the third screen. We can evaluate everything once we sift through these videos."

For the next couple of hours, Kenzo and Aleeya worked side by side, watching videos. The task was tedious, but necessary.

Another hour passed, and Aleeya snapped her finger,

getting his attention. "Look at this image." She zoomed in on a male figure carrying the child and running down a street that cut off the camera feed. "That's Jella, I just know it. She looks sedated. That took place on the day we were there. There's something about the figure that's familiar to me, but I don't know what. I wish there was a frontal view video."

Kenzo's stomach twisted when the figure turned slightly, revealing part of his black mask. "That mask looks like the ones my captors wore."

"We'll keep looking."

They continued until Jeeto made strange sounds in his sleep. Kenzo checked on his pet and discovered Jeeto was smiling in his dream. The Aurora Matrix must have given his pet some serious excitement. The animal had never slept this much before.

Kenzo's vambrace buzzed with a message from Tab. "I'm in Norak. I'm downstairs at Aleeya's building. Can you let me in?"

"You're here?" Kenzo's shock stopped Aleeya's research.

"Who's here? What's going on?"

"Tab's downstairs. Can you approve his entrance?"

Aleeya scratched the back of her neck, and the action reminded Kenzo of his suspicion that Tab was connected to Aleeya. Kenzo woke up before Aleeya this morning and researched his roommate. Tab had mentioned that he was a journalist who lived in Norak and his family had died. Could Aleeya be related to him somehow?

There wasn't much to find out about Tab in Norak or Delleon. Details about Tab and Aleeya ran through his mind. Tab and Aleeya didn't resemble each other. Tab's skin tone was darker than hers. However, the way they both pursed their lips in irritation mimicked each other.

Aleeya pulled up a screen on her vambrace and connected to the security in the main lobby. "You can let him in, thank you." She turned to Kenzo. "Did something happen in Phyllus?" She scratched her neck again. "Blackened Stardust. This device is irritating me again. I'll have to ask El Lara to refer me to someone she trusts."

Kenzo opened the door and Tab strode in, looking at Aleeya. "I'm sorry for stopping by unannounced, but it's urgent." He tucked his hands into his pants pockets, but not before Kenzo noticed the trembling.

Kenzo placed a gentle hand on his friend's back. "Are you okay? Come sit down." He led Tab to the couch. "Do you want something to drink?"

"Something warm would be great, thank you."

The anxiety and sadness in Tab's eyes reflected what he'd seen in Aleeya's eyes before. How had he missed this?

Aleeya sat across from Tab. "Don't worry about it. It's no bother. Did something happen in Phyllus? Did you locate Malixx?"

Kenzo brought a cup of tea over to Tab. Tab held the cup with both hands, sipped, and placed it on the coffee table. He scratched the back of his neck, and Aleeya picked up on the motion.

"Your neck itches too?"

Tab nodded.

"Just recently?"

He nodded again.

"Do you know why?"

"The chip inside your neck is activated when it's near mine." He inhaled a breath as he placed a hand over his chest, as if trying to calm an emotional storm. "You're my daughter, Aleeya."

TWENTY-THREE

Aleeya

Aleeya's corra dropped, rolled, and passed out somewhere between disbelief, hope, anger, and resentment. The muscles on her chest constricted as a sharp pain stabbed through her corra. She struggled for breath, even as the pain coursed through her, shredding her apart. She searched into the depths of herself for her warrior strength and shoved all the misery down. A vast numbness emerged, permitting her to stay present enough to face her immediate concerns.

In battle, moments of vulnerability were dangerous. They allowed the enemy to gain a foothold. She would not surrender to that. She inhaled deeply, fell back onto the couch, and crossed her arms in a defensive gesture that shielded her from unexpected pain.

She studied Tab. Could it be true? Could this star-being who sat before her with sad eyes under white eyebrows, a determined face, and dark skin be the father who had abandoned her? Did she look like him? She couldn't focus her wild thoughts because the war in her corra was too loud. She didn't know if she should feel rage or joy. A flood of questions overwhelmed her.

Why hadn't he come back for her before? And why was he here now?

A headache pounded at her temple, but she ignored it.

Kenzo sat down beside her and placed a hand on her back, providing comfort. He looked over at Tab and offered him a nod of acknowledgement.

Aleeya whipped her head to Kenzo. "Did you know?"

"I had my suspicions when I noticed both of you scratching your necks. The way you purse your lips in irritation is also similar." He jerked a chin at Tab. "I tried to research you, but I couldn't find anything." Kenzo's attention returned to her and sincerity filled his eyes. "I wanted to make sure I had the correct information before I told you anything. I didn't want to add more pain if my suspicions turned out wrong."

Irritated, Aleeya bit her bottom lip. His reasons made sense. But right now, the bonfire of emotions didn't allow her to think clearly. Distrust stepped to the forefront. "What else are you keeping from me?" The words came out harsher than she expected.

"Nothing." His hand stayed on her lower back, still giving her support. She scooted away from him. That action sliced him.

Tab looked at Kenzo. "You didn't find any information about me because my proper name is Tabori." His gaze slid over to Aleeya. "I know you have a lot of questions for me, Aleeya. But first, I want you to know that I *wanted* to come back for you. You're the only reason I continued living. I thought about you all these solar cycles."

Tabori. A part of her brain resonated with that name.

I wanted to come back for you. She'd dreamt of hearing those words for so long. But right now, they seemed distant, too far away for her corra to grasp. "Why didn't you?"

"I—I couldn't remember where I left you. I know that sounds irresponsible, cold, and awful, but it's the truth. My memory began slipping, and I couldn't remember certain things."

An unexpected fear reared up in her mind. Did she succumb to the same fate? Was that why she had trouble seeing his face after all these solar cycles? And that the image of her mother had blurred away. She could hardly recall the life she had before arriving at the orphanage. Where had she lived? What had her home been like?

"When I saw you the other day, I knew it was you. You look just like your mother. She's still in my memory. One of the memories I have left."

What other familial traits did she have with her mother? Aleeya had so many questions, she didn't know where to begin.

"What I remember is that I didn't want to put you in danger," Tab continued.

Her warrior's instincts kicked in. "What do you mean?"

Tab shifted, showing her the back of his neck. The rash resembled hers. "The metal chips have been activated. That's why they've been irritating us. The chips need to be removed. The information on them is evidence of brutality and other sensitive data that I don't understand." He took another sip of tea. "When the assassin killed your mother, he kidnapped your little brother—"

"I have a brother?" Shock slammed into her. She couldn't remember his face or anything about him.

"Adlar, he was only two solar cycles when they took him... and killed him."

"Who?" Her fingers curled. She had no memory of her

brother at all. Her body shuddered from the shock and sadness that rippled from inside out. It was as if her blood cells ruptured and shoved her organs out of their normal placements. Grief squeezed her muscles and cramped the side of her stomach.

"The star-beings wanted the data stored inside the chips. I located one assassin and killed him. The injury I gained was worth it." Tab rubbed a hand over his right leg, the one with the limp.

That statement hung in the room for a while. Retribution didn't offer satisfaction the way it should have. She would have done the same. But she understood the torment on Tab's face. "They deserved it. You prevented an awful being from hurting others."

Tab didn't reply, only scrubbed a hand over his face. Kenzo offered support to his friend with a friendly comment. "Do you want me to address you as Tabori or Tab?"

"You've known me as Tab. Stick with that."

"How did the chip get into my neck?" A crease formed between Aleeya's brows. "Who put it in me? When?"

"My friend, Garnu. He was a scientist who discovered the data. I was a journalist, so I had planned on a long article disclosing it. I never got that chance. Assassins came and killed Garnu's family, and they went after our family."

"Why didn't you alert the authorities? There's law and order in Norak."

"I did. I sent information to them and went dark. I didn't know who I could trust."

"What exactly is in this chip?"

"I only saw a bunch of codes. I couldn't understand them, but I trust Garnu. He had a brilliant mind, and he was like a brother to me. All I knew was that it held dangerous information."

"We'll extract the devices and decipher the data," Kenzo said.

Tab continued, "They sent assassins after me and Garnu. He broke the data into three parts. I gave him permission to hide the chip in me and Aleeya temporarily until things died down. He tested our frequencies, and they blended well with the devices, therefore hiding them better. I don't know where he hid the other chip. He never got the chance to tell me. He died and my memory began fluctuating."

"Maybe he hid it on himself." Aleeya flicked a glance at the man who claimed to be her father. "If he did, maybe the assassins already have that third piece. Or it died with Garnu."

"That could be a possibility. I never thought about that. But Garnu's frequency didn't jive well with the device. The chip kept hissing with his energy, but who knows, maybe he figured something out." Sorrow stretched over Tab's face.

Aleeya changed the subject. "He made the devices react when they're near each other?"

"Yes."

"Or perhaps the third piece of this puzzle has come alive and is functioning elsewhere, and these two devices picked up on its frequency," Kenzo said.

"Or maybe the two chips are malfunctioning. They've been underneath our skin for a long time." Tab added. "There are too many possibilities. We won't know until they're removed for examination."

Aleeya considered that and all the possibilities of why the metal chips could have activated. Were the chips related to Malixx and his insane experiments? Tab was right. They would have to study the devices and determine their components and functionality.

"Do you think Malixx did this? I've researched him, and

he's four hundred and seventy solar cycles, which means he could have had a part in it when I was a child." Aleeya glanced at Tab. "I can't remember your age…"

Regret filled Tab's eyes. "It's okay. I'm twenty solar cycles younger than Malixx. He's an intelligent scientist who has had a lot of time to hone his skills."

Kenzo tapped her back. "How old are you?"

"Two hundred and fifty solar cycles."

Kenzo stared at her and leaned in to whisper, "I've always been attracted to older women. They have so much wisdom and experience in areas that make a man weak and willing."

Still annoyed that he didn't share his suspicions with her, Aleeya ignored him.

"Damn, I'm only a baby at thirty-five years old."

"Human years are different," Tab said.

"I know, but when you spit out numbers like that, my logical mind doesn't differentiate human years, solar cycles, or different dimensions. They're just numbers and a two-digit number is *logically* smaller than a three-digit."

Tab released a half chuckle before his expression turned somber. "When I settled in Phyllus, I took random jobs while I tried to remember where I left Aleeya. A block of memory was ripped from me. It confused me, and I thought I was going crazy. I worked at Atrium's mail center because the hours were flexible, and the job was easy. I wanted nothing stressful because I was trying to regain my memory. As I got to know people, they told me things about the company, and I investigated. I thought Malixx was responsible for your mother's and brother's deaths." He looked at Aleeya. "I found no evidence of that. Instead, I discovered Malixx is creating these harmful products and selling them to the public. So I stayed there trying to gather data to take Atrium down." He paused and sipped more tea.

"Because of you, we got all the locations of those facilities," Kenzo said.

Tab scratched his white goatee. "Atrium has been transformed over the solar cycles. Malixx is now producing more medicine at an alarming rate. He's more radical; his experiments have escalated."

Aleeya contemplated everything about the metal chips, Malixx, Tab, Kenzo, Yarra, and herself. How were they connected? She absorbed the details as if she were conducting a covert mission, sorting out the specifics and cataloguing them in an organized way.

She tried to put herself in her father's shoes: the desperate situation of his family, the struggle to protect his children, and the memory loss. What would she have done? It was a lot to take in all at once. She understood he had to save her brother and couldn't take her with him. Leaving her at an orphanage was the way he kept her safe. He hoped to return to her. These were all points that flashed through her mind. But then he was injured after killing the assassins who murdered her mother and brother. The trauma of everything was probably the reason for the memory loss. The same trauma that affected her.

She comprehended the magnitude of his sacrifice, the terror, the grief, the vengeance—all the emotions that drove an individual insane. Still, her corra was stuck in the muddy place between resentment and forgiveness. She didn't know where she stood. All she knew was that she had to push these emotions aside to focus on the bigger picture. Norak was at stake, and Jella was still missing.

But the onslaught of emotions continued to batter her. Though she tried to suppress the emotional surge, it welled up into an enormous ball in her throat, cutting off her breathing. Her attention wavered, and she stopped listening to the conversation. She recognized the signs of a panic attack. With intention, she calmed herself, taking in slow breaths. Her apartment became too small. There was not enough air circulating, and the walls crowded around her, making her feel trapped.

"I need some air." She rose from the couch and left her apartment.

TWENTY-FOUR

Aleeya

Aleeya rushed outside and strode on the pebbled sidewalk. She didn't know where she was going. She just needed to move. She gulped in huge breaths of fresh air, letting them inflate her lungs. When she exhaled, she released the brick of pain that had been stuck inside her chest for far too long. It came out stale and bitter. She was so confused, so hurt.

She turned down a quiet street where there was a park with a pond. Nearby, two children chased each other around a playground while their parents watched. The lovely image squeezed her corra. That could have been her life.

Aleeya found a bench, sat down, and studied a patch of waterlilies that gave off sparkles in the air. Five pink and purple petal-flies swarmed the lilies, kissing one after another. Their colorful wings mimicked flower petals. Their delicate flutter from lily to lily calmed and cleared her mind. What were these insects thinking as they went about their day? Did they have goals? Did they have pain?

Of course they have, Aleeya. We all endure pain. It is part of living and learning, part of life.

She didn't know where that insight came from. But it brought her reprieve. That small window of relief offered her a new perspective. Everything was energy, and these adorable insects were no different. Like everything, their life consisted of difficulties too, but they made it appear so simple. That simplicity allowed them to achieve their goal, whether that be fluttering around playfully or gathering nectar for food.

Could she look at her life through that simple lens? She was trying her best.

An image flashed across her mind, and she saw herself as a child peering through the window, waiting for her father to come back. The uncertainty, fear, and loneliness ebbed and flowed around her like massive waves disrupting her corra.

Tears broke through her restrictions and flowed down her face. Moments ago, in her apartment, she didn't think she could cry. When she was up there with Tab, the shock had numbed her to where she had to reevaluate her ability to feel and express anything.

The familiar cautionary energy slammed into her, alerting her. It was more pronounced than in previous times. She jumped from the bench, glanced around, and avoided a beam of energy. A cyborg in gray uniform with a glowing blue chest charged at her with his blaster. She dodged his blasts, gripped her own, and fired back. Three shots went into the chest, and he dropped to the ground, but he wasn't dead. She fired three more into his blue corra.

Five more cyborgs appeared. With fear for the family playing nearby, she turned and shouted at them. "Go, get to safety!" They did.

She reached for Xmark and shot out her golden arrow. With her mind, she told them to aim for the cyborg's corra.

Then an arm wrapped around her neck, trying to choke her. She fired at his thigh and foot. He released his grip, and she whirled a fist to his face, cracking his jaw. Then she blasted him until his chest burst, revealing the blue corra. Did Malixx send these cyborgs?

She received her answer when Malixx appeared from the corner of her eye. The cyborgs recognized his presence and halted their attack. What happened to Malixx? He didn't look like the same being she saw at the convention. The red hair and green scales on his face and arms dulled like something siphoned the vitality from him. Soot emerged from pockets around his body.

"Leave my scientific breakthroughs alone." He lifted a finger at her. "Or you will die." A beam of electric fire shot out from his finger.

Aleeya jumped and avoided the blast. The cyborgs charged at her, and soot also emerged from pockets on their faces and bodies. Was the soot part of the scientific experiment? Or was this black magic?

She fired her arrows and killed the cyborgs. Malixx disappeared just as more cyborgs emerged. She sent several shots into their corras.

Peko rushed up to her. "Are you okay?" He blasted at the two cyborgs who attacked from behind. "What happened here?"

"I'm not sure what happened. They just attacked me." She waved the soot away from Peko's black hair.

"For no reason?"

She wasn't in the mood to disclose anything to anyone. Did Malixx send these cyborgs as retribution for destroying his facilities?

"I'll have to investigate this. How did you know there was a battle here?" Aleeya asked.

"I was on my way home and saw a frightened family shouting for help."

Shouldn't he be in Phyllus waiting on Elder Kai and El Lara? A thought bloomed in her mind. "Are Elder Kai and El Lara back in Norak?"

"Just El Lara, she skipped the last conference." He searched her face. "Are you sure you're okay? Did they hurt you? Let me check." He walked around her, scanning her body.

Peko's concern perplexed Aleeya. "I'm fine, really. You should go home. I'm calling the Crime Division Investigators. They'll need to clean this up and gather evidence. I'll stay here and give them my report."

"I can stay and help you. The CDIs will have questions. I can give them my angle."

Peko stayed and gave his version, which expedited the reports.

A few thoughts popped into her mind, but she needed clarity to sift through them before making a move. Right now, her emotions were in shambles. A warrior had to disentangle herself from the chaos before she could plan a strategy. Suspicion became a soot particle floating in her vision, giving her an idea of who she could be dealing with.

Would Malixx send more cyborgs to attack her and Kenzo?

TWENTY-FIVE

Kenzo

Where was Aleeya?

Kenzo assumed she ran down to the courtyard for some fresh air. He gave her time to be alone before he went searching for her. She probably needed someone to talk to. Given the impact of the sudden news, Aleeya must have been crushed. She composed herself well while she listened to Tab. He imagined the internal storm wrecking her.

The father who had abandoned her was now back. The father who was responsible for the trauma she probably developed as a child. Kenzo didn't have the experience, but he could assume. Trauma had a way of eating you. All he wanted to do was be there for Aleeya.

Concern coiled in his stomach. Kenzo sent Aleeya a message. *Are you okay? I'm sorry I should've informed you of my suspicions. I didn't mean to hurt you.*

He waited for a reply. When nothing came, he continued roaming the streets.

From yesterday's attack, Kenzo worried the individual could be back for him or Aleeya. He couldn't shake the feeling that someone was watching him. Was he being paranoid? Probably, but he had good reason. Kenzo should have gone after Aleeya sooner. He strode into the courtyard, but didn't see her. He went back to the street and surveyed the area again. So many tall buildings made of stones, metal, and innovation greeted him.

Where did she go? Maybe she was back home now.

As he turned and headed back to the apartment, Peko stopped his personal rider at the set of lights about thirty feet from Kenzo. Peko didn't look happy as he sped off.

A message from Aleeya popped onto Kenzo's screen. *I'm okay. I'm heading back now.*

TWENTY-SIX

Aleeya

A storm of emotions whirled inside Aleeya as she rushed back to her apartment. She tried her best to keep her feelings and fears contained. Kenzo met her around the corner. She didn't know why, but the sight of him was exactly what she needed. She understood why he kept the suspicion of Tab to himself. She would've done the same. He was just trying to protect her from unnecessary pain.

She barreled into his arms, and the emotional container broke free. She let herself go. The tears came, but they were more a release of pressure than anything else.

Kenzo tightened his grip around her. "What happened? Where did you go? I went looking for you."

She didn't speak and embraced him. The anxiety weighing on her slipped away. He asked no more questions, and they stood in silence for a while.

Aleeya veered back to look at him. "I know it was rude to leave abruptly. I needed to breathe."

He shrugged. "It's a natural reaction, an expected reaction. Where did you go, though?"

Aleeya told him about the attack from Malixx and his cyborgs, and how Peko helped her kill them.

"What?" His eyes steeled. "Did they hurt you?"

"No, they didn't. Malixx looks different. He's been altered or something. There were soot forming holes on his face and body."

"I saw Peko driving off just now. He didn't look happy. I'm glad he was there to help you. We need to be extra careful from now on. Malixx could send more cyborgs or some other assassins after us. This is retaliation for destroying his facilities."

"I agree, but first, I need to sit." She sat on the bench and prayed she could sit longer this time without fighting for her life. "I just need a moment to gather myself. Everything happened so quickly, I didn't have time to process it. Then the attack occurred, which threw me off and added another layer of stress. I know there are a lot of urgent things needing my attention, but right now, I don't have the mentality or the energy to take care of them." She closed her eyes, shutting out the world.

Kenzo relaxed beside her. "Take a breather. Rest. I need you well so we can be a team. Tab wondered how you were doing. I told him you're a warrior, physically and mentally. Nothing can break you."

Aleeya opened her eyes. "I feel like I'm in a million pieces right now."

"I'll help you pick them up, one at a time."

An eyebrow rose. "Poetry could be your side occupation when you need a break from bounty hunting."

That laugh again. She'd never tire of it.

"Life can be inspirational if you allow it. You've inspired me," he said. "I'm looking at things differently, Buttercup."

For some reason, that silly alias grew on her. He gave something simple—like a flower that no one paid attention to —purpose.

After a while, she asked, "Where did Tab go?"

"He's still in your apartment. He was tired, and I offered my room for now. I assume the two of you will need to extract the chips as soon as possible. Maybe you can have your priestess remove his too. He doesn't have any place to stay right now. If you're uncomfortable with him in your apartment, I can take him to get a hotel with me."

"No, it's fine. He can stay in the guest room. You can share my bedroom if you'd like." This time, she met his gaze.

"I would never refuse an invitation to your bed." His eyes gleamed. "Never."

Talking to Kenzo lifted her mood. Lila—the aura reader—was accurate. A family member did come into her life, and the idea of a long-term relationship was making itself more prominent every day.

Elder Kai's words also echoed in her mind. The reason she went to the GCOT convention in Delleon was because the suns and the moons urged him to take her. Had they all placed her exactly where she needed to be because of a prayer sent out a long time ago? How many times had she prayed to find her father? And now he was sleeping in her apartment!

What else did the Cosmos have planned for her?

Aleeya gulped in a deep breath and released it, the heavy burden no longer suffocating her.

"Tab's experiencing his own hell too," Kenzo said. "I don't know what I would've done if I had been in his situation. He did what he thought was best for you."

"I know. My mind understands that, but my corra needs time for it to sink in. I need time to forgive and heal. And I don't know when that'll happen. I can't force it."

"And you shouldn't. Let things flow at their own pace." He kicked a pebble, and it flew into the bushes.

A part of her blamed herself. "For the longest time, I detested him. I wondered why he had abandoned me. Did I do something wrong? Was I a rebellious child?"

"Those are normal fears." He squeezed her hand.

"Now that I know the actual story, I feel ashamed."

"You shouldn't feel that way. You were a victim, and so was he."

Aleeya glanced at him and a small smile surfaced on her face. "Did you learn psychology in military training? You're a good therapist, you know that?"

"Not a therapist, but someone who has seen it in others. I had extensive training to survive at sea, in the air, and on land. But sometimes the best knowledge is just experience. Trauma can blind us from common sense. It happened to me, which is why it's easier to help others than to help myself."

That explanation made so much sense to her. She'd never had a friend to just pour her emotions out like this. She had her warrior sisters, whom she referred to as "sistars" because they were her special entourage. But this connection with Kenzo was on a different level.

Aleeya let out a slow sigh. "I'm not sure where to go from here. Is there such a thing as starting over? It feels weird to start over with your father or any family member. I never thought about it. I mean, I looked for him because I needed closure, but it never occurred to me what would happen after I found him. I guess you're right. You *do* know what you're talking about. It is harder to see the common sense stuff when it's personal."

Amusement flashed in his eyes. "Say that again?"

"Say what?"

"Start with the part where you said: 'I guess you're right.

You *do* know what you're talking about.' I love hearing that from you."

She rolled her eyes, but a smile crept onto her face.

"Yes, you can start over. You're looking at a guy who started over many times. When I left my parents and chose my military path, I started life anew. When I was abducted, tortured, and escaped, I pushed myself up and began again. No matter how many setbacks and scars I acquired, I kept moving. I might not have a clear destination, but I know which direction I need to move in. That hunch has been my compass."

"That kind of intuitive detection wins all kinds of battles." This inner strength attracted her to him. The ability to make her feel safe and grounded was something she had never felt with anyone.

"I'm not unappreciative of what I have, or of what the orphanage gave me." She twisted her lips. "I just didn't know how heavy the resentment and blame were until they immobilized me."

"When you keep something that dark inside of you, it becomes a disease." Kenzo tilted her chin up to face him. "I was meant to meet you. I'm the connecting piece between you and Tab. I feel like I have to help you mend your relationship. I'm happy to be part of it."

Fate had sent her to him. Or was it Yarra? Something told her they were one and the same. Either way, she was grateful. "You're a gift from the Cosmos."

His stare intensified, making her corra jerk. "The feeling is mutual." He kissed her with such tenderness, she veered back to look at him.

She loved the juxtaposition of him; he was a contradiction in the most beautiful of ways. He was danger wrapped in poetry. He was what she needed and what she feared.

He was the air required for her to breathe. He was the air that suffocated her when it was no longer available.

"I admire your resilience and your persistence," he said, surprising her. "Many have used their difficult past as an excuse to rebel and cause harm onto others. They blame the world for their agony. You didn't. You carried your pain like fragile diamonds. They're precious to you even when they're rough and covered with dirt and grime."

She hadn't looked at her misery that way. But his words created such eloquent imagery that it glistened in her mind. "You should write a poetry book. Teegan will sell it at her bookstore."

Kenzo let out a laugh that soared through the sky. "No, thank you."

"You don't want to write a book about me?"

His gaze bore into her and mischief rose in his eyes. "If I write a poetic book about you, it'll be something you *don't* want your family or friends to read."

"Oh." Embarrassment washed over as her imagination went wild. "Let me know when you finish it. I'll give you my critique."

He chuckled. "I see you're feeling better. Tab resigned from Atrium. When he found you, he wanted to come back to Norak and start over."

A new beginning for her and her father sounded hopeful. She wanted to take it slow, so she didn't mess it up.

"What about getting information on Atrium's products?"

"We can still retrieve the info without Tab. I'll feel better knowing he's away from there. He's suffered enough, and I think his priorities have shifted to mending his relationship with you. Everything else can wait."

The lump in her throat shrank with the realization that she was a priority to someone, or rather, to two men: Tab and Kenzo.

"Malixx hasn't shown up for work. His employees haven't been able to locate him," Kenzo said. "The Phyllus officials are investigating every company that has ever worked with Atrium or their associates. Atrium is losing allies and businesses right and left. Detective Ahlex informed me that the documents Lila sent him ties Malixx to two Phyllus officials. I know Malixx feels cornered."

"Which will make him more erratic, more dangerous. If Jella is with him, I hope she's safe. I'll check in with Magnetti to see if he's found any additional information on her. We'll resume our surveillance review today. We'll uncover something soon."

Aleeya had to give her mind a rest if she wanted to look at the issues with clarity. But there was one thing she couldn't wait on. "El Lara is back in Norak. It's time to remove the metal chip."

TWENTY-SEVEN

Kenzo

Kenzo accompanied Aleeya and Tab to the Elseon Grove. Aleeya's spaceship flew past a long bridge made of rocks connecting two landmasses separated by a wide fissure. Underneath the bridge was a body of water. Curtains of energies flowed up and down from the sky into the land.

Aleeya docked *Sentra Five* in a small aero station outside of the grove. Jeeto jumped onto Kenzo's shoulder as he descended the energetic ramp and stood gazing at the incredible vegetation.

"The plant life here is more vibrant than Delleon's." He breathed in the mystery of the damp air and glanced at the trees with pink and purple leaves. A field of blue and purple bamboo swayed in the distance. In another section, enormous creatures loomed, with long necks, long legs, and narrow arms that drifted as they rearranged the vines and tree limbs that had fallen. Moss in various colors covered their arms.

"This grove feeds off energy from the Aurora Matrix."

Aleeya led them through a pebbled path with a fantastical view that belonged in a fantasy.

"I've heard of the Elseon Grove, but I've never had the chance to visit." Tab stopped and stared at a giant flower that produced gentle music. Kenzo joined him, peering into the flower. Two insects strummed the filaments like musical instruments. Jeeto hummed along.

Aleeya waved at a tall, lanky plant-being with large eyes driving an automobile made of metal, twigs, and leaves. "Hi, Plantiss."

The green-being with roots sprouting from his head and flower buds crowding his earlobes smiled. "El Lara's waiting for you. Hop on."

Aleeya sat in front with Plantiss. Kenzo and Tab took the back seats that were covered in green leather with veiny textures.

"This is my friend Kenzo. And this is... my father, Tab." Aleeya introduced them, her tone casual.

"Oh, what a pleasant surprise." Plantiss turned around to greet Tab and Kenzo. "Welcome to the Elseon Grove."

"Thank you," Kenzo replied.

Tab smiled with a nod at Plantiss and exchanged a warm glance with Kenzo. After Tab's admission that he was Aleeya's father, things had been awkward in her apartment. The father and daughter had stopped all conversation on the topic. Both needed time to adjust to their new relationship.

This was the first time Aleeya had addressed him as her father. Tab's eyes glistened, and Kenzo squeezed his shoulder. It was a good sign Aleeya was moving in a positive direction.

The plant-mobile stopped in front of a greenhouse with a large yard. Animals peeked in and darted off. A white jaguar rested under a flowering tree, peering over at them while plant-beings of various sizes tended to the bright vegetation around them. The air quality in this place stimulated his lungs, giving him more energy than ever before.

Kenzo's attention swerved to the magnificent floating islands beyond the greenery and at the enormous houses attached to each. He had seen several floating islands in Delleon, but none of them were as magical as this. These enchanted floating landscapes dripped with floral vines that dangled from the island like long beards. Colorful birds and petal-flies played with the vines.

The wide glass door to the greenhouse slid open and pulled him away from the floating islands. A stunning blue star-being emerged. Her long, white hair was streaked with purple. A star blinked from her forehead. She wore a soft green gown, and a live snake wrapped around her wrist like a bracelet.

Aleeya lifted her fist to her chest and tapped. "El Lara, thank you for seeing us so quickly. I know you just got back."

El Lara waved a hand. "It's no bother. I would have come back earlier if you had told me the urgency." She glanced over to Tab. "It's nice to meet you."

"Likewise. Thank you for taking care of Aleeya for all these solar cycles. I did some research, and I know that you often teach at the Cosmic Corra."

"Children are most important to me. They are the future. Society depends on what we teach them. When you teach love, love is what you'll get. We need to be there to support whatever they need."

Tab nodded, but he felt the sting from her words.

Feeling protective of his friend, Kenzo said, "I'm Kenzo, nice to meet you." He offered a smile.

The distraction worked. El Lara smiled in returned. "Same here."

From the back of Kenzo's shoulder, Jeeto peered over. "Hi, I'm Jeeto."

El Lara's stern expression softened. "Well, hello there."

Jeeto jumped onto her arm, the one without the snake bracelet.

"You can understand him?" Kenzo asked.

El Lara brushed Jeeto's blue hair. "Of course. He speaks the divine language of Yarra."

Kenzo and Jeeto exchanged a friendly glance.

El Lara's purple eyes gleamed. "You speak it too?"

"Yes, I didn't know I was speaking a rare language." Kenzo studied Jeeto as the animal made noises at the snake. The snake hissed. The two appeared to be carrying on a strange conversation. Nothing should have surprised him anymore, but this scenario delighted him.

"I can understand Jeeto too," Aleeya added.

"Hmm, interesting. You can tell me more about that later. For now, Sizzler would like to play with her new friend."

"Oh, I didn't know Sizzler was a female." Aleeya followed the Priestess down a hall and into a room filled with various sized crystals and plants.

"Today she is. Tomorrow is a different story." El Lara lowered her arm to a branch, and Sizzler slithered on it with Jeeto running after her.

Kenzo looked at Tab, who was also entertained by Jeeto's new friendship. Though the concept intrigued him, Kenzo didn't inquire about how his pet and a snake could become comrades so quickly. He feared the question would require a detailed explanation, and he wasn't in the mood for that.

El Lara turned to her guests. "Let's get to the reason you're here. Come with me."

TWENTY-EIGHT

Aleeya

When Aleeya introduced Tab as her father to Plantiss, the mental chains clanked from her. Her body and corra sighed in relief. She could recognize him as her father. The acknowledgment had stuck to her throat when she learned his true identity. Anger and resentment prevented her from accepting the truth.

But that was the truth. He was her father. Truth had many faces. Sometimes they were sharp and hard, and sometimes they came with an attachment that was unavoidable. When she faced her past for what it was, it could no longer chain her.

Her corra forgave him at its own pace. Nothing he did was his fault; she knew that. But like any wound that had gone untreated for so long, her wound had festered.

Give me time, she told him in her mind. *I need time to heal.*

Clearing her thoughts, Aleeya entered El Lara's laboratory. It had changed little. The same pastel walls greeted her. She sat on one examination table covered in a soft cloth, while Tab took the other. Kenzo stood beside Aleeya like a bodyguard, watching El Lara's every move. Aleeya discovered she liked his protectiveness of her.

"I tried to remove the metal chip," Kenzo said. "But there was too much blood, and I didn't want to injure a cervical nerve."

"I'll take a look. I assume Aleeya's insistence was why you took it upon yourself?" The Priestess gave Aleeya a sidelong glance.

"If you had a foreign object in you, you'd want it out as soon as possible."

"I understand, but the neck is a sensitive area. There are nerves that are connected to your brain. You don't want to risk that." A robotic table displaying all kinds of tools and various jars filled with bugs moved itself over to El Lara. She pulled on gloves and held up a jar of green ointment. "This will numb the area."

"I remember." This wasn't the first time the Priestess had treated her. Aleeya twisted her hair into a bun, giving easy access to her neck.

"You did a decent job sealing it." El Lara looked at Kenzo.

"Thank you, but I'll stay away from all surgical practices from now on."

El Lara lathered on the ointment, and Aleeya's skin prickled.

Seconds later, Aleeya remained as still as possible. "It's numb. I'm ready."

Tab came off his examination table to stand beside Kenzo, eyeing the procedure.

El Lara lifted a scalpel with an energy blade, letting Aleeya know what she was about to do.

"You okay?" Kenzo scanned Aleeya's face for any signs of discomfort.

His concern warmed her. "I'm fine. This isn't my first

wound or procedure. El Lara has stitched me up before."

The star on the Priestess's forehead glowed. "I'll take good care of her."

A slight pinch pierced her skin, but nothing painful. Aleeya sensed the extraction from her flesh. Her body sighed like a thorn was plucked from her body. A rush of fresh energy filled the empty space. Metal clanked into a container. From another jar, El Lara pulled out a yellow bug the size of her thumb.

Aleeya glance at it. "You again? I'd like to see this process. Can you turn on the screen for me, please?

El Lara activated two screens. One captured the procedure, while the other screen displayed it for Aleeya.

El Lara held up the bug for Tab and Kenzo to see. "It's going to stop the bleeding and sterilize the area."

The Priestess placed the bug on Aleeya's neck, and its size grew, covering the wound. When its yellow skin turned purple, El Lara removed the bug and dumped it into another jar, closing the lid. The bug crawled around, and purple gas seeped from its skin, shrinking its body back to its original size. El Lara sewed up the wound with an energetic stitch-up device, then sprayed it with a cool sealant.

While El Lara worked on Tab, Aleeya stared at the metal chip being cleansed by light beams inside the closed container. The chip was a quarter of an inch wide and one eighth thick. After so many solar cycles of having something stuck within her, her body noticed the changes. The heavy feeling she carried around flowed out of her, both physically and metaphorically.

"Both of you should take it easy for a couple of days. The tissues need to heal, and your body needs to adjust. Feel free to swim in the Star Lagoon to expedite the healing process. The water from the lagoon has healing properties." El Lara removed her gloves and turned to Tab. "Whoever inserted these devices performed an outstanding job on you and Aleeya."

Aleeya heard the unspoken word. "But?"

"But that chip pressed on an important nerve that connects to your brain. That could have happened during the early solar cycles when you were just learning how to maneuver as a warrior. Back then, you were jumping, climbing, and stretching various muscles. You could've pushed the device out of its initial placement. It's hard to keep something foreign so still inside your body."

Tab released a heavy sigh.

El Lara turned to Tab. "Yours misaligned as well. The body changes and shifts as part of maturity."

Kenzo's eye lit up. "Your theory could explain why Aleeya doesn't remember certain things from her childhood and why Tab had memory loss too."

"It could be." El Lara opened a closet door and removed a device that looked like a fashionable helmet. "This head scanner will give me a good reading of your brain health and frequency."

Aleeya made a face. "You don't want to see the mess inside my head."

"I do," Kenzo grinned, leaning in to whisper, "Maybe there are all kinds of sexy images of me."

Aleeya rolled her eyes. What was she afraid of? The Priestess wasn't trying to pry into her private thoughts. It was just a brain scan, not a mind scan. No machine could read her mind. Even she couldn't read her own mind at times.

"Let's do it." Aleeya straightened her posture, still sitting on the examination table.

"It won't hurt." El Lara placed the gunmetal helmet over Aleeya's head, covering her face.

Aleeya turned to the mirror on the wall. She looked like she was wearing a reflective egg. She could see through the thin glass flap. She tried her best to relax as energy swirled inside the helmet, massaging her scalp, forehead, and the back of her neck.

Her muscles loosened as the helmet administered a spa-like treatment.

A few minutes later, her session ended, and Tab got to experience the brain scan.

El Lara read the results from her virtual screens. She ushered everyone out to her kitchen. They sat around the table, set with trays of snacks and refreshments. "Eat and drink whatever you like."

Tab poured himself a cup of green herbal tea, while Kenzo opted for the blue water. He filled a cup for Aleeya and El Lara too.

El Lara met Aleeya's eyes. "The metal chip pinched a nerve that delayed blood and energy flow to the hippocampus, a region of the brain that's important for memory and emotion. The hippocampus acts as a memory sorter, sending out memories to the appropriate cerebral hemisphere for long-term storage. It retrieves those memories when necessary. Perhaps it was divine intervention that allowed you to forget certain things to help your growth. Would you have matured the way you did if you had remembered everything? Would you have made the same decisions if you had no questions about your life? These are things only you can answer."

Aleeya tried to imagine the Cosmic Gods rearranging her life by placing strategic roadblocks in her mind, guiding her along a mysterious map. They had shoved certain memories aside as a detour to assist her growth. Why were they bringing everything back? To see how she could handle them? What kind of twisted game was this? Should she be angry? Or should she appreciate what she had?

The vanished, or rather, hidden memories hadn't come flooding back yet. She didn't expect an onslaught, but feared how she'd react to them. How would all these "new" memories affect her? Would her personality change? Would she be a different person? Would she recognize herself?

Had she forgotten huge chunks of her life or just bits and pieces? Aleeya yearned to remember her mother's features, her voice, and her touch. Then there was Adlar, her little brother. What did he look like? These were critical aspects of her life that she had no recollection of.

The knee-jerk reaction would be anger, of course. But after all she'd been through, after all the suffering she'd seen in others who were worse off than her, she wondered if it was her destiny to experience pain in order to empathize and see the world with more compassion. The ability to choose her path had always been by her side. No one could take that right from her.

"I choose to believe that the Cosmos has my back. *Nona faiya, nona lux. Coma faiya, coma vita.* I've never given up on what matters to me. It's the Norakian warrior way."

No faith, no light. With faith, all life.

"I'm happy to hear that," El Lara said. "Norak is lucky to have you. Planet Terrakado is lucky to have you. You're an inspiration to so many females, young and old. You have a powerful belief system that's unwavering, Aleeya. I admire that. But I just want to remind you to be careful. Sometimes, that warrior strength can take its toll. I've watched you, Andara, and Zori develop over the years, and I'm so proud to be surrounded by such a respectable group of females. Your impact on adolescent females is exactly what is needed to ensure that they grow up strong, intelligent, and independent. You're the perfect example that proves your background *does not* matter. It has strengthened you."

"I'm sorry..." Tab murmured, shaking his head. "I never meant for you to lose your memory, for you to suffer the way you did."

The Priestess was about to add something, but Aleeya's

words tumbled out first. "It's not your fault. I don't blame you at all. Everything that happened has made me a better person."

"You had memory loss too," Kenzo reminded Tab.

"I understand now why I couldn't remember where I left you." He ran a hand over his bald head. "Life is so strange. It takes you around in crazy loops."

The raw pain on Tab's face tugged at Aleeya's corra. Like her, he had suffered. Without a doubt, she believed that if he had remembered her location, he would've returned for her.

"Maybe you can decipher the data on the chips now that they have been removed." Tab turned at El Lara. "I only know what Garnu told me. I'm not a scientist, so I don't understand the data or formulas."

El Lara placed her palms together in a thinking position. "I looked at the data. The chips were wired to each person's frequency, which was why your skin itched. The chip vibrated beneath your skin when it came near the other's energy."

Tab sipped his drink. "My gut tells me the third piece is still out there. After thinking about it, I don't believe Garnu hid the third component on himself. His frequency didn't blend well with it. He wouldn't have risked that."

Kenzo grabbed a pastry topped with floral petals. "It'll show up, eventually."

"Let's look at the data." The Priestess inserted the cleansed metal chips into a slit on her wall. A large virtual screen appeared with data flowing horizontally, then the abstract symbols changed to flow vertically and diagonally.

After a few seconds, a set of codes blinked among an ocean of letters, numbers, and symbols.

"Pause that." El Lara voiced a command to the screen. "This is a formula for a chemical that engineers organs. The data is intricate." Her eyebrows pinched together.

Aleeya whipped her head over to Kenzo. "That's it. That's

probably what Malixx used to alter his cyborgs and experiment on the children." She turned to the Priestess. "We discovered children with glowing corras. One child's corra exploded in front of us. Another was taken to the hospital yesterday."

"Do you see a code, an antidote, or something that can reverse the damages?"

El Lara zoomed the screens in and out. "I see a set of codes here. I'll need time to take a thorough look at them. I'll let you know."

"What else is on the device?" Tab asked.

"This looks like a regional map of facilities."

"We'll check them out. We'll need to send this map to other regions and alert them," Aleeya said. "This data is old. Some locations might not be relevant now, but it's good to double check."

The Priestess continued to analyze the data and gasped at the images flowing onto the screen. Images splashed with a junior version of Malixx experimenting on several humans and star-beings.

"Malixx started his atrocity early on." Tab pressed his lips into a tight line. "He looks about twenty solar cycles old."

El Lara moved to another set of codes, but it was incomplete. "The data is stuck." She reset the screen, but it didn't provide any additional information or images. "I'll have the tech team look at this. Maybe there's a glitch or the devices are defective."

"Can I get a copy of these images?" Kenzo asked. "This is extra proof for Detective Ahlex to make his case against Malixx and his company."

"Absolutely, I'll send you a copy right now." The Priestess pressed a button on her screen.

"Thank you." Kenzo typed on his vambrace. "Detective Ahlex will appreciate the information."

El Lara turned off the screen. "I need time to review the codes. You're welcome to stay here for a few days to rest up."

"That would be nice, thank you. The fresh air in Elseon is exactly what I've been missing. If you don't mind, I'd like to take a stroll around the lush yard." Tab jerked a chin outside.

"Please do and take your time. The air will help your body heal faster." The Priestess looked at Aleeya and Kenzo. "I'll be in my office if you need me. Rest up."

With the new information, Aleeya's mind spiraled with urgency. But the Priestess's words reminded her to take it easy. She didn't want to rip her wound or damage something that couldn't be reversed.

Aleeya and Kenzo remained in the kitchen a while longer.

Too many thoughts swirled in her mind. She remembered the cautionary energy that had alerted her about the cyborg attack. This energy was her friend, and she was grateful for it.

Did Magnetti find anything else about the Corra Spark? She checked her vambrace, but no messages appeared from him. It still baffled her that she had this information for the engineered corra and organs on her all this time. How many individuals had Malixx hurt over the solar cycles? Her fists clenched and rage boiled in her blood. She wanted to do something. She needed to be out and about, looking for clues. Her fury needed an outlet. But she forced her mind to calm. In battle, only a calm mind could see clearly.

Was Malixx hiding in Norak, or did he make a special trip just to attack her? Who was the individual with the mask and pink hair that killed those star-beings in the facility? She could walk to the Shopping Plaza and easily locate twenty star-beings with all shades of pink hair. Hair color was easy to alter...

Malastrom! She waited a beat to let her thoughts connect. When the clear image formed, she turned to Kenzo. "I know who has Jella."

TWENTY-NINE

Kenzo

"Who?" Urgency crept into his voice.

"Peko. The details began falling into place yesterday, but they solidified just now. Yesterday, I noticed his hair was black unlike the normal pink."

Realization dawned on Kenzo. "He dyed his hair after you released the description of the kidnapper to the media."

Aleeya nodded. "And when he helped me battle the cyborgs, black soot also came from his body. But it wasn't as obvious as the soot that came from the cyborgs or Malixx. I've been feeling this cautionary energy every time I'm near him. It's been warning me. I need to give Elder Kai a call and inform him, including an update with Magnetti. Elder Kai needs to stay away from Peko. I don't understand why Peko's working with Malixx."

"Maybe Malixx is paying him a lot of credits. Or maybe they're just both evil and insane."

Aleeya pulled up two screens. One for her to connect to

Elder Kai, and one for Kenzo to research Peko. While Aleeya informed her legion and told them to keep everything quiet, Kenzo retrieved Peko's address. With the facial recognition scanner, Kenzo found places Peko normally hung out. They needed to narrow down where he could be.

If Peko was the kidnapper with the mask, then he was one of the star-beings who tortured Kenzo and his brothers. Peko and Malixx both had a part in killing his brothers. Rage bubbled in him.

I hope you're enjoying your stay.

The fucker had mocked him. Kenzo remembered Peko's words that time he flew them to Norak from Delleon. Kenzo had thought the comment was strange since he told Peko he'd been living here for five years and not five weeks. Was Peko laughing at Kenzo on the inside?

Kenzo tamed his fury to do what was necessary.

Aleeya finished her conference. "Do you have his home address? He doesn't know we're onto him, so let's go get him."

"You just had surgery. You should rest. I'll go."

She rose from her seat, stubbornness radiating from her. "It was a minor surgery. I'm not staying. I have to go. You'll be there with me. We're stronger together, remember?"

Kenzo didn't like the idea, but he knew how important it was to her. Besides, this was her jurisdiction. He skimmed a knuckle down her cheek. "Okay, but please let me know if you're not feeling well."

"I will."

THIRTY

Aleeya

She took her cloud-mobile around Nouridan in search of Peko. He wasn't home at his address.

"Where to now?" Kenzo asked as the cloud-mobile hovered above a building that overlooked the Cosmic Corra Orphanage.

Aleeya's eyes trained on a cyborg who walked by the orphanage three times. She inspected him with her Zoomer device. The evening hours brought out crowds looking for food and fun. He wore all black instead of the regular gray uniform with the red vambraces. He had a long scar on his forehead.

"Monitor that cyborg dressed in black." Aleeya maneuvered her cloud-mobile, following him, but keeping her distance even though she was in the air. They remained inconspicuous amongst the small crafts out and about.

With the Zoomer, Kenzo kept visual of the cyborg as he turned a street and entered a building three blocks away from the orphanage. Aleeya stationed her cloud-mobile on the roof where a door allowed them entrance into the building. Kenzo melted the door handle with a metal-melter beam on his vambrace. He opened the door slowly, and Aleeya strode down the stairs. They moved in silence, and the cautionary feeling returned, confirming Peko was nearby.

Aleeya mouthed. "Peko is here."

They checked every floor as they descended. On the second floor, voices boomed from somewhere on the other side of where they stood. Kenzo opened the door and snuck in with Aleeya beside him. Three separate voices echoed in the wide room. Containers of Bliss aligned several aisles.

Aleeya moved past an area of boxes and slid into an alcove that gave her full view of Peko, Malixx, and the cyborg. Kenzo found another alcove near her.

"The orphanage is all set, boss," the cyborg said.

"Good." Peko whirled to Malixx. "I told you not to release the cyborgs so soon. Their corras were still too new. Why didn't you listen?"

Malixx snarled, soot flowing from him. "I don't answer to you. I took you under my wings and taught you what I knew. Don't tell me what to do. You were just an orphan who got kicked out. Don't forget what I did for you."

Peko pressed a button on his vambrace, and a bed made from a block of crystal rolled out from an adjacent room. A green-skinned star-being with long, orange hair lay on it. Her chest glowed bright yellow.

"Malixx, we've been partners for a long time. You should take my suggestions seriously. I helped engineer your wife's corra. Without me, Kalindo wouldn't be 'alive.' I helped you gather all those test subjects. I helped you improve Bliss and created the Corra Spark. I helped you achieve the scientific breakthroughs you've been working on for ages."

Like Aleeya, Kenzo studied the female star-being sitting on the bed.

Malixx's angry expression softened when his wife looked at him. She didn't speak. With glazed eyes, Kalindo placed her head on his shoulders.

Malixx whirled to Peko. "The scientific breakthroughs were all mine. I started this before you were born. You became an assistant I appreciated." He brushed away loose hair strands that blocked Kalindo's face. "It was my passion to innovate science. I sacrificed to achieve a better future for everyone. Now, I have the best engineered organs on this planet. Organs that have mind-control properties."

Peko pulled up a virtual screen, showing Jella sleeping inside some room. The walls appeared like this warehouse. Aleeya glance at Kenzo and made a gesture for Kenzo to search for Jella. Aleeya remained in her spot to monitor Peko and Malixx.

Kenzo pointed to her sealed wound. Aleeya smiled, reassuring him she was fine. His concern warmed her more than he could ever know. Kenzo snuck away, and Aleeya gripped her blaster as she returned her attention to Peko and Malixx.

Malixx placed a hand on Kalindo's shoulders. "You've been asleep for two hundred solar cycles, my love. You'll be renewed today. Your corra was sick. It made you leave me and love someone else. You couldn't love someone else. You didn't understand that I'm the *only* one for you." Love and pain tugged at his face. "So I engineered a corra just for you. It's going to keep you alive and allow me to know what you're feeling all the time. There will *only* be me inside your corra. Your corra will never be sick again."

Aleeya connected the dots. Malixx had started his cruel scientific experiments before he met Peko. His wife's cheating sent him spiraling out of control. Did Malixx kill his wife and keep her alive after all these solar cycles until he could refine an engineered corra to control her? Kalindo didn't express any emotion, looking like a corpse.

"Love is the only thing with the power to change everything." Malixx had lost his mind. He had a twisted version of love.

"That's one thing I can agree on. Love is the reason why I do what I do." Peko studied the monitor on Jella, turned it off, and faced Malixx. Soot particles emerged from pockets on Peko's face. "Jella's corra is reacting beautifully to the Corra Spark. It's the only one that survived this experiment. It's a strong corra."

"And that's why my Kalindo will be strong again. I'll remove the child's corra tomorrow and give it to Kalindo. I'll take tissue samples so we can harvest more strong corras."

Fear gripped Aleeya. She typed into her vambrace, contacting Kenzo. Did he locate Jella yet? They had to get her out of here. Aleeya feared if she attacked them, they would alert other cyborgs stationed elsewhere to go after Kenzo.

Peko's eyes darkened. "Aleeya's corra malfunctioned back then too. It was sick. She didn't know how much I loved her. I still love her. She needs a reminder. She needs to know she inspired me to better at everything." More soot emerged from his face. "My love for her is stronger than your love for your wife. You've been too focused on Kalindo, you've abandoned Atrium. The company is mine. I'll make it even more successful. I'll show Aleeya how she's motivated me. She'll be proud. We'll start a beautiful life together."

Malixx cursed. "You are not taking what belongs to me." More curses erupted.

"I already did." A sly smile grew on his face. He snapped his fingers, and Kalindo left Malixx's arms and strode over to Peko. Peko wrapped an arm around her, and she kissed his cheek.

"Kalindo! What are you doing?" Malixx shouted. "What did you do to her?"

Kalindo revealed no emotion, only looked at Peko.

"I just added a little enhancement to her Corra Spark." Peko smirked and pulled Kalindo into her arms. "You hurt my Aleeya, and I hurt your Kalindo. It's only fair."

Aleeya had no recollection of Peko's infatuation with her. Was that part of her memory loss?

Rage burned in Malixx's eyes. "Aleeya was never your wife. Kalindo was mine. You were just a loser that I took under my wing, Rellok."

Rellok? Memory slapped Aleeya awake. The orphan who tried to kiss her all those solar cycles ago? The orphan who had lived with Aleeya and her brothers and sisters at the orphanage?

Peko's face shifted, the blue skin darkened, and the thin face filled out with more flesh. The three ears became pointier, completely changing his appearance to be the Rellok she recognized. Soot floated around him like evil clouds.

Rellok had a childhood crush on her. He didn't train to be a Norakian warrior, he was more into science and inventions. She had been fifteen solar cycles old, and he was three solar cycles older, when he pushed her against a wall and forced his lips onto hers. If a teacher hadn't pulled him away, he would have done more.

Rellok had made his intentions known to her, and so did she. He didn't take rejections well. He was reprimanded for his inappropriate action but was eventually kicked out of the orphanage for his continued disobedience. She didn't know what happened to him after he left the orphanage. She assumed he had gotten on with his life.

Had Rellok held his resentment for the orphanage after all these solar cycles? Did he resent her?

Rellok lifted a hand. "You remember the story wrong. They didn't value my presence, so I *left*. There's a big difference.

You've taught me well, Malixx. But times are changing. It's time for me to lead, and for you to step back."

Curses flew out of Malixx's mouth. "You were not worthy then, and you're not worthy now. I gave you a job and taught you what I knew. And now, you want to take what's mine? Never!" He blasted an electric blue flame at Rellok.

The holes in Rellok's body increased and soot emerged with evil faces. With a twist, Rellok snapped Kalindo's neck, and she collapsed onto the floor.

Malixx screamed and a battle erupted. Rellok fired at Malixx with his blasters. But it was the dark soot from Rellok that strangled Malixx. Hellish sounds emanated from the clouds of soot. The cyborg darted somewhere.

Aleeya's vambrace buzzed with a message from Kenzo. "I have Jella! Heading to cloud-mobile now. Meet me there!"

With the news that Jella was out of harm's way, Aleeya tapped her vambrace and pressed a code, alerting Magnetti to this location with the soldiers. She whirled back to the battle. Where did the cyborg go?

Malixx gathered his powers and fought Rellok's soot. Malixx's electric blue beam sparked everywhere. Aleeya ducked to avoid it hitting her. Rellok got hit in his arms and legs. He cursed and increased his powers. The darkness from Rellok was stronger than the soot floating from Malixx. Somehow, Rellok turned Malixx's soot onto himself. The darkness devoured Malixx.

The force of power shoved racks and boxes around, destroying her hideout.

"If I don't arrive in two minutes, just go!" Aleeya stepped into view and spoke into her vambrace.

She had to prevent Rellok from catching up to Kenzo and Jella.

Rellok squinted his eyes. "Aleeya?" He made one step closer, staring at her in disbelief. "Is it really you, love?"

Indignation coursed through Aleeya. "Why are you doing this?"

His face beamed as he placed a hand over his corra. "It *is* you. You read my mind. Just minutes ago, I wished for you to be here. To witness my power. To see me overthrow Malixx. And here you are. You are the prize for all my hard work."

"I'm not your reward or anything. Why are you doing this?" she asked again.

"Because I love you."

"This is *not* love."

"Oh, but it is, Aleeya. Can't you see? Because of you, I've defeated Malixx. I'm indestructible. Atrium is now mine. It is *ours*. This proves I can have anything I desire." His eyes pinned her. "I desire you. Tell me you feel the same. I know you have me in your corra. I just know it. I feel it."

Rellok was too unhinged, too psychotic to understand anything she had to say. Would her words make any sense to him?

"But I don't desire you." She glared at the orphan who had distorted love into something evil. He was infected with an incurable darkness. "Love this." She fired her blaster at him.

Disbelief sparked in Rellok's face. The shot entered his chest and blood oozed. He didn't move. Why didn't he move out of the way? Soot filled in that wound just like the other wounds he'd gained from Malixx's attack. Though the blood stopped flowing out of him, he appeared weaker with the slouched posture.

"Your corra is still sick, Aleeya. I know you care for me. I feel it." He placed a hand over his corra. A string of soot snaked and slithered around him as if seducing him with falseness. "I'll fix you. I promise. You just need time to remember how you feel about me. I'll return to retrieve you. I'll give you a new corra." Soot burst from him and billowed into the room. Something crashed, and she rushed toward the broken window. Rellok had jumped out from the second floor and disappeared.

Aleeya alerted Magnetti about Rellok's escape. She also gave orders to her soldiers to search for Peko, also known as Rellok.

Then she fled toward the roof, hoping Kenzo was still there.

THIRTY-ONE

Kenzo

Back at the Elseon Grove, Kenzo and Aleeya stood watching over Jella. The child lay unconscious on a bed inside El Lara's laboratory. Her light blue skin paled to almost white. El Lara created a crystal grid that floated above Jella's body to harmonize her energy.

Aleeya released a sigh and ambled over to a chair and sat. Kenzo gathered her hair aside and reviewed her neck. Relief settled when the sealant on her wound looked intact. Concern for her elevated when he left her alone and went to search for Jella, who was just one floor above them.

"I'm fine." Jella's safety added to the gleam in Aleeya's eyes.

"I know. I just want to look for myself."

When Kenzo had found Jella and carried her to the cloud-mobile, he prayed his traumatic symptoms wouldn't cramp in that critical moment. His worry for Aleeya, the urgency of the situation, and facing his brothers' killers would have triggered his muscle spasms or something dire. Nothing came, and he thanked the heavens for that. One emotion rose to the top during the rescue: his love for Aleeya. He was in love with her. He believed that acknowledgement subdued his symptoms. In that moment, he feared he could lose her. Love liberated him, freeing him from the prison of the past. Loving Aleeya had illuminated a path for him that was previously dark. He had lived in darkness until she came. She healed him. Love healed him.

What if something had happened to her while he was saving Jella? Kenzo wouldn't be able to live with himself. She was the only woman who opened his heart. Tonight, these loving feelings seemed forbidden somehow. Like there were more important things at stake than his love for her. What was the point in living if you didn't acknowledge that which gave you purpose? Life was uncertain. The only certainty was the reminder that life could change instantly. Tomorrow could change drastically. He had to make sure the present moment counted. He needed to share his feelings with her. Show her how much he loved her.

Jella whimpered, and El Lara used a large crystal wand that calmed her corra, which glowed yellow and orange through the light-weight shirt. The energy of the wand soothed the brightness to a softer color.

"I sorted two reversal formulas that could help Jella. I'm adding a few other ingredients to ensure her safety. I'll prepare the solution and test it on my lab plants to see if it has any negative reaction. Once I know it's safe, we'll give it to Jella." She glanced at the monitors beside the bed. "Her vitals appear fine. I don't believe she's in immediate danger. You should go rest. I'll keep you posted on the reversal formula."

"Thank you." Aleeya rose from the chair.

"Do you mind if we stay on one of your floating islands?" Kenzo asked. "I've never been on one before."

"Of course. Have Mimic take you up." El Lara jerked her

chin toward the yard with glowing berries and fruits. "Tab is sound asleep in the guest room. It's good for him to rest. You should've been resting instead of out hunting. But I'm glad you rescued Jella."

Kenzo clutched Aleeya's hand and led her outside. The clear and quiet sky contrasted with the violence and darkness they had encountered hours ago. Aleeya glanced up at the moons and stars. He couldn't read her expression. She didn't look tired, more contemplative.

"What are you thinking?" Kenzo cupped her chin with his finger and thumb. "I'll give you all my credits if you tell me what you were thinking."

"No."

"And one of my arms?"

"No."

"Two of my legs?"

Laughing, she said, "No."

"Okay, then would you settle for my heart, my corra?"

She stared into his eyes, searching. Did his question catch her off guard? "Is that a new line for a poem you're going to write me?"

She didn't answer his question, but he'd give her time. He wasn't going anywhere. "Is that what you want?"

"Only if you're inspired to." She touched his face. "I was thinking about Rellok."

Kenzo's hands clenched at his name. Aleeya relayed the story about Rellok's intention with her when she was a teenager, what he did in the warehouse, and the threat that he'd be back for her. The only way Rellok would get to Aleeya was over Kenzo's dead body.

"I don't know how he could be infatuated with me. I didn't give him any encouragement."

"Psychotic individuals live in their own world. They don't

need a reason to cause harm. Life has a way of bringing justice to those we can't get to." That statement shifted something in him.

Though Kenzo didn't get a chance to kill Malixx himself, knowing that his enemy was dead closed that painful chapter in his life. Kenzo had never needed to be the one to kill Malixx for his healing to start. Aleeya already inspired his transformation.

He also believed in his statement; *life has a way of bringing justice to those we can't get to.* For the other criminals who had a part in torturing and killing his brothers, payment would be collected, no doubt. But the collection didn't need to be by Kenzo's hands alone. He was believing in a higher power now.

Aleeya offered a warm smile. "That's enough talk about the dark side for tonight. Let's get some rest." She strode off, looking for El Lara's purple parrot, Mimic, so they could get on the island.

Kenzo climbed onto Mimic, a huge parrot with soft, purple feathers. It was smaller than Magnetti's battle-bird, but large enough to support Kenzo and Aleeya. He sat behind her on a saddle with a high backing. Enjoying his position, Kenzo wrapped his arms around Aleeya's waist. Her hair gave off an enticing scent that slid into his nose and seduced his senses.

He recalled their mutual agreement that involved nothing more than sex. Too late, it was already much more than sex. Every moment with her was even more precious now.

"I like your new collar." Aleeya gripped the rope attached to the gold collar around Mimic's neck.

"Thank you. El Lara got it so guests could have something to hold on to when I fly them around." Mimic lifted them up from the ground.

Talking animals were wonders on this planet. They had feelings just like humans and star-beings. What would humans think or do if they encountered someone like Mimic or Jeeto?

He knew exactly what would happen. They'd be captured, caged, and used for testing or something drastic. Like the ruthless star-beings who abducted him and his brothers. Cruelty and brutality existed everywhere.

Kenzo focused on Mimic's flight as his body shifted in the saddle. He wasn't afraid of heights. He had jumped out of planes several times, but this sudden elevation and the flapping wings flipped his stomach sideways. Nerves churned for an instant before he regained his composure.

The flight wasn't smooth like a spaceship, yet it was liberating in its own way. He wasn't confined to a protected area. He was free. Free to fly with the wind, to be with the clouds, to see the world from all angles.

Mimic landed gracefully on a floating island with willow trees that sparkled from the setting suns. This island was far from the others. "There are guest pajamas, blankets, and toiletries in the cabin. If you need anything else, use the communication device, and I'll be over."

"We'll be okay, Mimic. Thank you." Aleeya stroked the bird's feathers.

"Thanks for the flight." Kenzo gave the bird a nod and received one of his own.

Kenzo strode over to the drooping willow branches with lilac leaves. He pulled a branch to him and released it. The branch swayed and created a lovely sound when the leaves kissed the other branches. It was a lot like a wind chime.

He followed Aleeya into a cabin made of wood and metal. Inside, the wooden floors welcomed him, and the soft colors offered a comfortable atmosphere. Purple couches with large pillows, tall crystal lamps, a crystal coffee table, and wooden art filled the living room. The high-tech equipment in the quaint kitchen and office made this the most luxurious cabin he'd ever been in. It wasn't big, but it had everything a minimal man like him could want.

He'd never considered a permanent home before. Now, the picture formed in his head. He whirled, expecting to find Aleeya elsewhere, but she stood staring at him with eagerness and passion. The energy from her slammed into him, seduced him, and *stripped* him. Tingles rushed down his body, waking every cell and muscle. The sensation came to knock on his heart, and that knock lit a fire in his soul.

How could her energy do that to him? How could his mind translate the movement of energy this way? It was as if he could see energy here and there in his mind's eye. Was that even possible? He'd contemplate on that later.

Right now, his brain and body were solely focused on Aleeya. If he couldn't understand the desperate look on her face, then he wasn't a man.

Somehow, this slice of heaven appeared prohibited, like they shouldn't be showing affection or acting on their needs. Would it be wrong to indulge in this precious moment with the only woman who opened his heart? Tomorrow was no guarantee, only this moment was.

"I could die happy from the way you're looking at me," he said.

The corners of her lips quirked as she walked up to him. Then she gasped and swayed.

Kenzo caught her. "You all right?"

Aleeya leaned into his body and took in big gulps of air. She stared blankly in front of her as tears streamed down her face, and her body shivered.

"What's wrong?" He brought her to the couch and set her down.

She didn't reply. He rushed to the kitchen and poured her some warm blue water. "Here, drink this." Could this be a delayed side effect from her neck surgery just hours ago? "Are you okay?"

She held the cup with two hands and sipped. "I remember." She placed the cup down on the crystal coffee table. "I remember them, Kenzo." Tears came again, and he offered her a tissue from a box on the side table.

"Remember who?"

"My mother and brother." Hope glittered in her eyes. "The images came flooding into my mind. My corra didn't know how to respond to the onslaught. I couldn't breathe. I remember what they looked like; I remember how they made me *feel*. All these feelings missing from my memory have returned." Her hand clutched her chest, and she released slow breaths.

When Aleeya collapsed into his arms, a ripple of fear he'd never felt before coursed through him.

"El Lara removed the chip from your neck, so there's no more obstruction to your memory. This is splendid news." He tightened his grip around her, and her head rested on his shoulder.

"My brother was such a cute baby. I wish I had more time with him." She swallowed. "I look like my mother. I remember playing with her long, white hair."

"I'm grateful for her because she gave me you."

Aleeya straightened up. "I'm so relieved, Kenzo. These were critical pieces of my life. It feels like I've just recovered from a long illness. I understand why I'm drawn to the soft yellow color. It was the color of my bedroom back then. I wonder if Tab... my father... has remembered anything yet. I'll ask him tomorrow."

Unlike before, her face now blossomed with color, and relief settled in him.

A gentle voice whispered in his ear. "Outside. Come outside."

Kenzo blinked and scanned the room. No one was there.

Aleeya's vambrace buzzed. She glanced at it. "I've got to quickly touch base with Magnetti."

Come outside. The voice sounded in his mind this time.

"Okay, I'll join you later. I'm going to check out the island."

Kenzo gave Aleeya time to discuss private Norakian matters with Magnetti. Kenzo could assist her with the video reviews later.

Come outside. The voice repeated.

THIRTY-TWO

Aleeya

She wanted to reply to Kenzo's question: *would you settle for my heart, my corra?* It should have been a simple yes or no. She wanted to share much more than a simple yes with him. But at that moment, a war of emotions roiled in her. After what she learned about Rellok, it shook her.

It wasn't the idea that Rellok could "love" her. It was the fact that he firmly believed her corra was sick and that she belonged to him. Genuine love didn't have this ugly side to it. The pure emotion of love did not comprise this twisted distortion, this falseness.

Both Malixx and Rellok "believed" what they were doing was right. They had spent solar cycles engineering a corra just so they could control their significant other. It was an illness Aleeya didn't understand.

Her mind wandered back to Rellok's threat that he'd find her. But how, when, and where? Aleeya didn't want to wait. The longer she waited meant the more time Rellok had to harm someone else or devise a dangerous retaliation. She had to make the first move.

Where would Rellok want to meet her? She remembered the cyborg wandering outside the orphanage. What had he been doing? Based on that fact, she formed a plan and shared it with Magnetti, who agreed on the scheme and set it in motion.

Aleeya had Peko's contact. Would Rellok reply if she sent him a message? Would he agree to a "date" with her? She had to play on the idea that he still cared about and "loved" her.

I'm sorry about what happened. You always knew what was best for me. I'd love to make this right between us. You've sacrificed so much for me, and I want to give us a chance.

It sickened her to type that message to him. But she had to lure out the enemy and kill him. She sent him the place and time and turned off her vambrace for the evening.

Tomorrow promised chaos and danger. Tonight, she just wanted to love a man who held her corra and didn't even know it. She loved Kenzo. With all the darkness surrounding her, he was her light. Because she loved him, she had to keep him safe.

Aleeya strode out to show him how she felt, because tomorrow she might not have that chance.

Come outside. A gentle voice echoed in her mind.

THIRTY-THREE

Kenzo

He strode through the back door and stood on stones that glowed from the moonlight. The night was so clear he could see the three moons glowing at various locations in the sky.

"I'm here. Who are you?" He waited for a response.

No reply came, but an energy entered from the crown of his head, rushed down his spine, and warmed his entire body. A plethora of stars twinkled at him as if they were alive. Bewildered, he remained still and let himself go. All his concerns faded, and he became a blank slate.

A wave of peace washed over him. The energy worked his body from the inside out. He felt the heat in his muscles and even in his cells. *Impossible.* How could he feel cellular movement? Somehow his mind understood that inexplicable thought. The muscles in his arms and legs tightened, and his heart contracted, perplexing him.

How could he feel an involuntary organ function, like he had control over its pulsation?

What the hell was going on?

"Your corra speaks to hers," the voice said. He couldn't tell if it was male or female. He didn't pick up any negative vibes from it.

Kenzo whirled, scanning the area filled with floral bushes and trees. "Who are you? Where are you?"

"Look up."

He glanced up, gasped, and fell two steps back. A giant moon loomed in his face, literally and figuratively. It glowed a soft yellow with a gold rim around it. It brightened the entire island. He reached to touch it, but his hand went through the image.

Abstract symbols in gold flowed out of it, circling him. One golden code came up close to him and slowed. The symbols were one abstract shape that flipped and spiraled at various angles, making them appear as though they were all different. He recognized the symbols as the ones he saw the night he escaped his torturer.

"I've seen these before."

"It's your soul symbol. You used to draw these as a child. I sent Jeeto to help you, remember?"

How did Yarra know he used to doodle this design? Had the moon been watching him since birth? These symbols had guided him to that dark alley where he found Jeeto, or rather, where Jeeto found him, and where Tab saved him.

Kenzo spoke to Yarra. "Why?"

"So you can join with your other half."

"What half? I don't understand."

"With all its pieces together, the key to everything will emerge."

The key to everything. Jeeto mentioned that before. What did that mean? Aleeya was right about the moon speaking in riddles.

Yarra zoomed back into the sky, still large but not so close to his face.

"Kenzo —"

Aleeya's sharply drawn breath drew his attention to her. She stood with a hand on her corra, staring at the moon. He wasn't imagining it after all.

The moon zipped in closer, greeting her. A colorful opening blossomed from its center like a spiraling flower. Like him, Aleeya reached her hand out to touch Yarra. But unlike him, her hand went into the spiral, and she sucked in a breath. The look on her face indicated she was seeing something that affected her. Something he couldn't see yet.

Aleeya

The glow of Yarra warmed Aleeya like a big hug from a forgotten family member. The spiraling energy from the center of Yarra held her hand, and unconditional love surged through her.

Emotions from the past and present stirred and stormed into a revelation that left her corra thudding with clarity. Images of her mother, brother, and star-beings she didn't recognize waved and smiled at her.

Your ancestors are always watching and guiding you. You are never alone. Never abandoned.

Aleeya's eyes glistened as a river of gold symbols flowed from the moon and twirled around her.

An image of Kenzo as a silver-skinned star-being flashed before her. Decked in gold armor with a sacred symbol engraved on his chest plate, he stood guard in front of a magnificent doorway of light. On the other side stood Aleeya, also in gold armor with a different unique symbol carved on her chest plate.

They glanced at each other and smiled. The love that emanated from them blossomed into her present moment. Her corra swelled in recognition. He was her starmate.

The abstract symbols lifted from their chest plates and intertwined together, creating a divine key-like image. Did Kenzo see what she was seeing? Aleeya turned to him, and his eyes told her he also witnessed the same phenomenon.

"You were both Guardians to the Doorway of Unity, where realities intersect. Kenzo, you represented the divine masculine energy, and Aleeya represented the divine feminine energy. But a distorted energy—a false light—snuck through the doorway during your guardianship. It has been your mission to find this false light. You have found it." The moon released Aleeya's hand.

"Where is it?" Kenzo asked what Aleeya wanted to know.

Yarra chuckled. *The moon actually chuckled.* It lightened the seriousness of the matter.

"Magic doesn't work that way. You need to do the work. You have met this false light. Identify it, alchemize it, turn it into light. Remember this, the Cosmos is multidimensional, and you are both still Guardians to the Doorway of Unity in another place, another time, another dimension."

Aleeya didn't understand the depth of Yarra's words, but she *felt* its truth in her blood. Her body and soul resonated with that statement.

"This is the key to love and truth. It is the answer to everything. This is the key that destroys the false light. The false light fears it." Yarra shrank and returned to the sky as a small globe, taking with it the magical bubble that had encased them.

Kenzo ran a hand through his hair. "That was unbelievable. I would have thought it was all my imagination if you weren't here talking to the moon with me."

Aleeya nodded, trying to settle and organize her emotions.

She saw her mother, brother, and ancestors. She had never been alone or abandoned. That acknowledgement freed her. Fear and doubts released her. The shackles clanked from her mind.

Aleeya ambled to a garden of iridescent aqua sand and crouched. With her finger, she drew the abstract symbol on the sand. "Draw yours."

Intrigue flickered in his eyes as he drew his symbol next to hers. Then they created a joined image of both symbols. Combined with hers, the symbol became a key, just like the image Yarra had shown her. The key looked like a divine sigil with elegant curves and strokes. One long stroke hung next to the shorter one, creating a balance in the image.

"Together, we're the key." He looked at her. "The key to everything."

With her vambrace, Aleeya snapped an image for safe keeping. "I have a feeling Yarra is referring to Rellok since Malixx is dead."

"I feel that too. We'll destroy him." Kenzo ran a finger down her cheek. "It's strange and incredible. I've never believed in mystical things until now." He faced her. "Now I understand why I want you all the time. My attraction to you goes beyond physical desire. There is nothing casual between us. There's only long-term from now on. Okay?"

Did she dare give her corra a chance to love under the stars? A warrior never retreated from a captivating challenge.

The soft light from the glowing leaves and berries rendered his face beautiful. Mysterious shadows occupied his face, giving him the perfect balance of light and shadow on his forehead, cheekbones, chin, and neck. This man—who had been her partner lifetimes ago—had chosen her again.

She only wanted the long-term with him too. "Why do you want me?"

He didn't hesitate. "Because my heart responds to you.

With you, I'm free." He tucked a loose strand of hair behind her ear. "You make me feel like I'm part of something bigger than myself. Something noble, something limitless. You healed my wounds. You removed the vengeance in me. Love is my life force. You are my life force. I love you, Aleeya."

Her corra skipped a beat. She tried to stop the emotions, but they leaked through her eyes. "I love you too. To answer your question, yes, I'll settle for your corra."

Kenzo flashed a grin that was brighter than the three moons combined. "I'm grateful for what Yarra showed me. We were guardians then, and we're guardians now. We're both on a mission for something beyond us. We promised to unveil the false light." He swallowed, and the veins on his neck pulsed. Desire flashed in his eyes. "There's one thing I know for certain. There's nothing false about how I feel for—"

Aleeya's lips crushed to his, muffling his words. A primal need soared through her. She growled with satisfaction, and he kissed her back with tongue, teeth, and temptation. In her mind, she saw their sacred symbols intertwined. He was the key to her corra, and she was his. She hadn't been able to understand her attraction to him in the beginning. But now, everything made sense. Their energies recognized each other from beyond time and space.

She had never gifted herself anything with value. Tonight, she would gift herself love.

Aleeya drew back and looked at him. His eyes scanned her face, and heat flamed her cheeks, illuminating her cosmic codes for him. She wanted him tonight, under the sky. She clutched his hand and led him around a row of tall trees. An outdoor bed beckoned with a canopy made of elegant tree trunks and vines with flowers strung like stars.

"The bed makes me want to do all kinds of things to you," he said.

"Show me exactly what you have in mind." Aleeya pressed herself to him, feeling all the hard lines, enjoying the sexual thrill in his eyes.

Tonight was different with Kenzo. Unlike the first time, where their union was a playful battlezone, tonight offered sensuality, sacredness, and truth. She loved him, and he loved her.

When Kenzo's mouth pressed to hers, heat burst from her core and singed its way around her body. She wouldn't have been surprised if her veins hissed. She gripped his midnight hair as the taste of him sent blood rushing into her head, one sinuous wave after another. His scent of sandalwood and pine seduced her.

As he devoured her mouth, he nudged her back into the tree trunk. The roughness of the bark bit into her back, offering more pleasure than pain. He dragged an open mouth over her jawline and down her throat as if marking her before claiming her. She moaned from his caresses, and her hands trembled, needing to find flesh. Clothes flew, armor clanked, and boots thudded to the ground while the sexual whirlwind took them both tumbling.

Aleeya fell onto the bed, her hair a wild mess on the silk sheets that kissed her skin. His eyes darkened as his chest rose and fell, taking in her body in a slow, amorous gaze. She flushed from the intensity of his passion and from the attention of his manhood. They both wanted her. He lowered himself, centering his arousal at her core, teasing and tormenting.

He pressed his face into her hair, breathing and nuzzling. "You smell like heaven."

Aleeya's nails dug into his back as need scorched her body and pounded inside her chest. The breeze sent the musical vines into a gentle rhythm, creating a lovely ambience that called for slow romance. But the desperation in her didn't allow for that. She fisted her fingers into his hair, dragged his mouth back to hers, and fueled the kiss with urgency, hunger, and impatience. Still, it wasn't enough. She needed more. Stars twinkled, and the moons glowed like they approved of this union.

Kenzo kissed her with unrestrained rapture that took her into another world. He tasted like untamed darkness where magic happened, where pleasure and pain blurred. Where she didn't know which was better for her, and she didn't care.

She let out a sigh of protest when he broke free from the kiss to nibble at the valley of her shoulder.

"Illuminate for me," Kenzo murmured as he licked a fiery trail toward her breasts. The cosmic codes on her body radiated from his affection. Smiling, he sampled one nipple. "Mine." She glowed brighter, and he feasted on one breast, then the other. Emotions tossed her into a well of paradise, and her body quivered with elation.

Nerves and need snapped together, forcing her corra to admit and accept that this energy flowing through her was love.

Aleeya loved Kenzo with every breath she took. Love looked her in the eye, and she looked back. Love was all she wanted. Kenzo was all she needed.

Sensations heightened to a level she'd never experienced before. Their fingers linked as they rolled over the bed. Dazed from the onslaught of ecstasy, Aleeya closed her eyes and surrendered to Kenzo's exploration as his kisses descended to her most sensitive area.

Her eyes flipped open when his lips landed on her core. She crooned out his name, then arched and moaned when he buried his face in her. Pleasure slashed through her, anchoring her to an exhilarating place between the edge of passion and release. She was like this floating island docked on the mountainside. She was the cliff clinging on with a thrill that made her feel like she was dying and flying at the same time. The combined emotions slammed into each other, and she had no choice but to let go. A stream of euphoria rippled through her body as she gasped out his name.

"That's my girl." Kenzo dropped soft kisses as he made his way back up her body and claimed her mouth.

Aleeya rode with the wave of exhilaration. She crisscrossed her legs, gripped his shoulders, and performed a warrior move that flipped Kenzo over. His muscular size didn't make it easy. He didn't resist and played along, and that made the experience sexy as hell.

Intrigue sparked on his face. "This is how men lose wars." He stared up at her while his hands cupped her breasts. His gaze challenged her, waiting for her to unleash her power.

She didn't give him time to wonder as she crawled down his body like a lioness eyeing her prey. Like a lioness ready to ravage.

"Victory is mine." She gripped the glory of him like a weapon in her hand. He sucked in a breath and met her eyes. With her hand and mouth, she unleashed her predatory skills and demonstrated how a skilled warrior conquers.

THIRTY-FIVE

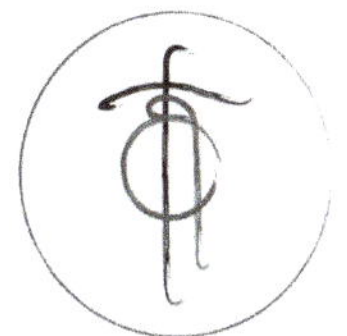

Kenzo

Kenzo woke with contentment in his heart. He turned to search for Aleeya, but an empty spot greeted him. Where had she gone?

After they made love outside under the stars, they continued the escapade inside the cabin after a late dinner. The giant bed with its fluid mattress and its ocean of satin sheets made him feel like a king. He performed positions he had once thought impossible. It was fucking glorious.

Though he got little sleep, he felt refreshed. Stacking his arms behind his head, he closed his eyes and relived last night's adventure. Love found him, or rather, he found love.

He was attracted to every aspect of her. It wasn't just her physical beauty, her compassion emanated from her heart. From the moment he met her, she projected truth and justice like an unyielding weapon. She cared for those in need. That empathy, that kindness, drove her to fight for what was right, what was just. Hell, she did this while her job and reputation were on the line. He admired and respected that.

He hadn't encountered many women who walked their talk. Not even men. Aleeya proved how rare she was. Her strength, her wit, and her heart were why he fell in love with her.

Love. That word terrified and elated him. Last night, he experienced both heaven and hell. Heaven was exploring and claiming every inch of her. Hell was knowing that she was a craving that would never be enough, an addiction that could shatter him.

His mind replayed his intimacy with Aleeya. She was a true warrior in bed, but she had done something no other female had done before. She'd opened him and melted the iceberg that kept him hard and cold. She took his mind away from his vengeful endeavors so that he could heal his soul.

Kenzo's admission to love wasn't because of what Yarra said about them being starmates and Guardians to the Doorway of Unity. That knowledge made their bond more special, but he loved her before that. Way before that.

He was a simple man. He needed little to survive, which was why his life had been here and there. But loving Aleeya anchored him to this place and made him yearn for something that lasted forever. For the first time in his life, he welcomed the idea of settling down. As long as he had her, he was content.

She was the lovely sigh to his contentment, the direction on his compass, the words to his poetry. She was the reason for all that he was.

His chest tightened as his vambrace buzzed on the night-stand, yanking him back to reality. He pulled up the message.

I have a date with Aleeya. She loves me. See?

Kenzo's spine stiffened as he straightened up in bed. *What the fuck?* All the ease left his body as tension and fear gripped him. This had to come from Rellok. It was eight in the morning.

An image of her message to Rellok appeared. At first, Kenzo's heart cleaved in two. After what they had shared last night, after the heartfelt confessions, how could she do this to him? He let the emotion roll through and out of him. It was a natural reaction from someone in love. But then his mind cleared.

Aleeya was luring Rellok into some plan. Where was she? Why didn't she share this with him last night? Didn't she trust him? Anger, disappointment, and worry tore through him. He'd deal with that later.

Kenzo didn't reply to Rellok's message. Instead, the fucking bastard sent him a new message. *Don't believe me? Be at the Cosmic Corra in two hours. I had fun torturing your brothers.*

Fury spiked in Kenzo. The need for vengeance replaced by a need to eradicate this evil in the world. Rellok was trying to enrage Kenzo, which he achieved to some extent. But Rellok didn't know that vengeance was no longer Kenzo's purpose.

Kenzo sent Aleeya a message. *Where are you? Are you safe? Is Rellok with you?* He jumped out of bed and got dressed.

When Aleeya didn't reply, he went looking for El Lara and Tab. He found both in the laboratory and checked on Jella, who was sitting up on her bed. Tab fed the child soup.

"How are you feeling, Jella?" Kenzo asked.

"Better." Her gray eyes bore into him. Her corra didn't show through her chest like last night, and her light blue skin grew more vibrant. "The Priestess said you and Aleeya saved me. Thank you."

"You're welcome. I'm glad you're safe. Your parents and brother will be happy to see you soon."

His military experience and his love for *The Art of War* planned a strategy in his mind. In warfare, it was best to act in accordance with a plan after full consideration of the consequences. He had to prepare for this encounter with Rellok. What did Rellok have waiting for him and Aleeya?

Why wasn't Aleeya replying to his messages? Was she safe? Was he torturing her?

While El Lara waved a large crystal wand around Jella, Kenzo gestured for Tab to the side. "Have you seen Aleeya?"

"She went out early this morning. I thought you knew."

"Did she say where she was going?"

"Taking care of business at the orphanage. She asked me to monitor Jella." Tab's eyebrows furrowed. "What's going on?"

Kenzo calmed himself and let his anger dissipate as he contemplated Aleeya's plan. She wanted to kill Rellok on her own. She wanted to keep Kenzo here, safe with her father. Kenzo's fingers clenched, even though he knew why she did it. She wanted to protect him. But didn't she understand that if something happened to her, his life would end regardless if he was with her or not? He'd rather be with her, no matter the outcome. He needed his starmate, and she needed him. That was how it had to work. Had she forgotten that they were stronger together? His stubborn warrior needed a reminder that love required communication and trust. She should have trusted him.

Kenzo didn't want to worry Tab. "Everything's fine. I forgot she had to go out early."

Tab's eyes gleamed. "I remember everything, Kenzo."

"You should share that with Aleeya. It'll make her happy."

"I did. Father and daughter had a lovely chat this morning. All is well." Tab's smile brightened Kenzo's mood. "Taking care of Jella is like taking care of Aleeya."

Tab returned to Jella when El Lara waved him over and showed him something on the monitor.

Then the Priestess strode out of the room with Kenzo. "Is everything all right?"

"Aleeya left for the orphanage this morning without telling me. She's trying to catch Rellok by herself."

"No, she's not. Magnetti is with her."

"She told you the plan?"

The star on El Lara glowed. "No, I pried it out of her. She didn't tell you because she wanted you safe. She loves you. I can see it."

Kenzo knew that and knowing Magnetti was with her settled his nerves. But still, his heart ached. "I need to keep her safe, not the other way around."

El Lara's eyes warmed. "She wanted you safe, and you wanted her safe. You would've done the same thing. Relationships are confusing. What matters is the underlying intention. Don't be angry. Go assist her."

"Did the reversal formula succeed?"

The Priestess nodded. "Only after I changed some codes. Jella will be fine. Her corra is strong and her healing abilities kept her alive."

Another sigh of relief escaped him. He glanced at his vambrace. He had one more thing to do before he headed to the orphanage. Though Rellok mentioned two hours, Kenzo would be there way before that time.

Kenzo's eyes landed on a flowering shrub. "What are those yellow flowers with the reflective petals?"

"Which one? I have a lot of flowers with reflective petals."

Kenzo ambled over to the bush and pointed. "These here. They look like buttercup flowers from Earth, but these petals capture and hold images."

"I didn't realize you were a flower kind of guy."

"I'm not. I'm only drawn to these because of Aleeya."

El Lara plucked a stem. "Not only do they reflect images, these Yellow Murmurs record messages too. They can record and play images like a video on their petals."

No fucking way. He watched as she spoke to the flower. The petals shifted and made a sound. The flower replayed the message with her face displayed on the petals. "That's incredible. Would it be possible to have a small pot of these? Please?"

"I'll get them ready for you."

"Please be discreet about it. I have something planned for her."

The Priestess grinned. "I understand." She grabbed a small pot from a table and dug up a section of the bush for him.

"I spoke to Yarra last night." Kenzo didn't know why he was sharing this with El Lara. "She showed me and Aleeya a key made from the combination of our symbols. I've been doodling this design since I was a kid. I just didn't know its significance."

"Can you show me the symbol?"

Kenzo grabbed a stick from the table and drew the symbol in the dirt.

El Lara placed a hand over her heart. "That's a cosmic key, a cosmic sigil. The Cosmos chose you."

"Yarra said we were starmates and Guardians to the Door of Unity. We're supposed to find the 'false light' and alchemize it. I don't really understand the magnitude of it, but I know it's important."

"The Cosmos works in mysterious ways that none of us can ever fully comprehend. But it is always working for the benefit of everyone."

He asked a question that might not have an answer. "What exactly is the Door of Unity?"

El Lara added dirt to the pot, patted it down, and cleaned the edges. "That door opens to a place where realities intersect. All dimensions and parallel universes exist there. No matter where we are, who we are, and what dimension we come from, in that space, we exist as one."

"That's hard for a logical mind to envision and understand."

"Worlds within dimensions are always developing. Terrakado vibrates within an eighth dimensional field. Earth exists in a third dimensional matrix, but it is slowly moving towards the fifth."

"How so?"

"By humans raising their consciousness. Simply by being aware of your existence, your presence." She placed the flowerpot in a box, closed it, and slid it over to him. "By knowing you have choices. When you *choose* based on that awareness, you shift dimensions. It is that easy, and at the same time, it's not. We're often attached to certain beliefs that hold us back. It's difficult to explain."

It was like love. The emotions were simple to feel, yet it brought on fears and complications that could prevent them from ever being acknowledged or appreciated. "I get it."

Jeeto's cheerful laughter snapped Kenzo's attention to his pet chasing Sizzler across the yard. The odd friendship made him smile. Things that didn't belong together somehow made the perfect combination.

The Priestess continued, "When a false light enters the Door of Unity, that 'false' energy can manipulate certain things. What happens in there affects everyone. The entire Cosmos. This planet, Earth, and others."

He thought about that for a moment. "As above, so below, right?"

El Lara beamed. "Exactly. What happens here spirals out to Earth too. We have chaos here too, just like everywhere else. We must stop the dark energy here so that it doesn't enter Earth's atmosphere. The density there makes it difficult to remove these kinds of heavy energies from the atmosphere."

Kenzo didn't know what to say. The concept was mind-blowing. People on Earth always wondered about life on another planet. Yet, they never considered the issues that occurred there, or how they related to Earth. Everything was connected, indeed. At least on an energetic level.

Knowing that, Kenzo was even more determined to kill Rellok. He was the false light. Kenzo didn't want it to enter his former home. His parents still lived there, along with billions of other innocent people.

Kenzo studied the box of Yellow Murmurs. "Thank you for this. I'll pick these up later. Thanks for the galactic education."

"Let me know if you need my help with anything else. We all serve the same thing." She pointed to the sky.

"Do you mind if I ask Mimic for a ride to the orphanage?"

"Go right ahead."

As he rode on Mimic to his destination, a warmth emanated from his right palm. He glanced down and the cosmic key—the fused sigil made from his and Aleeya's personal symbols—glowed like the sun. Gold energy burst from his palm like a geyser of light.

Why did the cosmic key appear on his palm now? Was it because they had spoken their hearts' truth out loud to each other? He remembered Yarra's words about love and truth. Both he and Aleeya had expressed that last night. Was her palm bursting with light too?

Kenzo asked Mimic to drop him off a block from the orphanage. What if Rellok or his cyborg were watching out for Kenzo's arrival? He had to play it safe.

Kenzo maneuvered around an elderly star-being with a hunched back. The elderly bumped into him and missed a step. Kenzo caught his arm, preventing a fall. A sharp pain stabbed into Kenzo's flesh and chills coursed through him. The elderly straightened his back, and the cyborg with the scar on his forehead grinned at Kenzo.

Energy zapped from Kenzo as consciousness wavered in and out. A war of energies battled inside him as the cyborg dragged him somewhere and tied up his wrists.

THIRTY-SIX

Aleeya

She arrived at the orphanage early this morning and added the finishing touches to the food and drinks. All the children and teachers went on a field trip far from the Shopping Plaza. Even Bound Together Bookstore & Cafe was closed for the day.

As she sat at the table with food and drinks, she replayed her interaction with her father this morning. She got the closure she needed. She had regained her memories and recalled the loving childhood she had with her family before things took their dark turn. Circumstances had created this gap between them, but love filled in that space.

She delivered these words to him this morning. His joyful face etched in her mind. "I know how sorry you are, and I'm sorry it took me so long to say what you wanted to hear. I love you."

The sadness and resentment she felt all these solar cycles slid off her body. She no longer carried that burden in her corra. She was free to feel. To love. To forgive.

Her father didn't abandon her. He kept her safe. She was a better person because of his sacrifice.

She ignored Kenzo's messages. She knew he'd be angry, but she needed him safe. That was her job as a warrior. She would not place him in danger. Her right palm heated with the cosmic symbol. It glowed a beautiful yellow, mimicking Yarra's color. Energy sizzled from her hand. What could this mean? Why now? Her mind wandered to last night. She and Kenzo made love under the stars and spoke words of love and truth. Revelation dawned on her.

The cautionary energy slammed into her. Rellok was here.

"You're more beautiful now than ever, Aleeya." Rellok appeared without a sound, as she had suspected. Soot flowed around him. Did he notice it? He had come through a secret pathway from the basement. Magnetti discovered the door to the basement had been tampered with. This was a door kids often used to play hide and seek. Magnetti left the damaged lock alone on purpose.

"Thank you. Have a seat, let's chat." She gestured to the seat across from her. "You've always wanted a date with me. Here it is." He didn't seem bothered by the injuries he gained yesterday. "You look well."

"I needed time to regain my strength. And you needed time to remember how you feel about me. You love me. Do you remember that? We're meant to be together."

Rellok had been living in his own world. His powers increased over the solar cycles, but so did his psychosis.

Rellok walked around the general room where children normally had lunch. "This is where it all started. Where I fell in love with you. Where you rejected me. You didn't know what your corra wanted then. I hope you know now. This place has sentimental value to me."

"I didn't realize how much you loved me. No one has ever

loved me that way before." That was the truth. Rellok's kind of love was twisted, dark, and evil. She stared at the false light in front of her. Soot particles flowed near her. Her right palm heated, and she clenched it tight under the table, away from Rellok's view. Did the cosmic key sense this darkness?

Rellok smiled, sat down, and surveyed the plates of food. "I used to sit across from you so I could look at you. I dreamt about you all the time."

The idea sent a nasty chill down her spine. She sipped the blue water. "These are all foods we used to eat as kids. Fowless balls and all kinds of pastries." She flicked a gaze at him, curious as to why he never attempted to hurt Elder Kai. Rellok would have died quickly, but still. "Elder Kai was disappointed when I told him about you. You deceived him."

Rellok's face softened. "He was like a father I never had. I admired him when he came to the orphanage to mentor us. But we are not here to discuss anyone else but us. We are the only ones who matter."

"Of course. That's why we're here."

He grabbed his glass of blue water and sipped. He didn't touch the food. His expression hardened. "If only I could believe you. Your corra is still sick, Aleeya. You will only be mine once it's been cleared of the male energies you've come in contact with." He flipped the table and the food and drink toppled to the floor. "Do you think I don't know what you're doing, my love?"

She composed her internal storm and delivered the truth. "I was never your love. I know you're angry because the orphanage kicked you out. But you didn't need anyone there to accomplish anything. You could have succeeded anywhere."

Images of Jella and those innocent people who were kidnapped and tortured flashed across her mind. If only Rellok had used his skills to benefit others, he would have become a decent member of society.

Aleeya got up from her chair and glared at him. "I will never love someone like you. What do you want?"

She knew what he wanted, but she needed time for the poison from the blue drink to kick in. His intelligence would have suspected the food. But because she drank the blue water, he probably assumed it was safe. Everything on that table was laced with poison, except for her drink.

From the window, Magnetti and his soldiers fought off a faction of cyborgs.

Rellok grinned at the battle. Soot emerged from his piercing eyes and the holes in his body. He didn't need to hide himself from her any longer. This Rellok had been devoured by darkness. The side of his face lagged and darkness seeped out from the pores. The face made of soot opened its mouth and made eerie sounds.

Rellok understood the hellish words. "I want the orphanage gone. I want all those teachers who reprimanded me to die." He stepped closer, and she stepped back. "I want you. No male may be with you, but me. I *love* you. I've been watching you all these solar cycles. I know who you dated, who you kissed, and who you made love to. You're in my head all the time. Everything I do is for you."

Aleeya understood love, and it was nothing skewed or dark. True love was light and hope.

"I killed all your lovers." He smirked, and soot escaped his lips like snakes.

She sucked in a breath as her chest ached.

"They weren't right for you, so I removed them. Do you see how much I care about you?"

Aleeya struggled for breath, for sanity. For a way to kill this monster in front of her. She clutched her blaster and fired at him. The beam slammed through him. It didn't affect him. His maniacal laugh took on a different pitch. It came from elsewhere.

Malastrom! Why wasn't the poison affecting him?

Rellok had killed all her previous mates. That was why she never heard from them again. They died because of her, simply because they were with her. She was culpable for their deaths, and that knowledge broke her.

Tears spilled down her face. "You're an evil monster, and I hope you suffer for all eternity."

Rellok flared his bloody nostrils. "Don't call me that! You're just angry. Do you remember Brock from Phyllus? He disrespected you, so I blew up his head."

Aleeya recalled the incident when she tried to interrogate Brock.

Rellok's voice chilled the room. "I have someone that would make you come with me willingly. Bring him in!"

The cyborg from yesterday emerged from the door. Her corra crashed to the floor. The cyborg dragged Kenzo in by a rope wrapped around his wrists. His steps wobbled and his head bobbed.

What did they do to him?

THIRTY-SEVEN

Kenzo

He heard Aleeya's voice and his heart beat faster, stronger. Her energy healed him and strengthened him. He let the cyborg drag him in, and though the drug warred inside him, Kenzo won the battle with the help from the cosmic code. Timing was everything.

"Let him go." Aleeya demanded with a firm voice. Yellow glow seeped through the seams of her fist. Kenzo saw it because he looked for it.

Rellok whipped his gaze toward Kenzo. "You were lucky that day I shot at you from the facility. You should have died that day." His attention returned to Aleeya. "Malixx wanted to test out his updated cyborgs and sent them after you. I told him no, but he didn't listen. I came to help you. Don't you see? I won't let anything happen to you."

Aleeya kept her gaze on Kenzo. "You and Malixx don't deserve to live."

Rellok walked up to Kenzo, whose head tilted to the side on

purpose. "I enjoyed killing your brothers. I took my time desecrating their bodies. Their screams were songs to my ears. That would've been your fate if you hadn't escaped."

Rellok's statement poured gasoline onto Kenzo's rage. Thunder roared in Kenzo's blood.

The fangs of vengeance snarled, and the golden light from Kenzo's palm broke the restraints.

"You sick fuck!" Kenzo straightened his posture and sent a powerful golden beam from his fist into Rellok's body. The beam took a chunk of shoulder off. Blood and soot poured from him.

Kenzo destroyed the cyborgs with another golden blast and rushed to Aleeya. "Are you okay?"

"Yes, and you?"

"I'm fine. But we need to talk to later." He lifted his right palm and showed her the glowing cosmic key. "We are the key."

Five cyborgs entered from the main door, but Magnetti killed them. "I'll take care of the enemies out here."

Rellok regained his composure and whipped out a blast of soot at Kenzo. With her right palm—the one with cosmic code— she blocked Rellok's attack. As she pulled back, the darkness from Rellok came out like thick yarn covered in dark mold. It smelled of death as it screamed hellish sounds.

Kenzo and Aleeya exchanged a mutual understanding. Aleeya yanked out the darkness inside Rellok. It wailed hellish sounds, not wanting to leave the host body. Kenzo blasted the monster with golden light. As Aleeya pulled out the darkness, Kenzo alchemized it, turning it into light. The repetition of pull and alchemy continued until flesh fell off Rellok's body. His skeleton stood screaming as more soot came from his bones. Darkness had seeped into every fiber of his being.

When Aleeya pulled out the last strand of soot, Kenzo sent a golden beam into Rellok's skeleton and alchemized him. Light sparkled everywhere. Aleeya waved their palms around the orphanage, yanking out any darkness that had lingered in the crevices out into the open for Kenzo to transmute it.

They rushed out to the back yard and soot steamed from the soil where the cyborg bodies had fallen. The darkness knew it was losing a battle, and it joined, creating a hellish monster.

Aleeya turned to Kenzo. "Together, we're stronger." She held up her glowing palm to his glowing palm, tapping cosmic key to cosmic key. A clicking sound vibrated throughout the area like a door unlocking. Now both of their palms glowed with gold energy.

They knew what to do, as if that attribute had been inside them for eons. Aleeya and Kenzo pitched golden energy into the monster of soot and alchemized every fucking particle of hell.

THIRTY-EIGHT

Aleeya

While Magnetti and the soldiers cleaned up the area in the backyard, Aleeya embraced Kenzo.

She looked him straight in the eyes. "I'm sorry I didn't tell you about my plan. I couldn't bear the thought of you getting hurt or dying. I didn't want to risk it. I love you."

Kenzo dropped a kiss to her forehead. "I know, and I understand. But I want you to promise me one thing."

"What is it?"

"Never do that again. Relationships are about communication and trust. I want you to trust me with all your plans, even if I may disagree with them. We'll work it out. But never leave me and place yourself in danger. If you're not beside me, I'd rather not live."

Tears spilled over her eyes. "I promise."

THIRTY-NINE

Kenzo

Hours later, the children and staff returned to the Cosmic Corra Orphanage. Magnetti and the soldiers had cleared the area of bodies. El Lara arrived with Tab and Jella and used her selenite crystal grid to harmonize the energy around the area.

Kenzo obtained a few minor injuries during the battle that were taken care of. Aleeya escaped with no new wounds, which he was grateful for. He glanced at the cosmic key symbol on his palm, still pulsing with warmth. The divine key reminded him of who he was bonded to: his starmate. Aleeya was where his heart and soul lay. They were the key to each other. With her, love and truth reigned supreme.

He never imagined he would possess this kind of magical power that existed in movies on Earth. What would his parents think when he returned for a visit? A smile grew on his lips. It was probably best to keep this part of life to himself. Certain things were too complicated to share or explain. Despite that, Kenzo welcomed the magic, accepted it, and would learn more about it. If he could use his power to keep Aleeya, Terrakado, and Earth safe, then that was his new mission.

In the library, Aleeya kneeled beside Jella. "I'm so happy you're feeling better."

Jella smiled. "Thank you for rescuing me and for not giving up." She threw her arms around Aleeya.

"You're brave, smart, and adorable. How can I not help you?" Aleeya rose and clutched Jella's hand. "Are you ready to go home?"

Jella's eyes beamed. "Yes, please." She rushed up to Kenzo, Tab, and El Lara, offering each one a hug. "Thank you for taking care of me."

Kenzo checked Aleeya's wound behind her neck. "It's healing well. I think the sealant will disappear tomorrow."

Aleeya ran a hand over the wound on his jaw. He clasped a hand over hers and squeezed. He had plans to share. He needed some alone time with her, but she had responsibilities to take care of right now. He could wait. He wasn't going anywhere. His heart was here in Norak.

She read his mind. "I'll be back soon. Stay out of trouble. I'm taking Jella back to Phyllus. Her family is eager to see her."

After Aleeya left, Kenzo went out to the backyard, where the children resumed their activities prior to the emergency evacuation. Laughter boomed as they played and climbed the obstacle course.

Magnetti came up beside him. "How are you doing?"

The messy blond hair spiked everywhere, making him appear like a lion that had just survived a battle.

With the files Kenzo sent Detective Ahlex, he shut down Atrium successfully. Two Delleon officials were charged with aiding Malixx and Rellok. They were heading to Asteroid Karma, where they'd spend the rest of their lives in prison. Based on the data received from the criminals' computers,

Detective Ahlex closed down three Corra Spark facilities in Delleon. Norak and Delleon were collaborating to locate other facilities throughout the regions. Nothing in the Cosmos could —or should—have the power to alter the heart. This sacred organ was magical.

Kenzo patted the sealed gash on his arm and gut. "Fine. And you?"

"Better now that the threats have been eliminated. This orphanage is as important to me as it is to Aleeya and all the children here." Magnetti faced Kenzo, and his green eyes sparked. "Thank you for helping me and Aleeya keep it safe." He tapped a fist to his chest, a Norakian greeting Kenzo appreciated.

"You're welcome. I can see how this place is a sanctuary for these children."

"They all possess something special that can contribute to society when they're ready. We need to ensure they have a safe space to learn and grow." He glanced at his vambrace. "I need to get going. I've picked up on a strange energy near the Gulf of Lindenai. With everything that's happened, I want to make sure there are no threats around." He cleared his throat. "Before I go, I have a proposal for you."

Part of Kenzo's plan had been to ask Magnetti, Captain of the Norakian warriors, if he could somehow work for the Norakian government. Kenzo wanted to be close to Aleeya because a long distance relationship wouldn't work for him.

"Just so you know, I'm officially retired from bounty hunting."

Magnetti chuckled. "Noted. Would you consider working for the Norakian government as a consultant? You've shown you can fight, and you have military knowledge that can help us. The Norakian warriors are honored to work with you."

It was true what they said about being in alignment with the

Cosmos. Everything worked out beautifully. He'd always wanted to be part of something big, something dignified, something beyond him. This opportunity gave him that and more.

"This offer means a lot to me. Thank you. First, I get to be close to the woman I love, and second, I get to serve beside warriors I admire. I accept your offer." Kenzo tapped a fist to his chest. "I hope I did that right."

"You did. Welcome to the Norakian warrior legion. You can let Aleeya know when she gets back. I'll introduce you to Kazstrom, the Prime General, when he returns from his trip. I've got to go now."

Magnetti left and Kenzo strode over to a bench, watching Tab work with the children. As he sat, Kenzo thought back on the events that led to this moment. Malixx and Rellok believed in the false light. The false light had many faces, and one of them was obsession. Malixx and Rellok were obsessed with a version of love that gave them false promises, lured them with distorted outcomes, and misled them down a dark path that eventually killed them. Their obsession allowed the darkness to live inside like a parasite. This parasite reproduced itself and took over their souls.

There was love, and there were imitations of that energy. What they deemed as love was in fact a distorted, false light. No one could rip out someone's heart—the core of their existence— and substitute it for an artificial thing. Or inject it with some chemical to change its natural ability and assume it would function properly.

What fulfilled for a moment wasn't worth the price of the soul. Kenzo understood this because he believed in this falseness for a while too. Vengeance was his excuse to obliterate the guilt and sorrow for failing to save his brothers. He allowed blame and unworthiness to reign within himself because he didn't know how to be otherwise.

He had been searching for the truth all his life. The truth of why he chose solitude, why he always felt the need to go his own way and search for his place in life. He had been searching for something he could fight for, something to be proud of. The truth for finding his brothers' killers. And in finding that truth, he also found love. Truth and love were similar energies.

The cosmic key represented truth and love. Once he found those attributes, once he understood them, he became the key. The key to love—to everything. He shuddered from the power packed in that wisdom.

Defying darkness led him to the truth. To agree to a false light was worse than to defy an ugly truth. He saw this in Aleeya too. She defied orders to stand down when she witnessed a crime that went against her belief system. That defiance led her to the truth. That process gave her back her memory, her father, her orphanage, her worthiness, and her heart.

She loved him and he loved her. So much power radiated from that fact.

Kenzo's heart thudded and the sigil on his palm sparked with warmth. This key represented so much more than his love for Aleeya. It possessed an ancient energy that knew what was best for him and how he could be of service. He glanced up at the three moons as they prepared to take over the evening skyline.

Yarra, the moon with the yellow aura and gold rim, pulsed. For a moment, its auric field produced a pattern around the sphere, creating various floral petals that baffled him.

You closed a powerful pocket of darkness, thank you. This is one step closer to restoring the light for what's to come.

A tunnel of light burst from Yarra, extending to the ground in front of him. Kenzo rose from the bench in surprise. He glanced around, but everyone appeared to be doing their own thing, not noticing what was happening. Was he the only one seeing this?

In a blink, Jeeto appeared at his feet, smiling. "I'm glad you're safe. I missed you!" His friend jumped into his arms for a cuddle.

"I missed you too, buddy. How are you?" Something felt different in Jeeto's energy. Cheeriness vibrated from him like a burst of uncontrollable joy.

Jeeto's emerald eyes and fur brightened from the light of the tunnel. "I'm feeling wonderful. My mission is complete. You're safe and you accomplished everything that was needed. I have to go home now."

Sadness clutched at his heart. Jeeto was his pet, his friend, and his savior all those years ago.

Jeeto placed a hand on Kenzo's face. "Don't be sad. You'll see me again. I'll come back to visit. But right now, Yarra has other tasks for me. There are others who need my help."

Kenzo embraced his little friend, who had given solace during his darkest times. "I won't forget you."

Jeeto's ears perked. "If you do, then we'll have issues. I won't forget you either." He rubbed his tummy. "I've never eaten so well as when I was with you. You fed all versions of me."

Kenzo chuckled. "What do you mean?"

"I exist in many places at once, so when you feed me, you feed other Jeetos too. I exist in a multidimensional matrix. Thank you for all the delicious foods."

Kenzo tickled Jeeto's fuzzy, round tummy. "You're welcome, my friend. Make sure you keep feeding this tummy. I'm going to miss my conversations with you."

Jeeto leaned into Kenzo's ear. "You can still talk to me anytime. I might not reply right away, but I will when I can. It'll be in here though." He tapped a claw at Kenzo's temple.

A gentle song emanated from the tunnel. Jeeto jumped into

its light, waved, wagged his tail, and disappeared with the tunnel. Though sadness gripped him, Kenzo knew Jeeto was safe, happy in another place, helping someone the way he helped him.

Tab walked up to him. "You're deep in thought. Is everything okay?"

Kenzo told him a short version of what occurred.

"Jeeto was your guardian," Tab said.

"So were you."

"We all have our roles in life. I knew there was something about you that needed tending to." Tab released a sigh. "I'm staying in Norak. I'll be working here." He jutted his chin toward a group of young kids playing in the obstacle course.

"You're great with the children." Kenzo had seen how Tab's face lit up every time a child came to him for help.

"I owe a lot to this place. This was Aleeya's loving home. I'd be happy to contribute in any way I can. The orphanage has offered me a teaching position. I'm good with words so I can put my journalism background to use." He met Kenzo's gaze. "Being with these children allows me to live all those solar cycles I missed with my daughter."

The glimmer in Tab's eyes revealed joy and peace. His friend deserved that and more.

"Life is so interesting. All the twists and turns bring us to where we need to be," Kenzo said. "The Cosmos is a sacred choreographer. The dance she comes up with can take our breaths away."

Tab shook his head and chuckled. "You going to write a book about that?"

Kenzo lifted a shoulder. "Never say never, right?"

After Kenzo shared news about Magnetti's offer, Tab went to referee a game between the kids.

Kenzo headed home to wait for Aleeya.

El Lara met him on his way out. "How are you doing?"

Kenzo showed the Priestess the cosmic symbol on his palm earlier, but she wasn't surprised.

"Yarra blessed you and Aleeya." The star on her forehead glowed. "I saw the tunnel of light earlier. Sizzler is sad that her friend's gone." The green snake snuck out from El Lara's sleeve, hissing. "Do you understand the significance of what just occurred?"

"That I closed a dark pocket of darkness and opened a portal of light?"

"Do you know how you did it?"

Kenzo wasn't sure. "Not really."

"Malixx and Rellok possessed a darkness that was interlaced with false light. I sensed the darkness leave when you alchemized the darkness into light. This darkness had rooted itself into the planet for a long time. It is an ancient energy that's powerful. It latched itself onto unstable souls like Malixx and Rellok, and from there, it twisted their minds into believing something that wasn't real." The cosmic codes on her face gleamed. "You and Aleeya annihilated that. You cleared the way for light to enter."

He and Aleeya were tasked to find each other and eradicate the false light that snuck through the Doorway of Unity. Did they dismantle all the deformity, distortion, misrepresentation, and falsification?

He knew the answer, but he asked anyway. "Do you think there's still false light around?"

"Always. It can take on different forms. It's intelligent, can shape-shift, is adaptable, and dangerous. It knows how to maneuver around light, and it's everywhere, even on Earth. All we can do is be aware of it, be conscious of it. The one thing the false light fears is truth because the truth is sacred. The truth doesn't lie. It just *is*. And the ones who fear that are the ones who will create chaos. They will get loud to distract you, and it's our job to stop the chaos."

Was it possible to prevent chaos? He imagined it'd be difficult. He couldn't control someone's mind or choices, but he could prepare himself for future battles.

"The portal of light you opened will feed the Great Vortex in positive ways."

"What is the Great Vortex?"

"It's an enigmatic area within the Cosmos that could bend time and space, warping realities, illusions, and energies. The Great Vortex is one big mystery to all of us. No one knows much about it because no one can get close to it. Its magnetic field is extensive, a power beyond anything I've seen. I believe this is an opportunity for all of us to work together. We are on a precipice of a new era. An alternative way of living that brings us all together. Darkness is the enemy of light, and it fears love and truth. The darkness pulls at this vortex, but so does the light. Which one will win? That's up to us."

Kenzo never thought about the galactic atmosphere in its entirety. He'd do what he could to help the light win.

"I saw Yarra's moon become a flower."

"It's a cosmic moon mandala, which means something critical is happening in the Cosmos. And this is the moon's way of keeping us aware and safe."

"Thank you for explaining all of this to me."

"You knew it in your corra, but sometimes it helps to hear it spoken out loud. I've been waiting a long time to see Yarra's tunnel of light come to life. I've connected to Farra, and now with Yarra. I'm looking forward to conversing with Jarra soon."

"You know when you're going to speak to it?"

The Priestess smiled. "Based on certain events, I can guess. Farra connected Kazstrom and Teegan. Yarra connected you and Aleeya. Each of you were fated to help each other.

Together, you gave something back to the moons. I wonder who will be next."

Kenzo pondered on that fascinating theory. Despite the seriousness of it, there was beauty to it as well. "It's romantic. I'm sure a lot of females would see it that way."

"It is."

"I'm going to head back to Aleeya's apartment. I have something special planned for her."

"Something 'romantic?'"

Kenzo's lips curved. "Something like that."

"You might have to wait awhile. Most likely, Aleeya will have to stop by Elder Kai's home to accept her punishment for disobeying his direct order."

Kenzo furrowed his eyebrows. "What punishment?"

"She defied a specific order from Elder Kai and me when she inserted herself into Phyllus's issues. We told her not to because it wasn't under Norakian jurisdiction."

He opened his mouth to defend Aleeya, but the Priestess held up a hand. "I know. In my eyes, her actions were justified. But in the grand scheme of things, she defied a direct order. She respects her Elders, and right now, she must make things 'right.'"

"She went after what she believed in," Kenzo said.

El Lara nodded. "Was she disturbing the peace or was she ringing a much-needed alarm? We both know the answer. We've seen what her actions have led to. Along with you, she saved this orphanage and all of Norak."

His woman was not only admirable, she was the epitome of love and justice. A warrior of truth.

What kind of punishment would Aleeya receive? "Is she going to be safe?"

"Of course," El Lara said. "Elder Kai is fair and appreciates all his warriors."

Kenzo flicked El Lara an inquisitive look. "Is it possible to get more of those Yellow Murmurs? I'm in the mood for poetry." His simple plan just turned more elaborate.

A smile bloomed on her face. "You can have as many as you'd like. Would you like Mimic to take you home as well?"

"I'd appreciate it."

FORTY

Aleeya

Aleeya waited for Elder Kai to finish his conference call and wandered around his courtyard. The last time she visited this place was after Kazstrom and Teegan defeated Moraku. It had only been one solar cycle ago. So much had changed since then. She'd connected with her father, understood why she had been left at the orphanage and why she had commitment issues. Most of all, she found love. Kenzo had been the key to her corra. Because of him, she found her identity, her self-worth, and her life's purpose. She lifted her palm and studied the cosmic symbol she shared with her starmate. With Kenzo by her side, Aleeya could battle anything that came at them in the future.

She glanced up at the three moons and thanked Yarra for the blessings, guidance, and opportunity to be of service. It had been her job as one of the Guardians to the Doorway of Unity. And she had fulfilled that service.

The yellow moon glowed, and flower petals grew around it,

creating a sacred mandala design. *Thank you, Aleeya. You helped us remove the false light.*

Then Jeeto's face appeared at the center of the flower. He smiled and waved at her. *See you later.*

Joy blossomed inside Aleeya. Was Kenzo feeling all right without Jeeto? She couldn't wait to start a new life with him.

The willow tree with blue leaves swayed in the breeze. A gentle song hummed as the droopy branches touched each other, making the leaves chime. She sat on a stone bench, closed her eyes, and got ready to receive whatever discipline she deserved.

She deserved punishment. She had defied Elder Kai and El Lara, which meant she had defied Norak. Her chest tightened at the thought. She loved Norak and its citizens. This was her home. Her defiance had been her way of clinging to what she believed in. If she couldn't protect that part of her, then what did she have left?

"How are you doing, Aleeya?" Elder Kai came up beside her. His long white hair hung like a serpent down his back, sectioned off by three gold bands.

Was he angry with her? Was he disappointed that one of his Norakian warriors had defied him? She'd let him down.

Aleeya rose and tapped a fist to her corra. "I'm glad Norak is safe from Malixx and Rellok."

The energy belt around his white cloak pulsed with power. "Thanks to you and Kenzo, the threats have been eliminated." Guilt grew on his orange, scaly face. "I'm also to blame for not seeing through Rellok's disguise. He worked for me through all these solar cycles, but I had no clue who he really was. I've always considered myself excellent at picking up on deception, and yet my pilot was the enemy all along."

She understood his pain and his guilt. "Sometimes it's hard to see the truth when we're so close to it. You take a chance when you trust someone. Sometimes it works out, other times you learn from it. Rellok was smart, and he deceived everyone. He probably invented some device that masked his energy. His actions aren't your fault. If anyone is to blame, it's me. I should have known he was more dangerous than he let on."

"You were a child when you met him," Elder Kai said. "And now, you're a warrior who could see through to the truth better than anyone I know." He released a heavy sigh as he stood glancing at the sky with his hands clasped behind his back. "I took you to the GCOT conference because I received divine guidance from our suns and moons. They never gave me a reason. I trusted them, and therefore, I have accepted the consequences of my decision."

Just like how she accepted the repercussion of her choices.

Every choice she made led her to do what was needed. "But that didn't give me the right to defy you. I'm sorry I disobeyed your specific orders to ignore the crime. I was listening to a part of me that kept 'me' together. And if I let that part go, I wouldn't have had anything left to fight for." Tears threatened her eyes, but she pushed them down.

"I understand." He gestured to the bench. "Sit with me. It's been a long day for you and for me. I have a few things to share with you."

Aleeya sat beside him.

"You know, Kazstrom had already approved your inquiry when you contacted him and Magnetti. He didn't tell you then. We both wanted to know where this would take you."

She whipped a surprised look at him. "He did? You knew?"

A small smile curved on his face. "Kaz discussed it with me. We saw the fire in you, we *felt* it. And the only thing that could extinguish that fire was the truth."

Warmth erupted all over her body. They knew her better

than she thought. They had supported her, even though it went against regulations. They bent the rules for her.

Elder Kai jerked his chin at the sky. "Did you know that I've traveled inside one of our moons and one of our suns?"

Was that even possible? He had to be joking. His eyes gleamed with wonder as he looked at the sky.

She understood that star-beings had access to multidimensional worlds, but she had never experienced it herself. Bewilderment filled her. "There are worlds *inside* our suns and moons?"

He nodded. "There are worlds within worlds. It's beautiful there. My corra beats for someone there."

That piqued her interest. Who was the being that had captured Elder Kai's corra? Why was he here and not there? Aleeya knew little about Elder Kai. He kept his personal life private.

"Your starmate?"

He didn't deny or admit anything. Instead, he smiled. "The reason I'm telling you this is that something is happening across the Cosmos. The individuals that live inside the suns and moons know this. And they need our help. You and Kenzo were chosen by Yarra. Kazstrom and Teegan were chosen by Farra. With your accomplishments, you have empowered them. Their energies are stronger to ensure that our galaxy will survive what is to come."

"What's coming?"

"I'm not privy to that knowledge. Some details are too sacred to be spoken out loud."

She had a million questions to ask him. Why wasn't he up there with his love? What was it like to be inside the sun or the moon? She imagined it must be difficult to pass through the fiery surface of the sun. As for the moons, she'd only seen images of their beautiful landscapes.

"Does anyone live on the moon? It's one place I haven't flown to. It seems too sacred for visitors."

"There's life everywhere, even on the moon. You'll see the beings when they want to be seen."

One day, she'd visit the three moons.

"I know you have a lot of questions, but there will be a time when you'll get your answers. Today isn't that day. Today is when we set things straight and true." Elder Kai faced her. "Yes, you defied my orders. Yes, I was disappointed, and no, I'm not angry. Everything you saw was there for a reason. That incident with those children propelled you to find your father, save Norak and Delleon from the horror of Malixx and Rellok. Most of all, it led you to your starmate, Kenzo. So your defiance was the key that unlocked these truths. How can I be angry with that?"

Aleeya didn't know what to say. He understood beyond her imagination.

"I know you feel you deserve a punishment because you're a Norakian warrior. Because your brothers and sisters are watching you, along with all those children at the orphanage who look up to you. At best, rules are guidelines. How true are we to our corras? That's a question many cannot answer. You stayed true to yours, and that has made all the difference."

Listening to her corra was the only thing she could depend on. Something lodged in her throat, making it difficult to respond to Elder Kai.

"My penalty is this: create an educational program for the Cosmic Corra that teaches the children how to listen to their corras, how to know the difference between right and wrong, how to understand the various consequences of their choices. Teach them to stand and fight for what they believe in. The corra is the sacred center of the soul. It's powerful and magical.

Teach them to be aware of their choices and how their actions affect others."

Tears spilled over her eyes. This was not a discipline. It was a reward, a divine gift that would continue the legacy of the orphanage, showing children it didn't matter where they came from; they could rise up and become their best selves. She could teach them to be their own warriors.

Elder Kai rose from the bench and strode to the willow tree. He held a branch in his hands, and the blades of the leaves glistened. "We need to teach the young ones to see the truth and help maintain the light on this planet." He released the branch, and it pushed against the other branches, creating a song that echoed on and on. "To be aware helps you prepare for what's to come. The fact that it can't take you by surprise allows you to respond differently. Your reaction is the difference between someone who leads and someone who doesn't. We need leaders in Norak, and I need you to help me achieve this."

Respect, honor, joy, and humility washed over her. She was still a warrior, but now she had another important task. She didn't take this responsibility lightly. It was something she believed in. She stood tall and proud. "I'll do my best."

"That's all you can do." Elder Kai tapped a fist to his corra. "Go home and rest. I'm sure someone's waiting for you. I'd like to meet Kenzo next week when both of you are well-rested."

With joy filling every cell in her body, she rushed home to be with her love.

Kenzo

Inside Aleeya's suite, Kenzo organized five pots of Yellow Murmurs. He hoped his Buttercup would appreciate his creativity. She'd either love it or hate it. At first, he had only planned for one pot. But after his conversation with El Lara, he wanted to give it all to Aleeya. She deserved it.

He placed one near the front of the door, so it was the first thing she'd see when she entered the house. He arranged the other four in a way that led her to the living room and out to the balcony where he'd be waiting for her.

Anticipation and nerves churned in his stomach. He hadn't felt this much pressure to perfect anything in such a long time. But then again, he'd never loved a woman before, either. If things worked out well, he'd take Aleeya to visit his parents one day. He was ready for the future.

The door opened and his love walked in. He'd drawn the curtains back to ensure he got the perfect view. Leaning on the railing of her balcony, he watched her every move.

Aleeya picked up the first pot, and the Yellow Murmurs recited with a cute voice, "Will you be my Buttercup." She let out a laugh that brightened the room. The flower petals fluttered with each word, and an image of his face and hers flowed from petal to petal. Thanks to the orphanage, he had received some recent images of her.

She laughed again and placed the pot down on the kitchen table. She made her way to the next pot. The flowers shimmied. "I have words to share with you."

Amusement sparked in her eyes as she met his gaze.

With an adorable voice, the next group of flowers said:

"If you were a flower in a field
And I was the soil embracing your roots,
We'd strengthen each other
With love and trust as absolutes."

The cosmic codes on her skin illuminated, and her eyes glistened. Her hands trembled as she reached for the fourth pot.

"Though you are a skilled warrior
And we are bound by fate,
I'd love and protect you
If you choose me as your mate."

Tears glittered in her eyes and a trembling hand clutched her heart. She ambled toward the balcony and embraced him.

"There's one more." Kenzo handed her the final flowerpot, but it didn't recite words. An instrumental song played from the flowers as images of them splashed across the petals.

Grinning, she placed the pot on the small table and kissed him.

He drew back and looked at her. "I love you. If I grew a flower for every time I thought of you, I would have a flower field called Aleeya. Do you want to start a new life with me? If you say yes, I'll do my best to write you more poems."

She laughed and cried. "Is that a bribe?"

He shrugged. "I'll do what I have to. Do you remember asking me this: 'Is that a new line for a poem you're going to write me?' I assumed it was a bribe too." He flashed a grin and worked his charm.

She forced herself to stop crying and took the tissue from his hand.

"How can I say no? How can anyone say no to you? After such an impressive presentation, you can have whatever you want. You're such a poet, and you should write a book. I'm not saying that because I love you. I'm saying it because I see talent. Give it a shot. The book doesn't have to be about me, although I might get jealous if it's about another female star-being. I'm just putting it out there."

Kenzo kissed her until her fatigue turned into vigor.

"Yes, I'll be your Buttercup. Does this mean you're staying here and moving in with me? It's the only way a long-term thing is going to work."

His heart thudded with joy and satisfaction. He told her he'd accepted Magnetti's job offer and about Tab's new role at the orphanage, which delighted her. She shared she received a visit from Jeeto. That made him happy that his pet also loved her.

"I'd like you to meet my parents when the time's right," Kenzo said. "You can disguise yourself, so they won't ask a lot of questions. I can show you around Earth. I'm sure your *Sentra Five* can get us back and forth quickly."

She cupped his face with her hands. "I'd love that." She

glanced back into the suite. "So what am I supposed to do with all these flowers?"

An idea came to him. "We can start a new garden at the orphanage."

"Something that will continue to flourish and symbolize our love."

Kenzo wrapped an arm around Aleeya as they glanced at the three moons and looked towards their future.

Jarra, the third moon, glowed as it prepared for the next step in the cosmic plan.

Thank you so much for reading! I hope you've enjoyed Aleeya and Kenzo's story! Magnetti's journey is coming soon!

Don't miss out on any new releases. Sign up for my newsletter! **https://callazae.com/newsletter/**

If you enjoyed this story, I'd love it if you'd consider leaving me a review on your favorite retailer website.

I invite you to join my Facebook reader's group, where I offer sneak peeks, giveaways, special perks, and other book news! **https://www.facebook.com/groups/callazae**

AUDIOBOOKS are available for my Soldiers of Saedo Series!

Suggested Reading Order:

An Alien Rescue (#1)

An Alien Crush (#2)

An Alien Dare (#3)

An Alien Storm (#4)

(An Alien Storm: Ebook available. Audiobook Coming Soon!)

An Alien Lore (#5) - Coming Soon!

"You weren't the only one who was rescued. We saved each other."

Emma is on vacation with her six siblings to ring in the New Year with everything auspicious and nothing to do with broken relationships, disappointments, and heartache. But what she got was an alien abduction.

Raeko, a beautiful green star-being, rescues her from horrific beasts that want her to reproduce for them. His protection and honesty stirs her heart in a way that echoes the love she has always wanted.

Is he Emma's New Year's gift? Or is he another male who's going to bruise her heart?

"A promise is sacred to me, and I had to fulfill it so I could woo you appropriately."

When a heroic star-being saves Sasha from horrific beasts, she develops a crush on him, sparking hope in her heart. But then he disappears. Taking matters into her own hands, Sasha tracks him down.

Maeson, a remarkable soldier who values his word, is attracted to Sasha, but a promise keeps him from her. In order to return to her, he must first fulfill his obligation to someone else and stop a dire threat from destroying them both.

Can Maeson offer Sasha what she needs? Or will he crush her heart?

"I love challenges, and you're the most captivating challenge to cross my path. I will unravel you."

Though excited to showcase her first galactic fashion show, Inga is stressed because she's desperate for one more model. A stunning star-being with the perfect body emerges, but his ego irritates her. Annoyed, she dares him to model for her, not expecting a challenge to her heart.

Osayik, an outstanding soldier with no interest in "strutting" down some runway—whatever that means—can't resist a challenge. Fascinated by Inga, he wants to know what lies beneath the beauty.

Does he dare listen to his heart? Or will pride get in his way?

"There's something different about you… Something untamed. Something mysterious. It's driving me crazy."

Battered and bruised from a previous relationship, Vanessa now prefers a quiet life as a chef on a new planet. But then a captivating star-being storms into her life and whips up a whirlwind of emotions that makes her heart yearn for things she has long forgotten.

Arkon, a skilled soldier who prefers numbers, charts, and anything with absoluteness is attracted to Vanessa. But she favors no rules and lures him out of his comfort zone. Having been scorned once, he fears she will burn him.

Is their union a recipe for love or destruction?

Ebook & Paperback are available for the Norakian Warrior Series. These are full-length novels within the Alarus Galaxy on planet Terrakado.

The Alien's Allegiance (#1)

The Alien's Defiance (#2)

"She arrived on this new planet with two hot suns, but it was this blue warrior who burned away all her doubts."

As Captain of the Norakian warriors, Kazstrom anticipates the upcoming competition that can promote him to be the next General of his legion. But a poisonous wound threatens to eliminate his dream. The hunt for a cure leads him to Earth, where he encounters an alluring human female who not only possesses the moonstone he desperately needs, but she also ignites something deep within him. Intrigued, he is compelled to protect her from enemies who are after the same moonstone.

Teegan, a second-grade teacher, is drowning in debt and doubt after a failed engagement when a stunning star-being asks her to go to his planet and heal him. With nothing to lose, she decides a mini out-of-this-world adventure with Kazstrom is the exact escape required to alleviate her life's issues. But her heart has its own plans and tosses her into an escalating romance filled with danger that will leave them both shattered if they are not careful.

As Kazstrom battles his worst enemy to protect his starmate, Teegan must find her warrior spirit to defend the star-being she has come to love.

For a complete list of my books, click here.

https://callazae.com/books/

ACKNOWLEDGMENTS

Thank you to Laurie, Carol, and Anna who helped my story shine. You are the shiny siSTARS in my galaxy. Thank you to my family who always give me everything I need to pursue my dreams. You are my entire Universe.

And thank you, dear readers, you give me a reason to keep writing. Without you, there's no one to appreciate the stardust within my creation. You have my utmost gratitude. Thank you, thank you, thank you.

ABOUT THE AUTHOR
CALLA ZAE

I love writing sci-fi, fantasy, paranormal, and contemporary romance novels. I'm an artist, and I love to create visuals to convey my stories.

I live in Massachusetts with my husband who keeps me grounded to Earth and two creative children who think I have my own secret planet. They're onto something...

facebook.com/callazaeauthor

instagram.com/callazae

bookbub.com/profile/calla-zae

amazon.com/author/callazae

pinterest.com/callazae

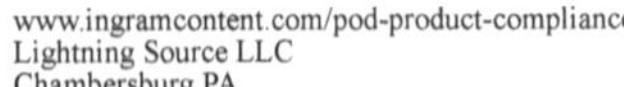